VAN BU
DECAT
P9-BAW-827

DISCARDED

By Amy Bloom

Lucky Us

Lucky Us

A NOVEL

Amy Bloom

RANDOM HOUSE
NEW YORK

Lucky Us is a work of fiction. All incidents and dialogue, and all characters with the exception of some well-known historical and public figures, are products of the author's imagination and are not to be construed as real. Where real-life historical or public figures appear, the situations, incidents, and dialogues concerning those persons are entirely fictional and are not intended to depict actual events or to change the entirely fictional nature of the work. In all other respects, any resemblance to persons living or dead is entirely coincidental.

Copyright © 2014 by Amy Bloom

All rights reserved.

Published in the United States by Random House,
an imprint and division of Random House LLC,
a Penguin Random House Company, New York.

RANDOM HOUSE and the HOUSE colophon are registered trademarks of Random House LLC.

Library of Congress Cataloging-in-Publication Data
Bloom, Amy
Lucky us: a novel/Amy Bloom.
pages cm
ISBN 978-1-4000-6724-4
eBook ISBN 978-0-8129-9600-5
1. Sisters—Fiction. 2. Abandoned children—Fiction. 3. Domestic fiction. I. Title.
PS3552.L6378L93 2014
813'.54—dc23
2013017648

Printed in the United States of America on acid-free paper

www.atrandom.com

123456789

First Edition

Endpapers: Deborah Van Auten, *Earthrise* (detail)

Book design by Susan Turner

7/14
Bет

For my sister, Ellen

Part One

1939–1943

1

I'd Know You Anywhere

MY FATHER'S WIFE DIED. MY MOTHER SAID WE SHOULD DRIVE down to his place and see what might be in it for us.

She tapped my nose with her grapefruit spoon. "It's like this," she said. "Your father loves us more, but he's got another family, a wife, and a girl a little older than you. Her family had all the money. Wipe your face."

There was no one like my mother, for straight talk. She washed my neck and ears until they shone. We helped each other dress: her lilac dress, with the underarm zipper, my pink one with the tricky buttons. My mother did my braids so tight, my eyes pulled up. She took her violet cloche and her best gloves and she ran across the road to borrow Mr. Portman's car. I was glad to be going and I thought I could get to be glad about having a sister. I wasn't sorry my father's other wife was dead.

. . .

WE'D WAITED FOR HIM for weeks. My mother sat by the window in the morning and smoked through supper every night. When she came home from work at Hobson's, she was in a bad mood, even after I rubbed her feet. I hung around the house all July, playing with Mr. Portman's poodle, waiting for my father to drive up. When he came, he usually came by two o'clock, in case there was a Fireside Chat that day. We listened to all the Fireside Chats together. We loved President Roosevelt. On Sundays, when my father came, he brought a pack of Lucky Strikes for my mother and a Hershey bar for me. After supper, my mother sat in my father's lap and I sat right on his slippers and if there was a Fireside Chat, my father did his FDR imitation. Good evening, friends, he said, and he stuck a straw in his mouth like a cigarette holder. Good evening, ladies and gentlemen. He bowed to my mother and said, Eleanor, my dear, how 'bout a waltz? They danced to the radio for a while and then it was my bedtime. My mother put a few bobby pins in my hair for curls and my father carried me to bed, singing, "I wish I could shimmy like my sister Kate." Then he tucked me in and shimmied out the door. Monday mornings, he was gone and I waited until Thursday, and sometimes, until next Sunday.

MY MOTHER PARKED THE car and redid her lipstick. My father's house was two stories of red stone and tall windows, with fringed lace curtains behind and wide brown steps stacked like boxes in front of the shining wood door. Your father does like to have things nice, while he's away, she said. It sure is nice, I said. We ought to live here.

My mother smiled at me and ran her tongue over her teeth. Could be, she said—you never know. She'd already told me she was tired of Abingdon, where we'd been since I was born. It was no kind of real town and she was fed up to here hostessing at Hobson's. We talked a lot about finding ourselves a better life in Chicago. *Chicago, Chicago, that toddlin' town . . . I saw a man, he danced with his wife.* I sang as we got out of the car and I did a few dance steps like in the movies. My mother said, You are the bee's knees, kiddo, and she grabbed the back of my dress. She licked her palm and pressed it to my bangs, so they wouldn't fly up. She straightened her skirt and told me to check her seams. Straight as arrows, I said, and we went up the stairs hand in hand.

My mother knocked and my father answered the door in the blue vest he wore at our house during the president's speeches. My father hugged me and my parents whispered to each other while I stood there, trying to see more of the parlor, which was as big as our whole apartment and filled with flowers. (Maybe my father said, What the hell are you doing here? Maybe my mother cursed him for staying away, but I doubt it. My father had played the gentleman his whole life and my mother must have said to me a hundred times that men needed to be handled right and a woman who couldn't handle her man had only herself to blame. "When I say men are dogs," she'd say, "I'm not being insulting. I like dogs.") Behind my father, I saw a tall girl.

"My daughter Iris," my father said. I could hear my mother breathe in.

"Iris," he said, "this is my friend Mrs. Logan and her daughter, her lovely daughter, Eva."

I knew, standing in their foyer, that this girl had a ton of things I didn't have. Flowers in crystal vases the size of buckets. Pretty, light-brown curls. My father's hand on her shoulder. She wore a baby-blue sweater and a white blouse with a bluebird pin on the collar. I think she wore stockings. Iris was sixteen and she looked like a grown woman to me. She looked like a movie star. My father pushed us to the stairs and told Iris to entertain me in her room while he and my mother had a chat.

"Picture this," Iris said. She lay on her bed and I sat on the braided rug next to it. She gave me a couple of gumdrops and I was happy to sit there. She was a great talker and a perfect mimic. "The whole college came to my mother's funeral. My grandfather used to be president of the college, but he had a stroke last year, so he's different now. There was this one girl, red hair, really awful. Redheads. Like they didn't cook long enough or something."

"I think Paulette Goddard's a redhead," I said. I'd read this in *Photoplay* last week.

"How old are you, ten? Who the hell wants to be Paulette Goddard? Anyway, this redheaded girl comes back to our house. She's just bawling to beat the band. So this lady, our neighbor, Mrs. Drysdale, says to her, 'Were you very close to dear Mrs. Acton?'"

The way Iris said this, I could just see Mrs. Drysdale, sticking her nose in, keeping her spotted veil out of her mouth while she ate, her wet hankie stuffed into her big bosom, which my mother told me was a disgusting thing to do.

"I'm twelve," I said.

Iris said, "My mother was like a saint—everybody says so. She was nice to everyone, but I don't want people thinking my mother wasted her time on this stupid girl, so I turn around and say that none of us even know who she is and she runs into the powder room downstairs—this is the funny part—the door gets stuck, and she can't get out. She's banging on the door and two professors have to jimmy it open. It was funny."

Iris told me that the whole college (I didn't know my father taught at a college; if you had asked me, I would have said that he read books for a living) came to the chapel to grieve for her mother, to offer sympathy to her and her father. She said that all of their family friends were there, which was her way of telling me that my mother could not really be a friend of her father's.

WE HEARD THE VOICES downstairs and then a door shutting and then the piano, playing "My Angel Put the Devil in Me." I didn't know my father played the piano. Iris and I stood at her bedroom door, leaning into the hall. We heard the toilet flush, which was embarrassing but reassuring and then my father started playing the "Moonlight Sonata" and then we heard a car's engine. Iris and I ran downstairs. My mother'd left the front door open and just slipped into Mr. Portman's car. She'd set a brown tweed suitcase on the front porch. I stood on the porch holding the suitcase, looking at the road. My father sat down in the rocker and pulled me onto his lap, which he'd stopped doing last year. He asked me if I thought my mother was coming back and I asked him, Do you think my mother is coming back? My father asked me if I had any other family on my mother's side, and I lay my head on his shoulder. I'd seen my father most Sundays and some Thursdays since I was a baby, and the whole rest of my family was my mother. I was friendly with Mr. Portman and his poodle and all of my teachers had taken an interest in me, and that was the sum of what you could call my family.

Iris opened the screen door and looked at me the way a cat looks at a dog.

We sat down to meat loaf and mashed potatoes and the third time Iris told me to get my elbows off the table, this isn't a boardinghouse, my father said, Behave yourself, Iris. She's your sister. Iris left the room and my father told me to improve my manners. You're not living in that dreadful town anymore and you're not Eva Logan anymore, he said. You're Eva Acton. We'll say you're my niece.

I was thirteen before I understood that my mother wasn't coming back to get me.

IRIS DIDN'T IGNORE ME for very long. She bossed me. She talked to me like Claudette Colbert talked to Louise Beavers in *Imitation of Life*, when she said, "We're in the same boat, Delilah," which showed that the white lady had no idea what the hell she was talking about, and of course Louise Beavers just sighed and made more pancakes.

Iris helped me navigate junior high. (A big, red-faced girl cornered me after two weeks and said, Who are you, anyway? Iris dropped a manicured hand on the girl's shoulder and said, Gussie, this is my cousin Eva Acton. Her mother has also passed away. And the girl said—and who can blame her—Jeez, what are you two, vampires? Don't walk past my house, is all I'm saying.)

I helped Iris prepare for her contests: elocution, rhetoric, dramatic readings, poetry readings, patriotic essays, and dance. Iris was a star. She had a lot of admirers at school, and some girls who didn't like her, and she didn't care. I pretended I didn't care either. I hung around the library and got A's and my real job, as I saw it, was to help Iris with her contests.

Things were not as nice at the house as they were the day my mother dropped me off. We didn't have fresh flowers anymore and everything was a little dusty. Iris and I cleaned our rooms and we were supposed to clean the parlor and the kitchen too, but we didn't. No one did. My father opened cans of salmon or tuna fish and dumped them on our plates, on top of a lettuce leaf. Sometimes he boiled six hot dogs with a can of beans and put a jar of mustard on the table.

I found Charlotte Acton's very clean copy of *Joy of Cooking* and I asked my father if I could use it. My father said that he wanted me to know that he and Iris would eat anything I deigned to make. Irma Rombauer said on the first page to begin by facing the stove. I put a bunch of parsley and a lemon in a chicken and put it in the oven for a couple of hours. We finished the chicken and my father thanked me.

On my thirteenth birthday, I made crepes, my father read "The Highwayman" aloud, and we had pineapple upside-down cake for dessert. Iris put the candles in and they both sang.

On New Year's Eve, our father went out and Iris and I drank gin and orange juice out of her mother's best cherry-blossom teacups.

"May the hinges of our friendship never grow rusty," Iris said. "I got that from Brigid, the maid. Before your time."

"Hear, hear," I said, and we hooked elbows and choked down the gin.

ONE NIGHT IN FEBRUARY, I woke up to Iris slapping me. It's true that Iris was not the sister I might have dreamed of. (Not that I'd ever dreamed of a sister at all. I dreamed of having a poodle, like Mr. Portman's, and for years I dreamed that my mother hired a private eye to find me and came crying to the doorstep of wherever I was living. I never let her in.) But Iris had never hit me before. I'd been in her house for more than a year and she'd never even set foot in my room. When Iris wanted to talk to me, she'd stand in the hallway and point and I'd go sit on her braided rug, next to her bed.

"You sneaky, thieving, filthy bitch." Her opal ring, the one from her mother, snagged in my hair, and we were stuck together, both of us crying. She yanked me out of bed and across the floor, until she got her hand loose. She threw everything I had, which wasn't much and most of it clothes she didn't want anymore, onto the floor. Oh, Christ, she said. I know it wasn't you. She lay down on the floor next to me, panting.

Iris said my father had stolen a hundred dollars she'd hidden under her mattress. He'd taken it all. It had happened one time before I'd come and then she moved her hiding place, but now he'd found it again. She had five bucks in her hand from tonight at the Pulaski Club, for one of her best speeches, "What Makes America Great?" and she was damned if Edgar was going to get it. She banged around my room, pulling all the books off my little bookshelf. She went into her room and came back with the big scissors we used to make some of her mother's clothes into things she could wear for her recitations. She cut the middle out of my copy of *Little Women*, page by page, from "Genius burns!" until almost the end, when Amy marries Laurie, which I hated anyway.

This is my Hollywood and Vine money, she said. That's my next stop. She put all of my books back nicely and she put my shoes and my clothes back in my closet. She brushed my hair. She folded up the cardigans that used to be hers, and my room and I looked better than usual.

It was amazing to me that Iris had made so much money from her contests. It was amazing to me that she thought it'd be smarter to keep her money in my room. I thought she was mistaken about my father stealing her money in the first place, but she wasn't. Iris was just being Iris. I don't think she was more observant or more intuitive than I was. I saw plenty, but I never knew what to make of it. Iris saw only what mattered to Iris, but she really paid attention, like a pilot watching for the flashing lights of the landing strip below. Her attention was the only thing standing between her and a terrible crash. Iris said I was more like someone with a crazy radio inside of me, and half the time the radio said things worth knowing and half the time it said things like, "Crops fail in Mississippi." Every time Iris won, from Valentine's Day to Memorial Day, she folded the money into her bra. My father waited up for her and every time, he'd ask her if she'd like him to hold on to her winnings. She always said, No, thanks, and went straight to her room, to throw him off. She was very polite about it.

THE DAY AFTER GRADUATION (me from eleventh grade, with the prizes in English literature and social studies, Iris from high school with a standing ovation and our father reciting "Gunga Din" at both places) Iris gave her speech about "The Fallen" for the Veterans of Foreign Wars. It brought down the house. Really, Iris said, I was great. And I was improvising. I said that she was better than great, that she was as good as Judy Garland, but prettier. Iris said that Judy Garland could cry at the drop of a hot dog and that she knew she had to work on that herself.

Iris did the Rotary and the Exchange Clubs and the American Association of University Women get-togethers from Windsor to Cincinnati, all summer long. She entered every contest within fifty miles, even if she had to hitch a ride and carry her dress clothes and shoes in a sack. She won them all. Sometimes, when Iris walked into the auditorium, you could hear the other girls sigh. She won a fifty-dollar bond from the Midwestern Carpenters Union for best speech by a boy or girl and she trounced the Italian girls with "Musetta's Waltz" at Casa Italia in Galesburg, where she also won in a walk for "Why I Am Proud to Be an American" at Temple Beth Israel, reciting as Iris Katz. The two of us did pretty well in the corn-shucking contests at the fairground. The corn wagons each held about twenty-five bushels and Iris and I did about sixty pounds together. We came in first in the Youth Group, Girls and we came in second for Youth Group, Seniors, right behind two boys who looked like they'd done nothing but shuck corn their whole lives. We pulled the silk off each other and had root-beer floats. The ten dollars went right into *Little Women*. Sometimes I opened the book just to look at Iris's money. At night, I sewed the sequins back on the outfit that was resting, or I basted the pleats on the sailor skirt or I put ribbon on her worn-out cuffs and waited for her to come home. The sequins came loose after every performance and my bed was always covered in them.

IT WAS THE DAY before Labor Day and hot and there were no contests anywhere and no party to get ready for. Iris and I walked down to Paradise Lake, the big pond at the edge of Windsor College. I dragged my feet to make dust devils. Iris took off her shoes and socks and put her feet in the water. She lit a cigarette and I lay down next to her. Iris took two beers out of her bag and I took out last week's *Screen* magazine.

"There's your heartthrob, Paulette Goddard," she said. "I can do what she does."

I thought Iris probably could. I kept watch for my father while Iris smoked, her eyes closed.

"Let's get wet," Iris said, and I ran back to my room to look for my bathing suit. My father was on his knees in my closet, one hand on my black party shoe.

"I thought you girls were down at the pond."

"I have to change," I said. "Iris's already down there. She brought her suit with her."

"Your sister plans ahead," he said. "You are more hey-nonny-nonny."

He tucked my shoe back into the closet and stood up, smiling a little absently, the way he did at breakfast, when I was talking while he was reading.

When I told Iris she said, "That sonofabitch. You have to do what I tell you."

I said I would, whatever it was.

IRIS AND I PRACTICED going up and down the honeysuckle trellis in the dark. My job was lookout. Iris packed her best outfits and makeup and the necessaries for me. She said we'd buy new clothes when we got to Hollywood. She said, What looks great in Windsor won't cut the mustard in Hollywood. Neither of us had really thought about new clothes for me, or where I'd go to school. I was going into twelfth grade, I looked eleven, and I'd skipped two grades already. If you asked either of us, we would have said that I needed more education like a cat needs more fur. Iris made sure we could carry our bags and purses without help; she said she could just picture the kind of wiseguys who would offer to give us a hand and that if she ever went to the ladies' room by herself for five minutes, I'd probably just hand over all our worldly possessions to some boob. I told Iris that no matter what my shortcomings, it'd still be better for her to have me along. I said I'd wear my glasses all the time and I'd wear the white anklets that I hated, and people would admire her like crazy for taking care of her sad-sack little sister. Men won't be asking you out all the time because they don't want to be saddled with me, I said. Old people will buy us meals.

It was exactly like I said. Iris threw her jacket over me when we got on the bus, and I slept for hours at a time, curled up with my head in Iris's lap, trying to look lovable and needy and keep my skirt tucked down over my knees, even when no one could see me. I hoped Iris was glad she hadn't left me in Ohio. It was sixty hours from Ohio to the Hollywood Plaza Hotel, which Iris found for us in the Windsor library's *Guide to California, 1941.*

WE WALKED FROM THE bus station to the Hollywood Plaza Hotel and Iris told me about hotels. She'd stayed at one in Chicago, with her mother. They'd gone for a weekend with her mother's sorority sisters and their daughters and they all had a big luncheon in the hotel, in a private dining room, with pink silk walls. They'd had shrimp cocktail and lobster Newburg and Shirley Temples. A doorman in a uniform had taken their suitcases. Iris and her mother called up for room service the first night. A man in a suit wheeled in a little table, full of china plates with silver domes. As Iris and her mother sat in pink armchairs, the man whisked away the domes and laid their napkins in their laps. The butter was shaped like rosebuds. After a chicken dinner and baked Alaska, Iris and her mother put on their nightgowns and robes, pulled back the curtains that the maid had closed, and watched the city lights.

The Hollywood Plaza was nothing like that hotel. It was a two-story concrete *u* shape, with chipped red roof tiles and the saddest little brown bush in the middle of the courtyard, where the weedy concrete paths split off to two short wings. An older lady stuck her head out of the window. Gruber, she said. First floor.

Iris finished eating her candy bar and wiped her hands on my plaid skirt. She spit into her handkerchief and wiped my face, which I absolutely hated. "Let's shake a leg," she said.

Letter from Iris

7 Queensberry Place
South Kensington, London
September 1946

Dear Eva,

I've been thinking about you. My show closed last night. I was good,
if not great, and a bunch of us working girls and a few sweet old
queens went out for Champagne and oysters. The war may be over,
but you can by no means get everything you want here (a decent
steak still requires more than I can manage). Happily, oysters from
the north are no problem. As I am tipping one down my throat, who
do I see but Mrs. Gruber, not in her housedress and broken loafers
but in a blue taffeta dress and matching pumps, holding a pink gin. I
almost choke. As it turns out, of course it's not Mrs. Gruber—who
might be dead by now and whom I can't imagine ever leaving the
Hollywood Plaza, let alone Hollywood. It was just Arlene
Harrington, a producer's wife, with a diamond brooch the size of the
Chrysler Building, and I did not say to her, My goodness, you look

like my long-suffering, extremely plain, possibly dead Jewish
landlady.

Do you ever think about Mrs. Gruber? As soon as she stuck her
head out the window you skittered up to her, breathless and shy,
the way you never actually were, and offered up the bus story
about our late papa and brave mama and our languishing midwestern fortune. I can't imagine she believed you but she liked
you and she didn't mind me. She took our money before she
handed me the key. One tiny room with two beds, a half-fridge
and a two-burner stovetop and the bathroom down the hall. I've
seen worse—so have you, I imagine—but back then, it was the
worst place I'd ever been. I knew we would have to struggle
when we got to Hollywood but I'd thought it would be a struggle like in the movies: five girls in a couple of rooms, everyone
putting their hair up in curlers and cleaning their faces with
Pond's and giggling when the hall phone rang and it was someone's sweetheart. There was no hall phone and the whole time
we were there, I never saw another person besides Mrs. Gruber. I
found a dead mouse in the corner when we moved in and when
you walked past, I gave it a little kick under the stove and I hope
you never saw it.

   Those three months were hard, but you were a trouper. You kept
the apartment nice and you made dinner on a dime. Do you
remember, I'd spill out my tips and we'd make piles, pennies, nickels,
dimes, quarters, and weren't we tickled when there was a half-dollar.
I still remember that night at The Derby. I did "You Are My
Sunshine" and I knew I'd nailed it. I could tell. You thought so too,
although you were such a little Doubting Thomas, you didn't want to
go for dinner until I was signed with MGM. And then Mr. Freed
called and you wore my old blue dress and I got a new one and a real
pair of heels and we went to Tubby's for steak. Six months, five
movies, three speaking parts: *Passing Through, Something Special,*

Evening Romance. (Do you remember the Nile-green silk nightie Harpo sent me? Still have it.)

Someone once said: God gave us memory, so we could have roses in December. Someone did not add, So we could have blizzards in June and food poisoning when there was nothing to eat.

Please write to me.

Iris

2

I May Be Wrong but I Think You're Wonderful

North Vine Street
Hollywood
January 4, 1942

Dear Dad,

Things are really changing around here.

THIS WAS AS FAR AS I GOT. I'D STARTED A DOZEN LETTERS TO HIM
and ripped them up and walked them to the corner trash can, while
our landlady watched. I don't know why I wrote at all. I didn't expect my father to rescue me. I didn't think I needed rescuing. It
seemed to me that if you had to have a mother who'd dropped you
off like a bag of dirty laundry and a father who was not above stealing from you (or your sister), you were pretty lucky to have that

same sister take you to Hollywood and wash your underpants with hers and share her sandwiches with you. Mrs. Gruber, our landlady and handyman, was excellent company for me when Iris was working. Mrs. Gruber condemned the fraudulence and the trickery of Hollywood but she knew, from personal experience, that some of that stuff was necessary for survival. She would say to me, Your sister will not be crushed by life, and we must admire that. Mrs. Gruber's own apartment was filled with duct tape and wrenches and half-pipes and wire coils. She wasn't much of a housekeeper. I thought she was a good cook, of the fried-egg-and-cheese-sandwich variety, which was what the two of us ate together every day. Mrs. Gruber had asked me about school and I told her the truth, that I loved the books and hated the kids, and she said she understood. She said she spoke four languages and had left school in the sixth grade. Where I come from, she said, six years is plenty. If you can read Turgenev, you're educated.

Mrs. Gruber loved President Roosevelt as much as my father and I did. She worried all the time that someone would assassinate him, until the warm day in December when the Japs bombed us at Pearl Harbor and President Roosevelt declared war on this date which will live in infamy. Mrs. Gruber and I sat still, and when it was over, we cried and read up on Japan in her encyclopedia. When we finished the article, Mrs. Gruber said, We must be glad. Mrs. Gruber said no one would hurt the president now because we needed him. She said she remembered when Republicans compared President Roosevelt to Hitler and to Stalin and to Mussolini. She said she used to see people wearing I HATE ELEANOR buttons walk past her on the sidewalk and she wanted to spit, she wanted to kill them. When she was a young person just arrived in this country, Mrs. Gruber said she would cry from rage and frustration, because she couldn't kill the people she wanted to kill. Sometimes, she said, men, who were often the people she wanted to kill, would misunderstand and try to comfort her.

So, we got no more of those hateful buttons, she said, but it's too bad—what's going to happen to Japanese people, here and in their own country? She said President Roosevelt was nobody's fool. Mrs. Gruber took her nap at two o'clock. I loosened her corset and shut her bedroom door. I read *First Love* or turned down the radio a little and listened to *Fibber McGee and Molly* or looked through Mrs. Gruber's old letters and photographs, which were mostly in another language. In one photograph, she's standing next to a short, wide man who has the Gruber nose and they're both wearing cowboy hats and chaps. Ah, she said when she woke up, we were getting ready for America.

IRIS GOT A CONTRACT. She had sung and shown her profile and her legs at every talent show in Hollywood and her screen test was a wow, she said, and now she was an MGM artist. She said that she'd be speaking lines before the month was out and she said we could move. I'd made Iris walk downstairs to Mrs. Gruber's to announce her contract and our improved circumstances and to celebrate with Mrs. Gruber's crème de menthe, which I knew we would have to do. Mrs. Gruber handed us each one of her three gold-stemmed liqueur glasses and sighed.

"You don't look happy for us," I said.

Iris finished her drink and examined her nails. She never had any trouble keeping her mouth shut. Plus, I could see she was done with the Hollywood Plaza. Mrs. Gruber had been tops, in her own frowzy, grumpy, foreign way but we were moving on to a nice one-bedroom at the Firenze Gardens on Sunset, and Greer Garson had said, Hello, dear, to Iris the second day on the set. The director had put Iris at the front of the crowd of girls walking down the sidewalk. Iris had pushed her hat forward a little and popped her collar, and after, the dresser said, Nice touch. For Iris, Mrs. Gruber was pretty much yesterday's egg sandwich.

Mrs. Gruber said that happiness was not something she aspired to, that when we had seen as much of the world as she had, we would know that what lies right behind the horseshit is not a prize pony, my dears, it's more horseshit. Iris smiled and stood up. She straightened her stockings and hugged Mrs. Gruber. Thanks for being so good to Eva, she said.

ONCE WE LEFT MRS. GRUBER's, I had no one to talk to. I made up sequels to the books I'd read: David Copperfield and his wife and three kids, living at the seaside; Jane Eyre and Mr. Rochester and their progressive boarding school for the blind.

It was still winter, but in Los Angeles the days seemed longer than at home. Iris was gone twelve hours a day. There were no old people and no children at the Firenze Gardens. I waited until three o'clock every day and went to the library, and after, I walked through the park with books on my hip, like a regular kid. I read through the lives of Joan of Arc (three versions, including George Bernard Shaw's, in which Joan seemed to me to be exactly the kind of bold, goofy girl you'd want for a best friend, voices or no voices) and Marie Curie, who seemed kind of crazy and noble in the same way. I read the biographies of Clara Barton and Florence Nightingale, and even in the books written for little girls, you could tell these women were so tough they'd take a bullet out of you with a fork and not blink.

The Firenze Gardens was much nicer than the old place, every apartment with its own toilet and a big and a little courtyard in the back, where people lay out on beach chairs. Once I lay in a beach chair too, in my shorts and blouse. I tied up my hair with a big bandanna and tried to look like a child actress, while I read about the great nurses. A real actress came over and said, firmly, that that was her chair and would I mind, and I avoided the big courtyard after that. Most of the people were up-and-coming actors, like Iris, working at Fox or MGM all day, with no interest in a flat-chested girl with glasses who wasn't in the business. I ate dinner whenever Iris got home, and sometimes she brought back sandwiches and cookies from the commissary, which sounded like heaven on earth to me. I would make Iris tell me everything that happened, on and off the set. For about a month, she went to makeup and costume in the morning and then she played a girl reading the newspaper in the bus station, then a girl in the bakery, handing out loaves of bread and making change, then a girl pushing a baby carriage down Main Street. After a few weeks, it was just as she said. The director from the bakery scene noticed how she did her hair ("Hair up, blouse down," Iris said) and he gave her a couple of lines, way ahead of the girls who'd started when she did. In the morning, I helped Iris pick out her outfit and talked about who she might see, and who might talk to her ("I don't just say, 'What's up, kiddo,'" Iris said. "I wait. And I'm helpful."), and she would practice saying her one line a bunch of different ways. Iris saw Miss Garson kiss Clark Gable. Harpo Marx patted Iris on the fanny and she ate cheeseburgers with pickles and relish ("Never any onions," she said, "because of the close-ups.") with women dressed like mermaids, who had to eat standing up, with their feet sticking out behind their tails, in sparkling green ballet slippers. Iris told me all the gossip that the hair stylists told her. The hairdressers told everybody everybody's business. Iris told me about Francisco Diego, who was the head of makeup and never gossiped about anyone. Francisco told Iris that she had not gone unnoticed and one time, after he did Lana Turner, he put Iris in his chair and did her face the same way. She had to wipe it off before she went back on set but everyone stood around her chair and Francisco gave her a brush and a jar of Ben Nye's special-blend face powder, for herself, for when she was shiny. When she had a day off, Iris put the Ben Nye powder on my face and a little red lipstick and the two of us went out for waffles. There was a high school about six blocks from Firenze Gardens and Iris and I steered clear.

I did miss Mrs. Gruber. I missed my father too. I refused to think about my mother, except when she showed up in my dreams, lost in the desert or dying by the side of a highway, every couple of nights. I kept writing to my father and tearing up the letters, even though I knew what he was and I knew he wasn't worrying about me. I knew he didn't give a tinker's dam—which is what he said all the time, and he'd explained that it wasn't a curse, it wasn't "damn," it was "dam," which was a very small piece of something you use before the soldering of tin takes place, and so I used the expression all the time and felt that I was cursing like crazy—but secretly. I wrote him once a month, and saved the pieces until my feelings passed, and then I threw the pieces away.

3

Dirty Butter

Iris wasn't sure what kind of party it was. Two women in matching pink silk jackets and long black dresses stepped in front of her, up the stairs to a big house. The doorman or butler was a very large Negro man, in a white satin suit from the eighteenth century and a white powdered wig tied with a black ribbon. He had two gold teeth and he acted like he was not just pleased, but completely delighted to see every woman who walked through the door. He held the door open for Iris and winked.

The women in front of Iris handed their jackets to another man in a white powdered wig and white satin suit and Iris followed them into the larger room. She kept her face still. This was a living room the way Cleveland Stadium was a baseball field. Three girls wearing white satin tap pants and white satin court shoes, and no tops, with pink ribbons around their necks and pink bows in their towering white wigs, walked past Iris, offering pigs in blankets and scallops wrapped in bacon. The girls had little mouche marks near their eyes and rouge on the tips of their nipples. Iris followed the two women in the long black dresses past big satin poufs on the floor and the pale-pink satin divans. ("My goodness, those things'll stain like crazy," a girl standing behind Iris said.)

Two tall men in white breeches held giant horns of fruit. Iris guessed they were blond under their white wigs, because their chests were smooth and their eyes were blue. They were barefoot. A woman in front of Iris took a grape and pinched one of the fruit holders' nipples until he winced a little. Iris gasped. "What a nice party," the woman said, and she reached under her dress and un-snapped her garters. The woman looked around and put her black pumps and her stockings and panties under one of the divans.

Four dwarves in white turbans and bright-pink vests and matching sultans' pants came through with jeweled hookahs. They sat down on the big poufs, and women crowded around them on the floor, smoking and laughing. Iris was pretty sure she heard Tallulah Bankhead laughing. A pale woman, beautiful like a silent movie star, with black-lined eyes, black spit curls, and a long, backless silver dress, pulled on Iris's hand. She asked Iris if she was new and who she'd come with. Iris told her that yesterday, when she was having her makeup done by Francisco Diego, Patsy Kelly's assistant came by handing out invitations, and she'd given Iris a thick white envelope. Patsy Kelly's assistant kissed Francisco and said, No invite for you, and he'd laughed. Patsy must have spotted you, the pale woman said now. Iris smiled. I'm Sylvia, the woman said. Iris, Iris said. Sylvia waved her hand and a dwarf wearing a white fez and no vest came by, carrying a tray of pink ladies. Sylvia handed one to Iris. Welcome to Paradise, sweetie pie, she said. Iris and Sylvia sat down on a divan.

A woman came up to them and leaned down to kiss Sylvia. Sylvia introduced Iris and the woman kissed Iris too. She trailed a feather along Iris's shoulders. Iris sat very still until the woman walked away. Another woman came by and took a sip of Iris's pink lady, watching Iris over the rim. She finished the drink in a swallow, and she and Sylvia walked away. Iris felt a hand pulling on her hem. A woman was sitting on the floor beside the divan, putting her hand under Iris's dress and sliding it up her thigh. She brushed her fingers over the inside of Iris's thighs and over her panties. Iris sat as still as she could. This was not the kind of party, like the ones in Dellie Bryson's finished basement back home, where you could have a little fun and slap someone and go back to having fun, on your own terms. Iris heard a woman scream in another room but it didn't sound like a person offended or injured, and the hand was still there, flicking in and out of Iris's panties. It was possible that in this big house, with all these beautiful women (and the ones who were not beautiful were built like goddesses, and the ones who were neither looked clever and powerful), there was someone whose hand Iris would actually welcome. Iris said, "Thank you," to the woman sitting on the floor, although that seemed ridiculous, and she walked into the next room, where the buffet was.

Food was lined up, from dinner to dessert—which was a pretty girl with whipped cream and strawberries, laid in thick waves, from her chest to her feet. Women in their slips and high heels, in their cocktail dresses with the backs partially unzipped, were filling their plates. A quartet played all the popular songs, and on the far side of the buffet the two women in long black dresses were doing a slow fox-trot. A brunette in a scarlet kimono and black silk pants was eating steadily from a plate piled with lobster tails. I love lobster tails, she said. I mean it—I think they are the greatest thing ever. Her voice was throaty and warm and she sounded like an American girl, but a little softer and sweeter at the edges. Rose Sawyer, she said, and instead of shaking hands, she gave Iris a lobster tail. Let's find a spot, Rose said, and they walked to where more women were dancing. She sat Iris down on an empty couch. What a crowd, Rose said. You stay here, beautiful girl. She came back with more lobster tails and an unsteady tower of oysters on the half shell, blinis with caviar piled like flapjacks, and two Champagne flutes tucked into her bodice.

Iris put her hand to her hair to fix it, and the dwarf with the white fez came by. Champagne? he said. Oh, please, Iris said. Rose looked at her. Well, here I am thinking, Look at this little bumpkin, and here you are, having your way with Armand and who knows what else. Shame on me, she said. Oyster? Iris opened her mouth.

This was not the kind of party where you said, Oh, I've never eaten oysters, or, Oh, gosh, they look wet and disgusting, which they really did. If oysters were the path to parties like these and beautiful, dazzling, dark Rose Sawyer, Iris thought she could toss back oysters like cold beer on a summer day. She managed two and chased them with Champagne.

"Aren't you a pro," Rose said.

"Not really," Iris said. "I'm from Ohio." There was no reason to lie to Rose.

"Of course you are," Rose said. "You are my beautiful American baby. Dance?"

Iris had never danced with another girl, except bumping around the room with Eva, to practice for a party or a show. Iris always made Eva lead so she could work on her steps, but then she had to put up with being led by Eva, who was fierce and wrong-footed on the dance floor and only came up to Iris's collarbone. Rose Sawyer was about an inch taller than Iris.

"Who should lead?" Rose said.

"I could," Iris said quietly.

"But you don't want to," Rose said, and she put a strong arm around Iris's waist. All Iris's dancing, her show routines, waltzing with her father, the senior-year parties with Harry Bledsoe and Jim Cummings, who were the best dancers in Windsor, faded away. She was dancing for the first time, right now, her face against Rose's smooth, powdered cheek. Breast to red silk breast, thigh to black silk thigh. They did two promenades and a slow twist, as if they'd been practicing, and Rose pulled Iris back to the divan. More Champagne appeared.

Look, Rose said. *Shmundies* on parade. Iris didn't know the word but she got the idea. There were naked women everywhere, drinking and eating and smoking and dancing, all naked and nearly naked. A chubby girl lay over the back of one of the divans, her head almost touching the floor. A woman sat underneath her, kissing her face and neck and cradling her head while another woman pulled the girl's legs over her shoulders and buried her face between them. All Iris could see was the girl's pearly, round stomach heaving, and the back of the other woman's head, her smooth platinum hair pulled up with combs shaped like tulips. A woman in a pale-pink chiffon toga walked by and waved to Rose. Her toga came only to her thighs and it was held together by one big ruby starburst at her shoulder. Her small breasts and her large, bushy and bright-orange triangle were not at all covered by the chiffon, just softened, as if by candlelight. A Negro girl, in silver lamé pumps, danced by herself, near the piano. She wore her hair up, rhinestones twinkling in her chignon and more rhinestones sparkling like dewdrops in her dark, curly pubic hair. Iris saw an unfortunate olive-skinned girl near the oysters, with dark hairs around her nipples and a thick cloud of darker hair growing up from the middle of her thighs, like moss climbing a tree and spreading up and across her stomach, almost to her navel. Iris thought the girl was going to feel terrible when no one picked her. Iris wondered if the girl would just eat a few oysters and head home to cry. A tiny blonde, with a big white bow in her hair and a pair of white Mary Janes on her little feet, skipped over and put her face between the dark girl's breasts.

"A lid for every pot," Rose said. She spilled a little of her Champagne on Iris's breast and licked it off, like a cat. The Champagne soaked Iris's bodice, down to her lap. To her *shmundie*.

Iris thought the top of her head would come off, shooting through the room like a cannonball of dense, rocketing pleasure. The room did not spin, the way it did when there was too much beer at a party back home. It opened like a flower, the walls falling back to contain the smoke and scent and *shmundies*—and another one appeared, an inch from Iris's Champagne flute, blond, dyed blue, and shaped like a heart. The walls yielded and began to melt from every kind of body heat. Even when Iris was much older, even after years of Champagne and cigarettes and silk underthings and a wonderfully varied and pleasing parade of *shmundies* in her own life, she could recall every single minute of the Hollywood orgy with Rose Sawyer.

WHEN SHE GOT HOME, damp but fully dressed, from garters to gloves, Iris lay on her bed, a few feet away from Eva's bed. Eva gave a little sniff, about the smokiness in Iris's clothes, and she turned toward Iris, ready to listen.

"I met a girl," Iris said. "I'm in love."

Iris thought it was to Evie's everlasting credit that all her little sister said was, That's nice.

Letter from Eva (Unsent)

Firenze Gardens
Hollywood
February 1, 1942

Dear Dad,

Things sure are changing fast around here. We moved into a really nice apartment, now that Iris is under contract at MGM. Mr. Arthur Freed signed her—after just one audition on Sunday night at The Derby (and another at the studio, later). We're pretty sure Iris is going to be a star. She has a new friend, Rose Sawyer, who you might have seen in the magazines. America's Sweetheart Rose is what they call her. Rose is showing Iris the ropes, as much as she can, and Iris has already gotten two speaking parts, one in *Evening Romance* (she gives Robert Taylor a cup of coffee) and one in *Something Special*. They didn't make her change anything for that movie, which says a lot. (The girls here change their noses and their names and their eyebrows and everything. One girl has to pad everywhere, front and back and even on the sides. A girl Iris works with had to pluck every hair out of her hairline because they said she had to make her forehead bigger.) Iris doesn't have to do much. They put some more red in her hair and Francisco Diego, the makeup man, who is really becoming a friend, told her to wear pink-orange lipsticks, not blue-red, because that's for real brunettes (like me, he said).

4

My Blue Heaven

ROSE RUBBED SUNTAN LOTION ALL OVER IRIS. SHE SQUINTED IN the sun and gave each toe a dab, and each ankle two whirls around and then up and down the shins. Inner thighs right to edge of the white bathing suit. It was a great choice for Iris, Rose thought. Iris stood out in that suit, like a diamond, and the suntan lotion made her fair skin and tiny blond hairs gleam pale gold all over. Rose always saw the best and prettiest parts of every woman she met and she'd point them out and tell how they could look even better. At the studio, she sometimes dressed girls she hardly knew, hat to shoes, just because it pleased her. She didn't have dolls, or friends, growing up.

Rose smeared cream on Iris's face ("Don't wind up with a red nose," she said. "Mr. Freed'll kill me.") and her chest, to the wired edge of the suit, slipping her fingers under the shoulder straps. She told Iris to turn over so she could do her back.

"Oh, this is nice," Rose said.

"Yes."

Rose could hear Iris breathing loudly in her ear. Rose massaged her shoulders, stroking her arms. She pulled gently on Iris's fingers. Rose had never had a massage but she'd heard two women talking about massages at the commissary. They said Hedy Lamarr had one every morning for her lymph nodes and that was why she looked so amazing. Everything drains out of you, said one of the women. Rose wanted to drain everything out of Iris. She splashed oil on the backs of Iris's legs and pulled Iris's legs apart. Everything that was draining now swelled up and came back in little waves, up one leg, then the other, rushing up Iris's spine and down her calves. Iris's feet flexed under Rose's hands. Iris buried her face in the beach blanket. Rose had brought everything she could think of: sandwiches, oranges, hard-boiled eggs, soda pop, a beach blanket, and the slick gold oil for Iris's skin. The sun had started to drop, just a little, still bright orange above the horizon, and the beach was still warm. A little girl with pigtails, wearing just her underpants, did a couple of cartwheels through the waves, and her parents gathered her up in a big towel. Rose and Iris watched the three little figures trudge to the parking lot, and then the beach was empty.

Rose lay back and untied the straps of her suit. Iris said nothing. Rose unrolled her suit top to below her breasts. No one's here, she said. Look.

Iris looked carefully in every direction. After the orgy, Iris told Rose that she'd hardly seen breasts until that night, and that they'd never mattered to her. She said that she'd seen her mother's a few times and she saw Eva's little nothings, a pair of fried eggs, all the time—how could she avoid it. Walking to the beach, Iris said to Rose, Love looks not with the eyes but with the mind, and that's how I look at you.

Rose kissed Iris's nipple. She pulled Iris's hair and kissed Iris on the forehead, on the cheek, on the lips, on her neck, behind the ear. Iris kissed her back. Rose pushed Iris off and stood up. Rose pulled down her bathing suit and stretched, the sun glowing behind her and through her legs.

"You too," she said.

Iris kicked off her suit and they clasped hands and ran into the water.

"Geronimo!" Iris yelled.

They swam like seals, and before it got too dark, they ran out of the water and dried each other off. Rose packed everything up and carried the basket on her head like an island woman.

PUDGE NEVER DROVE OVER the speed limit. It took him less than an hour to drive from Hollywood to Malibu and only ten minutes to park his car and trail the two girls walking from Tim's delicatessen to the beach. He walked north, close to the road, where no one on the beach would notice him. After twenty minutes, he had all the photos he needed. And he knew the pictures were perfect. You can't really go wrong with a C3 range finder and two beautiful naked girls cavorting on the beach, is what Pudge thought. He didn't have to do a thing to the pictures. The redhead's pretty mouth on the brunette's tit. The brunette and the redhead (not a real redhead, he noticed) taking off their suits and running into the water, their asses bouncing like happy peaches. Pudge did the negatives and the contact sheet and he didn't wait for the six prints to dry. He laid them on a couple of dish towels on his backseat and drove them over to Hedda Hopper's office. She made him spread the photos out on her secretary's desk and she put on her glasses. Hedda Hopper told her secretary to give him fifty dollars.

"Thank you, Mr. Rustin," the secretary said.

"They're good pictures," Pudge said. "You can see everything."

ROSE KNEW WHO HEDDA Hopper was. Hedda Hopper was not, in Rose's opinion, the worst person in the world or in America, or even just in Hollywood in 1942. Hedda Hopper hated FDR and she wrote some bad things about Jews that never came to much and she was famous for saying that the civil rights movement was bad for Negroes. Thirty-two million people read Hedda Hopper.

On Tuesday, Hedda Hopper called Rose at her bungalow and invited her to lunch the next day. Rose took off her red nail polish and put on pink. She wore an ivory gabardine suit and a hat and gloves. Hedda Hopper had iced tea and a Cobb salad. Rose wanted a club sandwich but she ordered the same thing. Hedda Hopper passed Rose the *Los Angeles Times*, folded in half. Inside the fold, there were three photographs of Rose and Iris at Malibu.

Rose said, "If that photographer had stayed another minute, he would have seen me slapping her face. I was never so upset in my life."

Hedda and Rose looked down at the photographs together. Hedda put the picture of Rose kissing Iris's breast on top of the pile. She sipped her iced tea and Rose sipped hers.

Rose said, "Honestly, Miss Hopper, I didn't even know girls like that existed. She asked me if I wanted to go the beach. I thought we were friends. I didn't know what to do."

Hedda Hopper didn't say a thing. She moved her hand so her rings caught the light. She ate a few bites of her salad.

Rose said, "I think girls like her are just ruining Hollywood. They're just not . . . not the right kind of people."

Hedda asked for a little more dressing.

Rose clasped her modest, pink hands in front of her.

"I admire all you've done to clean up Hollywood, Miss Hopper. I do. Just the other day—before this, this awful, mixed-up thing, I was saying to Buck, Buck Collins—my fiancé; did you know we're engaged? We've been keeping it a secret, not that we think someone like you would be interested in our little romance—I always say that everyone in the business has an obligation to support the right kind of movies, and the right kind of people."

Rose called her agent to say that she hoped that something

would come of her romantic feelings for Buck and then she took her phone off the hook and was sick for two days. On Thursday, Rose's picture was in the paper. It was a studio picture of her and Buck Collins, smiling at each other and holding the reins of his beautiful horse, Star. On Saturday, the studio drove her and Buck and a photographer to a bungalow not too far from the Malibu beach and on Sunday, there was a full-page spread of them in front of the bungalow and in front of St. Thomas the Apostle Episcopal Church. Rose held on to Buck's hand. On the drive back, Buck said, We really should have dinner. We will, Rose said. She put her head against his thick shoulder.

In the article, Hedda Hopper quoted Rose as saying, "When you're in love, why wait?" Miss Hopper wrote, in the next line, "Why indeed? These lovebirds are ready to bill and coo in their new nest and we wish them all the best!" In the middle of Monday's column, Miss Hopper wrote: "There is always going to be an unsavory element in Hollywood, women—we certainly can't call them ladies—of a certain stripe, who may lead young girls into the shady, dangerous parts of our little town. Do the right thing, Mr. Mayer."

Rose read every word. The head of public relations at MGM would call a man, who'd call a man, and by the time Iris got to the set on Tuesday, she'd be turned away at the gate. The guard would hand her a paper bag with some bobby pins, her slippers, and her silk robe inside it. Iris was about to turn nineteen, and her career was over. Rose had seen it happen to other girls.

She knew better than to call Iris. Iris would apply for all the waitress jobs at the places near the studio, where everyone knew her and liked her, and the manager would give her a free cup of coffee and a slice of pie and Iris would know what that meant. Iris would apply at Ohrbach's and Bullock's and the salesladies would take the application and put it on the pile, without a word.

———

FRANCISCO DIEGO THOUGHT OF HIMSELF AS AN ARTIST. HE'D been putting makeup on beautiful women and pretty girls and some very attractive men for thirty years. He'd done the deep-red Cupid's bow lips, the delicate pink flush, the Betty Boop eyes, and narrow, penciled-on eyebrows one hair thick, and then the full, slick brows and Maybelline lashes and the big, raspberry eat-me-now mouth. He'd worked with beet juice and talc when he'd had to and he'd drawn stockings on his own sisters' legs when they couldn't get nylons. He'd met Max Factor. The late Max Factor had showed him a very good time in a couple of Malibu bars, and, in return, Francisco showed the man a better way to sponge on foundation. He could still do the Charleston with the starlets and arm wrestle with the boys. He loved the girls who, when he cupped their little chins, pointy or round or square as a sugar cube but still charming, their eyes welled up with gratitude. He had made them beautiful when they had just been pretty. He made the rare beauties unforgettable. He had made a sweet stick of a farmgirl into an Egyptian princess and watched her glide onto the set, knowing she now knew who she was.

He loved the boys who would let him love them, who let him fill in the little ginger mustache or the lopsided brows or slip a pad onto the left shoulder and knew he had given them their careers. He even liked the ones whose vanity was legion. A tailor once called him after a big star came in to have the waist on his pants taken in. The star told everyone about his tailoring needs and the tailor told everyone that the problem was not the small waist, but some smallness a little farther south. To be that vain was to be as vulnerable as a woman, is what Francisco thought. He had solved the problem by looking like everyone's Mexican grandfather. He didn't color his hair, he didn't watch his weight. He smoked one cigar a day and he got his cigars from the same place Mr. Thalberg used to. He had seven gray smocks and seven pairs of black linen pants and seven pairs of black espadrilles and dressed up for no one. For some of the actors, coming into the makeup room after six months of unemployment or suspension or being lent out for some piece of crap at First National Pictures, finding Francisco in his trailer, cleaning his brushes, was like catching sight of the lighthouse after months at sea. He took some of the sailors home with him, gave them refuge in his quiet bungalow, in his big lap, in the home-cooked meal, and in his affection, which he made sure had not a single dot or thread of envy or competition in it.

HE'D NOTICED IRIS ACTON on her first day. There were always a dozen of her kind, even prettier, on the MGM lot on any day of the week, but she was quick and clever, and it was possible she could act. Someone had taught her good manners. She watched what everyone did and didn't do. She didn't throw fits. She didn't make eyes at the movie stars. She was never late. He suggested she take in the back of her dress about an inch right over the roundest part of her rear, and the next day, the girl had put a dart in every dress she had.

After Hedda Hopper kicked Iris's ass, and no one on the set would even say the girl's name, he drove over to the Firenze Gardens. He went because he was, as his younger sister liked to say, a big fat pile of pity for every stray dog and mangy cat that crossed his path. Iris was a starlet on the way up for about six months and now she was a stray dog, and she probably didn't even know it. He had a soft spot for young people. They had no idea what was coming and how much of it was just dumb luck. They thought every asset they had would last forever and that their flaws could be concealed under fabric or false names or foundation until the lights were turned off. If you can feel sorry for a starving mutt, Francisco thought, you should certainly feel sorry for the young and beautiful.

Iris opened the door, her eyes as red as cherries. She didn't invite him in.

"It's so nice of you to come by, Mr. Diego," the little sister said. She brought him a glass of water and put him in the only armchair.

"I came to invite you girls to dinner," Francisco said.

Iris flinched.

"That's very nice of you," the little girl said and she wiped her glasses on her skirt and settled them back on her square face. Iris looked out the window.

"Everyone likes my cooking," he said.

He made them dinner three Tuesdays in a row, waiting for Iris to tell him what he already knew, so he could help her make a fresh start somewhere. The little sister ate two plates of everything and told him the history of the X-ray and the iron lung. He told the girls about his childhood in the San Fernando Valley on Rancho El Escorpión and how it became the Platt dairy ranch, and how that was pretty much the history of Southern California. He told them about the one-room schoolhouse and riding home on his palomino and his discovery of his feelings for handsome ranch hands and his understanding, at nine, that when he finished high school, he would need to run, not walk, to a big city. He told them about his mother, who was every flashing-eyed, hot-tempered Mexican heroine in history, and her three quiet husbands, all of whom died after fathering Francisco and his two half-sisters—now in New York and prospering, he said, and about as Mexican as salami on rye. He gave Iris a hundred chances to tell the truth, and Iris lied through every meal. He admired the way she talked about leads and interviews. She lied when he handed around the empanadas and she lied right through to the butter-pecan ice cream. She lied while he played cards with the little sister. She lied patting him on the cheek, to say goodnight, and Francisco caught her hand. Next time, he said, it's your turn to have me over for dinner, just to be nice and, and afterward, we're playing To Tell the Truth.

5

If You Ain't Got the Do-Re-Mi

No one returned my sister's calls. I made Kraft macaroni and cheese most nights, with variations. Iris kept looking for work. I know your face, dear, one of the women at Ralphs Grocery told her. Everyone who read the newspapers and the movie magazines knew Iris's face now.

"It's like I've got the plague," Iris said. "It's like being Typhoid Mary."

I said, "You're not actually killing people."

The next morning, I went by Mrs. Gruber's to see if our old place was available and Mrs. Gruber asked why and I gave her the short version, as I understood it. Mrs. Gruber said, What a bitch, that Rose Sawyer. She said, *Azoy gait es,* that's how it goes. Which I'd heard her say so many times, I'd started to say it myself. Mrs. Gruber poured crème de menthe into the gold-stemmed glasses for the two of us, and she said, Of course, you girls can have the room, at your old rate. She said she'd throw people out if she had to, and we clinked glasses. Mrs. Gruber said, Fame and beauty. Believe me, *Alle ziben glicken.* It means it's not such a gift, *ketzele.* You stick with the big books and the little glasses.

BECAUSE OF THE SITUATION, I didn't want to go out. I didn't go to the park. I didn't go down to the Firenze Gardens courtyard. Iris didn't ask me to stay in with her. She didn't ask me for anything. She did her exercises and touched up her hair and washed our clothes in the sink. She began packing our things and she told me that we'd move in a week. You don't need to mention this to anyone, she said. Who would I tell, I said.

Iris did her vocal exercises every morning. She ironed all of our blouses and skirts in silence and generally acted like a person who lived alone, which I understood. I understood it and I tried to act like I didn't even notice and I hoped that Iris wasn't thinking about leaving, which I would have been. I wouldn't have hung around for everyone to crap on and I wouldn't have wanted a fourteen-year-old girl, who looked twelve and did absolutely nothing but cook food from a box and worry and read, for my sidekick. I sat in the armchair near the window and read *The Picture of Dorian Gray,* which I'd stolen from the library, and the old *Photoplay*s that were in the apartment when we got here. When I finished the magazines, I found a Bible. I skipped over the slow stuff, the begats and some of the more disgusting parts, but I liked the New Testament, which was full of green hills and blue skies and forgiveness and similes and metaphors. In the Old Testament, there were no metaphors—bushes actually burned, walls fell down, seas parted, and any rational person would dive for cover when that happened. In the Old Testament, God delivered people. He rescued them from their enemies, from the wicked, from famine, from the grave. He waltzed them out of Egypt with a mighty hand and a bag of crackers, and that's what I had in mind.

. . .

GOD'S BURNING SERAPH, OR someone, was leaning on the doorbell while Iris packed and Francisco and I were washing up, after I made us a hot-dog supper. After I dried the last plate, we'd play cards, and after that, I was pretty sure Francisco would stick ten dollars under Iris's pillow for the move to Mrs. Gruber's. The bell rang three times. We stood there. We were ducking the manager of the Firenze Gardens. We could pay him for last month or we could pay Mrs. Gruber for next month and have something left over. Mrs. Gruber and the Hollywood Plaza Hotel were our future. Francisco looked at Iris.

"It could be Rose," Iris said, and I cut in front of her to get to the door. It would not be Rose and I didn't want my sister to spend even one second thinking that it could be Rose Sawyer, whose name was now my private shorthand for true evil in the world. Rose Sawyer made my mother look *good.*

"Oh, little Evie," my father said. He had a white bakery box wrapped with red twine swinging from one finger, a bouquet of sunflowers crushed under his arm, and a suitcase in his other hand.

"Christ, what ugly flowers," Iris said.

FRANCISCO FOLDED THE DISH towel and moved over to the door. He put his hand on my shoulder. My father looked elegant and exhausted, and I thought that if Francisco couldn't beat the shit out of him, which he probably could, Iris and I could pile on.

Iris sat down on the couch. Francisco kept his hand on my shoulder. I came to and said, My father, Edgar Acton, our dear friend Francisco Diego, and I was very pleased with myself. They eyed each other. No one made claims. No one asked anyone for money. No one offered Edgar a cup of tea or a drink or leftover baked beans. No one told to him to come inside and no one told him to beat it.

My father cut the twine with his pocketknife and passed around the box of cookies, in silence. I ate six and Iris ate two. Francisco put his hand on his belly and declined. My father ate the rest of the cookies. At ten o'clock, I stretched out on the couch, next to my father. He made room for me and rested his hand on my shoulder. Iris closed her magazine and stood up.

"I'm beat. I'm going to bed." She unpacked one of the blankets and put it over me and went into her room.

My father said, "Terrific poise."

Francisco said, "Superb."

In the early morning, I found the two men heaped on the floor, sofa cushions under their heads. An empty Scotch bottle was next to the coffee table. I sat on the couch and watched my father and Francisco sleep, and when I started to cry, I stood up and got into bed with Iris.

"Never a dull," she said.

IN THE MORNING WE went to the diner for breakfast. The men walked ahead. My father ordered eggs and toast and he said that breakfast was on him. He said that he was very, very proud of Iris, that not a lot of girls could do what she had done. Iris said, Don't bother. You're too late. My father said that he was sorry he hadn't come sooner but that he had had to tie up his affairs in Ohio and my sister said, We're broke. Oke-bray. Francisco said that Iris was telling the truth. He said that no one even remotely connected with the movie business, not a restaurant, not a dress shop, nor a beauty parlor, was going to hire Iris after what happened. My father asked, What happened? and Francisco and I watched Iris, because it wasn't for us to say. I got caught kissing another girl, Iris said. Miserable, puritanical sonsofbitches, my father said, and he patted Iris's hand. That's all? he said to Francisco.

We walked back to the apartment and Iris whispered that Edgar would be gone soon. There's nothing for him here, she said. Francisco went down to the courtyard to make a call and the three of us looked at one another.

"What's your plan?" my father asked.

Iris said that we were moving back to Mrs. Gruber's and she'd keep looking for work. I said I'd do some dog-walking. My father raised his voice.

He said, "You've suffered an untoward blow from which you are not going to recover quickly. You can't pay the bills you have and you've no expectation of paying bills in the future. You must see that you will be taking advantage of poor Mrs. Gruber. One does not, if one can possibly help it, take advantage of one's true friends."

I started to ask exactly how that worked for him when Francisco came back into the room, beaming.

"What do you do for a living, Edgar?"

"Oh, poetry and prose. I was an English professor. Now retired."

"Must be nice," Francisco said. He turned to me and Iris.

"You know my sisters in New York," he said. "Encarnación and Beatriz. Carnie and Bea. The girls say they know about a job for Edgar, being a butler"—he didn't look at my father—"and for you, Iris, teaching some little kids. Let's say, a governess."

No one even looked my way.

My father shook Francisco's hand (There are no words, he said) and came back a few hours later with a 1938 Chevy station wagon. Nothing to it, he said. We packed up everything we owned and a few things the Firenze Gardens owned, and Francisco brought over his two suitcases and his huge makeup box. I ran down to Mrs. Gruber's and brought her back with her bottle of crème de menthe. We all took a swig. My father kissed her hand. Mrs. Gruber said, Good-bye, all of you. She kissed me on the lips and walked away.

"And, wheresoever thou move, good luck shall fling her old

shoe after. That's Tennyson," my father said and slid into the passenger seat.

Iris and I crammed into the backseat, with a Firenze Gardens lamp at our feet. Francisco winked at us. My father clapped his hands. It was, pretty much, his finest moment.

6

Every Day's a Holiday

WE SANG EVERY MORNING. MY FATHER SANG "IT'S COLD WITH-out Your Trousers" and "A Little Bit of Cucumber." Francisco and my father sang "Hey! Stop Kissin' My Sister," snapping their fingers, my father yelling, "You swine! To the pigpen!" Iris and I sang "You Must Have Been a Beautiful Baby" and "You Made Me Love You." We drank watery coffee. Iris and I ate fresh doughnuts, the oil still spitting in them (and bismarks and bear claws and brown bobbys, whatever the local pastry was, since, finally, briefly, my father was paying) and my father and Francisco ate ham and eggs and blue-plate specials. We all had our assignments. Francisco drove all day and haggled for gas every morning. Six nights, the four of us slept in a motel room. No one blinked at us. It was the war and people were showing up in all sorts of fatherless, motherless, husbandless combinations. Francisco got a bed, Iris and I got a bed, and my father took the floor and a bedspread. In Kansas, he taught my sister how to drive, just to pass the time. In Missouri,

Francisco turned straight north to Illinois. My father said he'd like
to see Missouri. Francisco said, Not with me, you won't. He said
Missouri was like the South and the only part of the South he
planned to ever drive through was South America.

I knew that we were near Windsor, Ohio, before I saw the
highway signs. There was the comforting flatness, the pleasant
brown haze, the solid houses that looked like the solid people. I
thought that we hadn't left much behind. I had my father and my
sister and Francisco, who seemed like a part, a better part, of our
little family. The only thing I missed was my nice room at my father's house and Mr. Portman's poodle. Iris poked me and said, Our
house isn't that far, and I poked her back. My father never said a
word. He read until dark and in the morning, we were out of Ohio
entirely.

My father read up on butlering. (Or buttling. Edgar and Francisco argued, many times, about what it was called. My father said
that whatever you called it, it came down to arse-licking and silver-
polishing.) My father had snagged an Emily Post book and my job
was to ask him questions, to try to stump him. (Mustaches on man-
servants or no? No. Who is the head of the table? The wife. Val-*et*
or val-*ay*? Val-*et*, which seemed awful to me. My father promised
me that he would refer to any valet he met as a "val-ay" and that he
would not wear a mustache—or a flower in his buttonhole, which
was quite a concern on page 297.) Occasionally, there was a memo-
rable line or warning in Emily Post, and Francisco would sing it
out, like opera. All through western Pennsylvania we warbled, "Better to be frumpy than vulgar." I bet if you walked up to my sister
today, she could quote you chapter and verse of Emily Post.

Iris's job was to become a governess in six days. According to
Emily Post, governesses were better educated than nannies and
better paid. They were supposed to teach the children something
until someone thought they were old enough for school. How old
are these kids, Iris asked, and how many are there? Francisco
shrugged. I think there are three, he said. I could be wrong. Iris said

she didn't know how to pretend to be a college graduate; she'd scraped through Windsor High and no one had expected her to do anything except star in all the shows and help out at ceremonies. My father said that she was officially twenty-one and a recent graduate of the Windsor College for Women. He said that he'd take care of her letters of reference. Iris said he should make her Phi Beta Kappa in that case, and my father sighed. He said he didn't care for her overreaching. My other job was to sum up Shakespeare's plays and recite crucial passages to Iris.

My father handed me a pile of the Little Blue Books on English literature and then, when he got tired of butler questions and Francisco stopped doing his Arthur Treacher imitations, my father made me quiz Iris on the Shakespearean plays and the sonnets. You don't have to actually know, he said. You only have to know more than they do. A little self-discipline is all that's required, he said. One hour before bedtime to stay ahead. Same for you, he said to me, but I didn't know who I'd be staying ahead of.

I peppered Iris every day. Who was Beatrice? Why was she so mean to Benedick? What was *The Tempest* about? When Iris stumbled, my father would roar whole soliloquies at her. When we couldn't stand it anymore, I'd read aloud from one of the other Little Blue Books.

The Little Blue Books were little marvels. *The Art of Reading. The Egypt of Yesterday. Balzac's Short Stories. A Guide to Aristotle.* My father said that there was not a single thing an educated man—even a gentleman—needed to know that was not in one of the thousand Little Blue Books. Emanuel Haldeman-Julius created the Little Blue Books, my father said, and he was a genius. A Jew and a socialist and a genius. He was not one of Nature's aristocrats. When you hear that phrase, my father said, they mean the peasant who did them a favor, some gobshite by the side of the road whom they'll never see again. Believe me, darling, they do not mean the Jewish gentleman whom we have just invited to join our country club. Later in my life, in fact, for my whole life, I've relied on the

Little Blue Books to finish my education, and I saw why my father loved them so.

Every night, in the motels, I wanted to take a shower and wash my hair, and I couldn't bring myself to do it while the other people sat in the next room, listening and waiting. My father and Francisco used the bathroom. My sister used it for hours and came out, her face lit up with cold cream, her hair in tight pin curls. I could sit there just long enough to pee.

On our last day on the road, I turned fifteen. I waited for someone to remember and then, finally, around the middle of the day, I said, during a lull, Oh, happy birthday to me, and Francisco pulled off the road. My father got out of the car and hugged me and my sister and Francisco kissed me on both cheeks and right in front of a Burma-Shave sign, they sang "Happy Birthday." My father said that we needed to celebrate and we stopped for lunch, which we usually didn't. We all had Coca-Colas and the house special, which was ham sandwiches on homemade bread. ("Those are our own pigs too," the waitress said. "Marvelous," my father said, and he winked at me.) My sister put her silver barrettes in my hair and Francisco went into his makeup box and gave me a tube of red lipstick. My father said he would wait until we got settled to give me my birthday present. I thought maybe they would spring for two rooms and dinner out but my father and Francisco went to an all-you-can-eat chicken dinner ("And they watch you like hawks," Francisco said) and lined their pockets with waxed paper and napkins. They came back to the room with chicken legs and drumsticks and squashed biscuits and Iris and I ate everything, sitting on the floor of the motel room. We slept the way we always did, and in the middle of the night, I woke up and saw my sister leaning next to Francisco on the floor. I tiptoed to the bathroom, bumping the wall as I went.

"We can see you, birthday girl," my sister said.

I said I didn't want to bother them.

"Oh, it's fine," Francisco, said. "We're just passing the time. Iris is in mourning for her life!"

"Not a chance," she said. "Turn me loose."

Iris cozied up to Francisco and my father slept on. I went back to bed.

OUR LITTLE PIECE OF Hollywood hadn't been much like Windsor, Ohio, but East Brooklyn was like Mars. I kept my head out of the window to get a good look at the apartment buildings fifteen stories high and the wide boulevards, the sidewalks crammed with people in a hurry, buses and trains running right through and across the city, restaurants with awnings, Chinese food and Greek food and Polish food and Italian food, nice houses like my father's in Ohio, and small shabby houses so close to their neighbors they could pass each other breakfast. It had a hat factory, now making helmets for the war, an elevator factory, and a carpet mill, women in pants going to and from the factories, and thousands of people minding their business, which was definitely not show business.

We walked up two flights of stairs, and Francisco's sisters threw themselves on him, like he was back home from the front. They hugged Iris and me in a friendly, mechanical way and they eyed my father.

Looking back, I forgive them everything. They took in a skinny fifteen-year-old girl with thick glasses and a stubborn look and her sister, a stuck-up former starlet (with a former starlet's ways) and a snooty Englishman with fancy manners and nothing else. They gave us beds and dinners and they stayed out of our way during the next days' fierce cram session for the job interviews in Great Neck. When Bea suggested that my sister would look more governess-y (whatever that was; we were six people who had never seen an actual governess or a home that required one) with less red and more mouse brown, the two of them went up to Bea's apartment and my sister came down looking like Olivia de Havilland. I'd never seen a husband, but I thought that both sisters were married, because they both wore wedding rings. Iris said I was an idiot and that anybody, including me and Francisco, could wear a wedding ring and no one could prove them a liar.

It's the great thing about the war, she said. Anyone can be anyone.

BEA ASKED ME IF I wanted to get out and walk around the neighborhood while Francisco and my father did the last round of Emily Post's rules for modern living and my sister recited Shakespeare and the forty-eight states. Carnie gave me twenty-five cents to go. I walked up to the corner store and bought some Turkish taffy. I walked around the block a few times and crossed the street, over toward some bigger houses and bigger trees and past a big brick building the size of a hospital or a high school. It had a big Jewish star over the tall white doors and Hebrew letters carved into the corners. The white wooden sign said PRIDE OF ISRAEL ORPHAN HOME. Around back, there was a playground, with a slide and a jungle gym and a teeter-totter. There were fifty kids playing in it. There were a bunch of boys around my age, playing baseball. The leather flapped when they hit the ball. It rolled toward me, and one of biggest boys, tall and blond, scooped it up and eyed me, then threw it to the pitcher.

"You ain't in school," he said. I walked to the corner of the building, leaned one hip against the brick, and ate my long roll of taffy. When the tall blond boy caught the ball again and tagged some short, fat kid out, he pushed back his hair and looked at me again. I took an actress pose, leg bent against the brick, arms folded. I put my glasses in my pocket and let him see my profile.

I walked past the orphanage every day. I kept my eyes open for the tall blond boy. These were my people: the abandoned, the unloved, the phenomenally unlucky. Plus, they were Jews, and my age, and their cousins were being slaughtered every day in Europe. Germans could even come and invade and slaughter them here in Brooklyn. They, like me, must be worrying all the time. Sometimes I liked thinking about how brave I would be if I were facing Germans. I knew that it was disgusting to contemplate my own bravery and, even worse, I knew the brave one would be Iris, flirting with the Nazis, stuffing passports into her bra to save the old people and the Jewish babies. I'd be sitting on some staircase somewhere, with my nose in a book, squeezing against the banister when they came running past me.

7

Dream a Little Dream of Me

WE WERE EARLY. WE STUDIED THE TORELLI HOUSE FROM ACROSS the road, parked underneath a big oak tree. There were no sidewalks and the driveways were so long, the houses were a quarter mile past the stone walls or wrought-iron fences. A big forsythia bush draped over Carnie's car. My father thought this was good camouflage.

He said, "Mediterranean style. Naturally, they're Italian. I like the red tile. I imagine there's a pool."

Iris said, "It's like Hollywood. They have houses like this all over Beverly Hills."

My father said, in his quoting voice, "'They were careless people . . . they smashed up things and creatures and then retreated back into their . . . vast carelessness.' *The Great Gatsby*." Iris got out of the car to smooth her skirt and I got out to help her.

Francisco said, "I don't think these people are careless. This money, they just got their hands on it. I tell you what, I bet Grandpa

Torelli was running a fruit stand when this guy was a baby. Look at it, the bushes, the driveway, that's a lotta Belgian block. Everything new."

My father said, "All those in favor of the new and costly?" and Iris and I lifted our hands. We looked and looked at the lovely house, from all angles, trying to see into the rooms. We studied the white balcony on the second floor and the long gray cobblestone drive winding through the sea of green lawn. Francisco sprayed my sister's hair again and told my father not to wear a hat, and after they disappeared up the driveway, Francisco and I sat back in the shade and played conquian until they came out.

Letter from Iris

27 Portobello Road
London
January 1947

Dear Evie,

I remember spying on the Torellis through the forsythia. Francisco
did my hair in a chignon.

I thought the Torellis were very sweet people from day one.
(Well, Joe Torelli looked like he'd been loading trucks all day. He
smelled like provolone and he did love his family. I think I've just
written everything I ever knew about Joe Torelli.) I remember the
twins, Catherine and Mary, and the little boy, Joey, and Baby Paulie.
The baby was known, pretty much, as The Baby, and he was not my
responsibility. You probably liked him.

Mrs. Torelli answered the door. Edgar introduced us and came
up with some impressive horseshit about his experience and mine,
and he offered dignified silences, and barely stifled sounds of
admiration for the furniture (big, dark) and the views (long, green).
He offered his letters of reference and mine and I did everything he

did, because my experience at MGM was not for naught. He put his hands behind his back and slid over to a big picture window. I slid right behind him. We watched the Long Island Sound while Mrs. Torelli read our letters (written in a beautiful script by Francisco) and then handed them back. Mrs. Torelli indicated that *butler* was maybe not the exact word one would use, that maybe the Torelli household did not really require someone of Edgar's stature. Edgar was unfazed. He was gracious. Majordomo, he suggested. One might, he said, do whatever driving is required for Mr. Torelli and the family, and serve on more formal occasions, and run the household in a general way. Mrs. Torelli was not a poker player. She beamed. She wondered what they would be calling him and Edgar said that Acton would suit him fine. Mrs. Torelli tried out Mr. Acton and Edgar stiffened, fractionally. Just Acton is suitable, madame, he said, and put his hands behind his back. She was wisely reprimanded, happily forgiven, in thrall. Between you and Edgar, I'm surprised I ever got on the stage at all. Mrs. Torelli was not formal, and not used to being rich, but she was European and she understood class differences, even if she'd been mostly on the short end of them before. This move to Great Neck was as much of a leap for them as it was for us.

We were never anything except Miss Iris and Mrs. Torelli. She'd gathered the children around her in an Old World tableau in the vast burgundy living room. The two girls were round and pretty in navy-and-white sailor dresses, with black curls heaped up and down, and Joey was a stick of dynamite in navy shorts and a vest and a half-done bow tie. The baby was in a domed lacy bassinette fit for a little prince.

"The girls start school next year," Mrs. Torelli said. "I'm not gonna bother with the kindy-garden. They'll start first grade. I want them to be . . . they need to be . . ."

"Prepared," I said.

She nodded and put her hands on Catherine's (or Mary's) hair. We were in business.

I felt bad that I was selling her this shoddy bill of goods, myself, when what she wanted was the best for her girls, so that the other girls, whose mamas were slim and blond-streaked and casual in their shirtwaists and Cadillacs, would play with her Cathy and her Mary. She walked us through the house and I made the same kinds of noises Edgar did. There was nothing not to like. The kitchen was fit for a good restaurant, with miles of marble and a pair of bright-yellow refrigerators. It was a sun shower. Very cheerful, madame, Edgar said, and Mrs. Torelli said whatever she said and I said nothing because Reenie walked in then, holding a bag of groceries, and I thought I would pass out.

Do you remember how she looked? I don't think we ever talked about how she looked. If she were a man, I would have said to you, What a dreamboat, what a catch. You don't say to your little sister, Oh my God, isn't the Torellis' cook the sexiest thing you've ever seen? Isn't she a dish, with that wide Madonna forehead and big eyes and big red mouth, everything wonderfully big and nothing too much? And even an infidel like me could see she had the soul of a saint, all goodness. No, you don't say that. And I know you didn't see in her what I saw.

I hope I never love anyone again.

Hoping to hear from you,

Iris

WE MOVED INTO THE CARRIAGE HOUSE, ALSO KNOWN AS OVER-the-garage. The Torellis had two cars, a black Cadillac and a black Lincoln. We settled ourselves and it wasn't really that different from back in Ohio, except the carriage-house living room was smaller, the food was better, and we didn't have a piano. I was apparently never going back to school, and I had a pool to swim in when the Torellis weren't home. My father and my sister went to work on the other side of the swimming pool every day and I stayed out of the way, or went to Brooklyn to visit Bea, Carnie, and Francisco, who now had three apartments in the same building, and Bea and Carnie still had invisible husbands. Four days a week, I got myself to East Brooklyn (I could do it in my sleep: bus to the subway station, train to Flushing, subway to Gates Avenue station, turn left, and walk six blocks to Bea and Carnie's salon, La Bella Donna). For fifty cents a day, I swept up hair, folded towels, cleaned the bathroom, and made lunch for Bea and Carnie and me. Bea was teaching me to shampoo (Don't pull, never rub, use your finger pads), and the ladies liked the feeling of my small hands. Carnie introduced me as a niece and they told everyone, like my father had told the Torellis, that I was a genius, and a little small for my age and had already graduated high school at just fifteen. No one asked why a genius like me was the maid-of-all-sorts at a beauty parlor. I took notes about hair color and eyebrows, matching lips and tips, and beauty parlor rules. (You do not say, Hey, your roots are showing. You say, Maybe a little touch-up. You don't say, Holy Mother of God, what happened to you? You say, Maybe Evie could get you a cuppa tea or a Coke.) I worked my way through Charles Dickens and I kept up with *Photoplay*. I walked past the orphanage, on my breaks, watching for the tall blond boy.

．．．

AND IRIS WAS WATCHING Reenie Heitmann. Irene Lombardo Heitmann. Iris sat in the Torelli kitchen for six months, pretending she wanted to learn all about roasting chicken and the many interesting things you could do with green beans. She brought the Torelli girls into the kitchen and made cookies with them. She sat at the big table in the middle of the kitchen, after dinner, and offered to dry dishes or bring Reenie a glass of water, and if I came in for a snack, Iris looked daggers at me and I moseyed along. I couldn't see it, about Reenie. She reminded me of one of the ladies on a spaghetti-sauce jar, but with a better figure. To give Iris room, I stayed in Brooklyn a couple of nights a week, on one of the couches, and once in a while, if Reenie went home early, Iris joined us. And talked about Reenie. She talked about what a special person Reenie was, and what a great cook, and what a beautiful soul, and her pretty eyes and the beauty mark right near her left eye and how unhappy Reenie was with her husband, Gus, because they couldn't have a baby, but how good she was to him. Bea and Carnie didn't say a word about any of it, and before it got too late, Francisco would walk us to the subway. One night he said, Iris, make a move, or move on. You've officially become the most boring dyke in America.

Iris listened to him. When Gus came for Reenie after dinner and the washing up, Iris told them that we were bored silly in the evenings and wanted to get away from the Torellis. (There was no reason to get away from the Torellis. They gave us platters of leftovers from Reenie's four-course dinners, they put a washing machine in our house, and they made Catherine and Mary go to bed at eight. In the three years we were there, they never expressed an opinion about what we did after hours and they never knocked on the carriage-house door in the evening.) Iris said to me, Gus is a nice guy—spend some time with him. Play cards.

Gus Heitmann was what people called a man's man. He fixed

things and he had a deep laugh. He looked like he could carry you out of a burning building and he looked like the kind of man who would go back in to get your poodle. And even though he made fun of his own looks (Gable's ears and Durante's nose, he said), I liked his face. He looked like a big, wise animal, the kind that saw you before you saw it. There were no card games Gus didn't play: poker, five-card stud, blackjack, gin, and even the crazy ones like Egyptian cut-ups and palace of my fathers, which I still don't understand, except that you can hold twelve cards at any given time. Reenie and Gus drove us to their house on the other side of the train station once a week, and the four of us sat around and played cards and had a couple of beers. When Reenie wanted a late dinner she didn't have to cook, Gus made spaghetti and meatballs, German-style, with cream and dill, and he did the dishes too. He was nice to Reenie, and always polite, but even I could see it wasn't love. I asked him once how they met. We were both at a dance in the city, he said. She didn't like the guy she was with, and I didn't like the girl, so in the middle of the dance, I said, Maybe we should switch part-ners. So we did. The other couple, they're married, three kids. Woulda been nice, he said.

When Reenie left the room, Iris's face fell. Gus's face didn't change a bit.

After a couple of beers, Reenie would start to talk about how she wished they could have babies, or that she was tired of cooking Italian all the time, and then she'd say her feet were killing her. Iris would give me the eye and we'd split up into Iris and Reenie, Eva and Gus. Reenie and my sister would go outside for a smoke in the backyard or Iris would take Reenie into the bedroom and rub her feet with almond oil and then Reenie would give Iris a manicure and peace would prevail. Once in a while, Reenie would call out, How you guys doing out there? and Gus and I would say, We're fine. Sometimes Gus said, Enjoy your hen party, but he said it in a nice way. Gus and I would play cards for another hour without them.

Gus asked me if I was interested in cars and I said I wasn't. He asked me if I was interested in people and I said that people were pretty much the only thing I was interested in, and he told me stories about his customers. Sometimes he'd say, What do you make of this one? And he'd tell me about the widow lady with the bad carburetor and her three sons and the fact that the third son wasn't hers—he was the child that her husband had with the lady's sister, before he passed away—and even so, that was the child the lady loved the best. He told me about the priest with the pale-blue Buick and the soft brakes and his girlfriend, who stood across the street from Gus's garage every Wednesday at four and always acted like they had run into each other by accident. I said I thought that maybe the man wasn't really a priest in that case, and Gus said, He's a man, kiddo. Gus asked me, Do you want me to tell you he wasn't a priest? I told him that I appreciated hearing the truth about things and Gus said that I shouldn't think that the truth was just ugly.

One time, he asked me how old I was and I said almost sixteen and Gus put his hands over his face. When he looked at me again he took my hand and turned it palm up. Let me tell your future, he said. You're not going to be working at the beauty parlor for the rest of your life. You're going to meet some boys here and there, and he pretended he was looking very closely at my palm, so his nose was almost touching it. I could feel his breath in the valley of my palm. Not as many as I'd expect, he said, but boys can only think with one head and we're slow learners, as a group, so no one should be surprised about that. And then you're going to meet a good guy, a stand-up guy, a guy who loves you like crazy, and you'll know he's the one.

I put my other hand palm up too, in case there was more. Yeah, he said, you'll know he's the one because when he says he'll do anything for you, he means it. Don't you fall for the big hearts and flowers, acting like it's the movies. Bunch of bullshit, he said. Pardon me. You want the guy who'll get your medicine in the middle of the night, even in a blizzard, even after twenty years. You want the guy who shows you every day, shoveling the walk, carrying your groceries, shows you how much he loves you. It's not about talking the talk, Eva. You must have met my father, I said.

On the drive back home, Iris would curl up in the backseat and Gus would ask me about Bea and Carnie and La Bella Donna (he said it was his favorite soap opera) and he'd talk to me about college. One time he said to Iris, You don't think Eva ought to be going to college, smart as she is? Iris said that it was entirely up to me.

THE LAST NIGHT WE were over, Reenie and Iris had been in the backyard for a long time. Gus laid down another winning hand and told me I was down a thousand points. He asked me if I wanted a beer and I smiled. He said, They treat you like a grown-up. Why should you get all the grief and none of the fun? We split a beer and then he yawned and asked me to get Iris, so he could drive us home.

I went out to the backyard. It was a perfect spring night. The air had just gotten warm and I could stand outside in just my shirt and blue jeans and feel the breeze and the damp grass. Even in the dark, things were green, from top to bottom. I couldn't see Iris and Reenie and I didn't want to yell because the people next door had a baby. I crept around the edge of the yard, near the boxwood, like I had when I was a kid, playing Indians. I could see their bodies heaped together in the darkest corner of the yard. The streetlamp touched Reenie's white hair ribbon on the grass. It touched Iris's white socks and Reenie's white bra. Reenie must have seen me creeping, because she screamed and then she muffled it.

"Hey," Iris said. "Don't trip over us."

"Okay," I said. "Gus wants to take us home. He's beat."

Iris lay down in the backseat. She said her stomach was killing her. Gus and I talked about baseball, which was more interesting to both of us than other sports, and he told me that he'd seen the Girls Professional Baseball League and it was our loss that they'd fold up when the men came home. I looked at Gus's big wrists on the steering wheel and at his dirty nails. He smoked while we talked about the war, about his bad leg, about my going to college. He said that his bad leg was no one's fault but that if I didn't go to college, he'd hold it against my father and my sister. I said that it was up to me, and he said he'd heard that opinion and he admired my attitude but that I was mistaken. I turned around to look at Iris when we went through the lights on Middle Neck Road. She lay with her arms around herself, crumpled on her side. She looked at me and she held a finger up to her lips. She was crying so hard, her whole shirt was wet. She had Reenie's hair ribbon tight in her hand.

Letter from Iris (Unsent)

South Ken, London
England
March 1947

Dear Eva,

You would think it'd be hard to get a man plucked out of his everyday life on Long Island and shipped off somewhere. You'd think it'd at least be awkward. You had read that whole article about Ezio Pinza aloud at breakfast. Famous opera singer, basso cantante, and before this, famous only for his voice and for his first wife having sued a soprano at the Metropolitan Opera House for alienation of affection. According to you and *Time* magazine, he married another American girl (not the alienator of affection) and they had a daughter. The article said he was released after two months at Ellis Island and that he went back to singing opera right away. That's what stuck with me. The man didn't spend a day in jail. He wasn't even arrested. He just went away for two months. Do you know, at the end of the war, Ezio Pinza sang "The Star-Spangled Banner" for General Patton and

General Doolittle and the man who had ordered his arrest? This, also courtesy of *Time* magazine.

I was so scared, I thought I'd vomit on the bus. I walked past the railroad station, to put enough distance between it and me. I always ran into people I knew at that end of town. I had a handful of dimes in my bag. I put a handkerchief over the receiver. A man answered and I thought that they must all sound like J. Edgar Hoover, with his high, flat voice. I couldn't remember the agent's name five minutes after I hung up. I'd made up a character for the phone call. I was a single lady from Hartford, Connecticut, visiting friends in Great Neck. I worked in a bank. I told the man that Gus Heitmann might be, maybe, a German spy. I said that I knew that everyone had to do their part in the war effort. My voice shook like I was on a train. I said I hoped I was doing the right thing. The man did not say, You lying bitch. He said that I was doing my duty. He repeated Gus's name and the address of his repair shop and he thanked me, twice. I was sweating like a whore in church, not surprisingly, and I wiped my face with my mother's blue lace hankie and I threw it in the trash can at the train station.

I knew that if there was a God, I would be punished for this in unimaginable ways. My life would be like one of those medieval paintings, where misshapen devils climb out of the brain and across the body, with their tiny black pitchforks and sharp, silvery tails. I can only say I was unprepared. Love for Reenie had knocked all the sense out of me. What I'd had with Rose was lust (with great lighting and some terrific moments, but still, just lust) and what I felt for Reenie was a million times that. I was dancing in the street and singing in the shower. I'd walk into the empty kitchen, my heart hammering away, and find a note in Reenie's schoolgirl script, saying that she'd gone home early, or driven to the grocery store with Edgar, and I'd stumble down to the water and cry like I had two weeks to live. I tried on three or four outfits every morning, before I walked over to the Torellis'. I applied all the face masques Francisco recommended, sometimes three at a time, and used salt scrubs on my arms and did the exercises I used to do in Hollywood. I sang Edgar's old songs while I did them, because I knew that one of these days, Reenie would see me and love me and turn her life upside down for me.

I didn't know a thing. I watched Reenie with Gus and their kindnesses to each other and their mild companionship and sometimes I despised them both and mostly I just despised myself. I worried when Gus made Reenie laugh and the night he tied one of her scarves over his head and did his Judy Canova imitation, I hoped Reenie thought he was a fool. You laughed your head off. I worried when he made Reenie tea and patted her shoulder as he walked by. I had in mind a fight to the death with a depraved brute. He would have strength on his side and I would have true love on mine and I would take him down like David took Goliath. It was terrible that Gus wasn't a brute and after a while, I decided that was his strategy. His cleverness was to appear kind and decent, so she would never see how he stood, like the Rockies, between us. I made you distract Gus, so I could get close enough to profess my love in their dark backyard. I tried to be cleverer. I flirted with Gus and suggested that a man with his skills and wit could move out into the wider world. I made fond, damning remarks about Reenie, that she probably couldn't keep up with a sharp customer like himself, and Gus said only, Don't kid a kidder. Do you remember one morning, you got up early and you made me banana-stuffed French toast and you asked me if I was all right? I said that I was fine and you took my hand and you said that if I was dying, I should tell you, because there was an awful lot to do, if that was the case. I did eat that French toast. I hope that I did.

I found Reenie in the kitchen and, having failed at strategy and seduction, I sat on the floor and put my arms around her knees, until she pulled me up to her. (What can I say? I wasn't a man, so I couldn't go down on one knee and I did think that some abject pose was right for the occasion. I certainly felt abject.) I cried on Reenie's leg and then on her shoulder and I tried to give her a pearl ring from Lutzmann's on Madison Avenue. Reenie put the box back in my pocket. She backed away from me. I begged Reenie to open the box, and when she finally did, those beautiful brown eyes filled with tears. "I'm not stupid," she said. "I know what this means." I put the pearl ring on her finger and she took it off. She wiped her eyes and she stood there, sensible and kind, as if she hadn't cried. "What would I say? Come on, Iris, you can't give me a ring." I took it back to Lutzmann's and gave Reenie the silent treatment for two weeks.

I had failed, worse than in Hollywood. On the other hand, she had cried over me.

Every day, I threatened her with the loneliness and heartbreak of what we could have had, and I'm sorry to say that I made some noise about doing away with myself (I can see the look of disgust and disbelief on your face), at which point poor Reenie said she'd go work elsewhere. I made Reenie cry sometimes, for that dark pleasure, like pressing a wound, and then I begged forgiveness, which I got. ("I know," Reenie said. "It's okay. I know why.") Edgar would pass me at the Torellis' and roll his eyes.

Finally, finally, we got there. I came up close to her, the way I did whenever I had a chance. I pressed my lips to the back of her neck, where the black curls were pinned up, and this time she turned toward me, not away, and the door that had been between us swung open. The Torellis were all at Mass and we took advantage of the guest room. That became our time. During the week, we whispered to each other in the kitchen and in the rose garden and she said that she loved me. She said she loved me with all her heart, that when we held each other she thought at last, her life was beginning. She said she couldn't turn her back on her wedding vows and her hope that a baby would come. She said she had made a promise, not just to Gus, but to God. I kissed her because she never said that she loved Gus. She said that she would love me, just me, until she died. I said I understood, because I did. I said that I would always love her, and I would always be there for her. We both lay on the floor of the guest room, crying like broken things.

After I made the phone call, I hung around the train station for a while and then I started walking home, waiting for one of the Middle Neck Road buses. It was a warm night, for May, and people were glad that summer was coming. Everyone had their front doors open. Men were smoking and drinking coffee and reading the paper, in their shirtsleeves. Women were doing the dishes, wearing their aprons. Everyone had the radio on.

Iris

Letter from Gus

U.S.A.
May 20, 1943

Dear Eva, my Yankee Doodle pal,

On May 4, while I was checking out Millie Brown's carburetor, after I gave Sticky the afternoon off because things were slow, who should come into the shop but three guys with ties and jackets and machine guns. Well, kiddo, I didn't know whether to shit or go blind. They tore up the shop, including the girlie magazines (what can I say— Reenie asked me to keep that crap out of the house, so I did), and they read through all my bills and threw everything out of my desk. They banged around my tools for a little while, like my crescent wrench was going to turn into a Nazi flame-thrower, and I sat there, on the bench, hands cuffed.

I don't remember exactly what I said, but you could call it inflammatory. It got me nowhere. I changed my tune. I said, How can I help you, fellas? And the biggest guy hit me in the gut and ground my face in the floor pretty good before he put me back on the bench. That was that.

Why aren't you in the military? the little one said.

Possibly because of this, I said, and I pulled my pants leg up to the knee and showed them my left leg. I said I'd been limping since I could walk. I said that being sucker-punched just now hadn't helped but he shouldn't blame himself—the limp was really the fault of poliomyelitis and possibly my mother, who was pretty lax about hygiene. Surprising in a German, I said.

Next thing I know, I'm in a car with two of the bastards. They drive all day and night, in shifts. Wherever we are, it's goddamn flat. After that, I'm in a cell for two days. No one says nothing. The hearing is four new guys, dressed like the ones who dragged me out of the shop, but not a weapon in sight. There are two American flags, in case you thought that somehow you had left the U.S.A., and a big sign behind them that says United States Department of Justice. I tell you what, you ever walk into a room with a sign like that, you run right out and keep on going.

Me and the four guys palaver. They say, What is your relationship with Standard Oil, and I say I worked for them for a year, 1934. They say, How did you come up with the capital to open your own shop? I tell them I bought out Gibby Schmidt. That's like a fart in church, another German name—now it's a goddamn conspiracy. How about your wife? one of the assholes says. I tell them Reenie is Italian-American on her father's side and her late mother was Irish and now we're doubling down on Reenie's gene pool. I mention her father was an American war hero in World War I and her brother is a priest. I say that her father's Medal of Honor should balance out her innately untrustworthy Italianness. We go back to why I sometimes work at night and what kind of shortwave radio do I have. They won't say who dropped the dime on me. They tell me that decent Americans everywhere are keeping their eyes and ears open for threats to America, especially threats within our own borders.

I tell them that if they think a fat, gimpy mechanic with a German last name is a threat to America, I am more worried about this country than I was when the Japs hit us. (Later, I'll tell you about the Japs at this camp. They garden and the men wrestle. You haven't really lived until you've seen some little Nip drop-kick a two-hundred-pound Bavarian and leave him facedown on the canvas. We do have some times here.)

The Alien Enemies Act of 1798 turns out to be important. I should have paid attention in school. You may ask yourself, Exactly who were our enemies in 1798 beside a bunch of Indians, but I don't say a word. The old guy at the table tells me that under the terms of the Enemy Alien Control Program, they can offer me two choices: stay in beautiful Fort Lincoln in Bismarck, North Dakota, or be repatriated to Germany. Back to Germany, one guy keeps saying. I say to him, I've never been to Germany. My father didn't speak German at home because he wanted us to be real Americans. I tell them the German I know—"Shut up, the kids are listening" and "I'm going give you an ass-kicking you won't forget." The old guy shakes his head slightly, like it's too bad I'm such a fucking ignoramus but the big man in the middle brings his hand down like a gavel and says, Mr. Heitmann, at this time, you will be residing in Fort Lincoln, enjoying the hospitality of Uncle Sam, while we keep America safe.

You know me. I'm capable of brooding. I've spent a lot of time thinking about who did this to me and what I'm going to do to him when I get out. I think I got shopped by Louis Ringer, an auto mechanic at the edge of town. The little wall-eyed bastard never liked me. It happened I took a couple of customers away from him, probably because his shop was such a goddamn pigsty. At night, I picture Louis Ringer, in bed with his big, soft-looking wife, and I see Mary Ringer in a pink nightgown with a ruffle at the neck, her tits showing through and bright-red lipstick on her doll mouth. I drag Ringer out of bed and I punch him in the jaw. He goes down but I pull him back up. Then I drive one right into his gut. Mary's kneeling on the bed, opening and closing her red mouth like a rainbow trout. He gets in one punch and that's all I need. I finish him off. I leave him on the bedroom floor, his wife crying and begging me not to kill her too. There's more, but you were always a girl with some imagination so I'll leave it there.

I hope life at the Cut 'N' Curl is going okay. Say hi to those hot tamales, the Diego girls. If you get this and you see Reenie, tell her I'm sorry. Tell her I wish her luck.

Gus Heitmann

Part Two

1943–1945

8

You're Not the Only Oyster in the Stew

CLARA WILLIAMS HATED THE TIME BETWEEN SETS AT THE NITE Cap. The whole half hour was sweating and setting and refinishing her skin. Her vitiligo never took a night off. Clara drank one big glass of water and one hot tea with honey in the nasty dressing room and she sat at the bar for only two minutes before she went back onstage. She did notice that when she made herself up as white, she was more conservative all over. Light-pink lipstick, pearl earrings, a-tisket, a-tasket. She hadn't gotten as many chances lately. Since the war started, people looked at one another more carefully. Negro and white people looked twice at dark-skinned white people, at Chinese and Japanese people, at people with accents. Before, if you said you were white, by God, people took you for white, and if you said you were Negro, people certainly took you for Negro. Clara thought that it might be pushing her luck to impersonate a white woman too often, although she had an itch, every now and then, to bust out her Doris Day and she had the tight pink sheath and white gloves to do it. In Reno, she'd done Doris Day for about a week, with a white quartet behind her.

That Reno trumpeter wasn't really a man. He was a tubby, sweet-faced little guy and no one mentioned to his wife or three sons—and Clara had wondered about those three strapping boys—that he was really a tubby, sweet-faced gal who could swing all night on the trumpet and had decided that her chances were better if she wasn't a woman. Sometimes, in spite or annoyance, when the band stayed half a beat behind her all night, Clara'd imagine swiping a lipstick across the trumpeter's round face or pulling his pompadour forward into a pixie cut. It would take only one gesture and she would never be he again.

Sometimes, when Clara filled in her face, connecting all the blank seas and inlets of the vitiligo to the smaller and smaller brown islands of her real color, it was hard not to feel that she was impersonating a Negro. The dark, arched eyebrows. Ruby-red lipstick shaping her pale, streaky mouth. Her nose, which was sometimes a contouring challenge when she was white, was a comfort. It was a Negro nose. When she was Negro, she sometimes put a little beige cream down the bridge to broaden it, in case someone failed to notice. Clara understood that race was more than a matter of appearance, but it was also a matter of appearance. Like Rudolph Valentino's nose. How did people not notice that schnoz everywhere? Clara saw that nose on fancy white men from Philly to Boston. She saw it on half the Italians in New York, every other Tony and Guido. She saw it on almost every handsome colored flying ace, in newsreel after newsreel. That bony arch and hawklike tip. How did people not see that it was the same nose? It was probably the same dick too. Clara knew a girl who had met Errol Flynn in Hollywood and she said it was no longer than your forefinger but as wide around as a biscuit, and Clara had heard the same was true of many Italian men and of the Tuskegee Airmen too.

Pond Road
Great Neck, New York
18 June 1943

Dear Miss Williams,

I am writing to you after an evening at the Nite Cap. I am the
chap who bought you a stinger between sets, but you have so
many admirers that that description may not help my cause. Your
performance tonight was splendid. I think that Lena Horne
herself would have applauded your "Stormy Weather," and your
version of "There Are Such Things" was truly beautiful. I will be
at the Nite Cap next Sunday. If I may, I will again buy you a drink
between sets.

Yours, in admiration,
Edgar V. Acton

Edgar wrote the note ten times. He didn't write, I am the white
man who bought you a drink, because it was possible that there'd
been other white men at other shows, although he hadn't seen any.
Edgar felt that the letter had more Jeeves-and-the-country-house
than he'd intended. He'd never used the word "chap" in his life, but
he was an English butler in a Negro nightclub and he thought that
foolishness might be his trump card.

HE HADN'T THOUGHT ABOUT how it would be inside the Nite Cap.
He had a free Saturday night, which he rarely did. (Saturday night,
the Torellis usually had twenty or thirty relatives over for dinner
and Edgar tended bar, served the priests, supervised the buffet, and
drove the resentful cousins he had not been able to keep out of Joe
Torelli's Scotch back to the Bronx. "From whence they come," Joe
Torelli said.) The Irish bars of Great Neck were rough and charm-

less, and Manhattan was a big pond, after Ohio. He wanted a place he could listen to jazz, where no one knew him and no one wanted to. Inside the Nite Cap, Edgar was not invisible. He shone, and not in a good way. The bouncer was Negro, the tall, creamy coat-check girl was Negro, the broad-shouldered, bald-headed bartender and all of the men and women around him were Negro. At Windsor College, he was often the only man in a room full of women and it never bothered him. To be the sole man was not unpleasant; sometimes it was charming. Nice women rarely turn on a man they know, and even if they do, they're women; their weapons are words. The Nite Cap was filled with tired cleaning ladies and baby nurses who worked hard for their living, and a few working girls and men with nicked, thick hands and cut faces; laborers, cooks, truck drivers, fighters. After Edgar had sat ten minutes at a rickety table, a waiter brought him a gin. He let go of Edgar's glass reluctantly, not opening his hand until Edgar gave him five dollars and told him to keep it. The waiter moved a little more briskly, as if service could now be expected. Edgar's first impulse was appeasement. If he knew what would make these men smile, and these women forgive him, he would offer it. He would soft-shoe across the small stage, make fun of his own accent and pallor, demonstrating his essential harmlessness, so he could stay in the Nite Cap, and not get hurt.

Pond Road
Great Neck, New York
1 July 1943

Dear Miss Williams,

It was a pleasure to see you again. I fear that I may have interrupted your conversation with your colleague the drummer, and I apologize. I'm delighted that you remembered encountering me outside the Silver Star Diner. I certainly remembered you. Would you consider joining me for a late supper at Gino's this coming Wednesday evening? I understand that Mr. Circiello is quite a jazz fan and I'm sure he would be honored to have you at his restaurant.

Yours,
Edgar V. Acton

There would be difficulties in courting Clara. He was almost twenty years older. He was white. He wasn't rich. He wasn't certain that even by the standards of a Negro jazz singer on Long Island, he qualified as good enough. He gave a lot of thought to which places would be welcoming to them as a couple and he felt that Greenwich Village was his first choice. From what he'd heard from Earl, the bartender at the Nite Cap, there were a few nightclubs in Harlem that would be a distant second.

Clara, having been born and raised in America, didn't give it another thought.

"Do you have your own home?" she said.

THEY WALKED DOWN HUDSON Street. It was a cool night and Clara pulled her shawl around her. Dinner at Gino's was what Edgar had hoped for. The food covered the plate, the tomato sauce was mildly spicy and thick, and one could imagine a warm-hearted, chubby woman, who was not like Edgar's mother and probably not like Clara's, stirring a pot in the kitchen, humming some Neapolitan tune. Mr. Circiello didn't welcome them with any special attention but he didn't raise an eyebrow and he gave them a good table and he did say, Good night, *signorina*, good night, *signore*. It was a tremendous success. They had been seen and served and thanked. Edgar drove them back to the house Clara shared, to the room she rented from a cousin of the drummer. They sat in the car. Edgar put the radio on.

"Like a couple of kids," Clara said.

"You, of course, are a spring flower," Edgar said. "I should be bringing you to The Ritz."

Clara sat still.

"You think if The Ritz was handy, I'd let you take me there?" she said.

Edgar's sympathies were all with Clara.

"Clara, I'm too old for you and I'm not rich. I want to take you out every evening that we are both free and I want us to go to the best clubs and eat dinner at places like Gino's, which I can hardly afford on a butler's salary. If I follow my impulses in this matter, I will have to steal the Torelli silver, pawn it at that place we passed tonight, and, unless I am very clever, spend the rest of my quiet life in the state penitentiary. Breaking rocks."

"I see that," Clara said. "I see you on the chain gang. I see you singing 'In the Jailhouse Now' from can to can't."

"I do know 'In the Jailhouse Now,'" Edgar said.

"You do not."

"I may struggle with the tune," he said, and he sang, not badly and in no accent but his own.

He's in the jailhouse now. He's in the jailhouse now.
I told him once or twice quit playin' cards and shootin' dice.
He's in the jailhouse now.

Clara smiled and shook her head.

Edgar said, "Oh, I know. I cannot impress you."

He leaned forward and kissed Clara on her neck and her cheek.

He wanted to lick off her makeup, to kiss the perfect, bare Clara underneath.

CLARA THOUGHT THAT IT would be good if he did; it would be cool water on her blistered heart if he did.

9

Pennies from Heaven

THE TORELLIS WERE MY FAIRY-TALE FAMILY. I BELIEVED THAT their house was so much nicer and their family so much sturdier because they were better people than we were. My mother and I had been the worst people, so we'd had the worst home. We had had the worn-out first floor of a worn-out two-family and I saw, the day I was left on my father's porch, that everything we owned had been shabby and just cheap to begin with, including my clothes and my person. At my father's house, which was really Iris's mother's house, things were lovely. My father didn't really qualify as a lovely person but he did rescue us from Hollywood, is how I saw it.

Everyone told me Iris's mother, Charlotte, had been wonderful, and I thought that her perfection had probably made up for my father's shortcomings. I believed that the Torellis, unlike my family, had souls, and their souls, if you'd hung them on the clothesline behind the carriage house, would have billowed bright white and sheer, smelling like sunshine. Mrs. Torelli, as I saw her, took motherhood seriously. She talked to Reenie about what her children liked to eat, she talked to Iris about their feelings (their "crazy ideas" is what she said, but still, she was interested), she told everyone about Mr. Torelli's digestive problems, which little Joey had inherited, and when Baby Paulie had a bumpy, purple rash on his fat little neck, Mrs. Torelli made Dr. Fishkind come to the house to treat it. She could not have left a child on the front porch of any house, anywhere, ever.

Mr. Torelli talked to me once in a while when I was snitching something from the kitchen early in the morning or when he passed me at the end of the day on the walk from the garage to their house. Sometimes he patted my head and said, How's the genius? Sometimes he just started talking the way you do to a dog, and I'd follow him up to the kitchen door until he went inside.

The Torellis liked daily naps for their children and big meals of good food. They liked large, clean cars, a clean kitchen, and nice clothes, with no stains or tears. As long as we made this possible, the Torellis didn't bother us. (Reenie dropped the "Heitmann" when Gus was taken away and went back to "Lombardo." She moved into the carriage house with us, and my father only said, Well, aren't we Opéra-Bouffe-by-the-Sea.) Mrs. Torelli did say to me, over her morning cantaloupe and Baby Paulie's rice cereal, which covered half her silk housecoat, that it was good that we had taken Reenie in. That poor girl didn't know which way was up, Mrs. Torelli said.

Reenie and Iris shared a room now and Iris went into the city to audition twice a week. (I meant to tell you, she said. I took my mother's maiden name. Reardon. We're still sisters. People do it all the time.) When Iris was catching the morning train, she asked me to take her place with the little girls, and we'd play Geography and I Spy, which seemed like very educational games to me. Sometimes we would act out our version of *Little Women,* in which Beth didn't die and Joey played the March family dog. Mrs. Torelli didn't mind.

She managed her household with one chubby white hand and the help that really mattered was my father and Reenie. Iris called my time with the kids "enrichment." Now that the girls were in school, Mrs. Torelli focused on the boys during the day, and she let them run around the garden until they were wet and dirty and hungry. When I was home, I brought out sandwiches and apple juice. Iris's absences bothered only Reenie, I think. Iris invited us both to see her onstage. Reenie said, "I don't have time to do that. I'm working." "Me too," I said, and it gave me some mean satisfaction to let Iris know that this time I had better things to do than sew the sequins and wait in the wings.

When Iris was gone two days in a row, which happened more and more, I'd rehearse the Torellis' children one evening and have them perform the next. We did *Cinderella*, with Catherine as Cinderella, then with Mary as Cinderella, and always with Joey as a madcap pumpkin. We did an abbreviated *Tempest*, mostly storm and rescue, with Mary as Miranda ("You're the princess"), Catherine as Ariel ("You're a magic fairy," I told her), Joey as Caliban ("You scare the crap out of the girls"), and Baby Paulie as Prospero (carried by me, his lines uttered by me—that long drive to East Brooklyn had not been for nothing), and I made my father, Mrs. Torelli, and Reenie watch.

They clapped and Mrs. Torelli took the kids upstairs. My father said, Interesting experiment, and walked back to the carriage house. Reenie sat weeping at the kitchen table.

"I'll never see Gus again," she said.

I said that we didn't know that.

"I'll never have children," she said, and I thought that was about the shortest mourning period on record.

"Do you think he was a German spy?" Reenie said.

"Do you?" I said.

Reenie wiped her face with a dish towel. "Of course not. He was a good man."

I said I thought so too, and Reenie got up and took off her apron.

"You could write to the government to find out what's happened to him," I said. "Or I could."

"I did that," she said. "It's not as easy as you think. None of it."

Reenie put on her coat and picked up a dish of fruit compote she'd made for us at the house, bits and pieces of fruit that were starting to go bad, all stewed together with cinnamon and white wine. Iris and I ate bowls of it.

"Iris worries about him," Reenie said.

Like fun, I thought. Reenie wanted a baby and Iris wanted Reenie and it seemed to me that the only person who heard Gus's big laugh, who missed his sharp look and those thick, quick fingers shuffling cards like a croupier, was me.

CLARA WILLIAMS WAS THE next morning's surprise. My father introduced her to me, pretty much the way he had introduced me to my sister, back in Ohio. When it came to immediate family, Edgar was all for plain talk. Oh, Evie, glad you're up. Iris has been in and out. This is my very good friend Miss Clara Williams. We hope she'll be visiting us quite a bit.

Miss Clara Williams, pale and dark, put out her pretty light-blue suede glove (my mother would have killed for those gloves, with the tiny, flat pleats at the wrist and two blue pearl buttons) and I took her hand and mumbled. She smiled and the dimple in her left cheek was deep as a dime. I wanted to make her smile again. She sat down and pulled off her gloves. I saw her hands, speckled with white patches and dots of white skin. She said that maybe I'd stick around and have a cup of coffee with her, if I wasn't too busy. I poured two cups. My father put on his butler's coat, patted my shoulder, and went to the door.

"For God, for country, for Joseph Torelli," he said, and left.

Clara stirred her coffee and sat with her spoon hovering an inch above the table.

"I'm sorry," I said. I put down the two scorched linen napkins my father had taken (rescued, he said) from the Torellis' laundry pile.

"Isn't this just fine," she said. "Fine." In East Brooklyn, there was an Italian café my sister and I liked, and for a treat, we would order affogato, hot espresso poured over vanilla ice cream, the dark streaming into melting ivory pools. Like that.

"Are you in school?" she said.

I went through my song-and-dance, which began with my implying that I had already graduated and ended with me saying I really was giving a lot of thought to City College.

"Your father says you're the smart one."

"Not the pretty one," I said. I was mortified.

"Oh, you can fake pretty," she said.

CLARA CAME TO OUR house most nights after that, and she stayed in my father's room. In the morning, I'd wake up early to watch the light-blue cab come for her and see her run down the stairs with a dress over her arm and her enormous crocodile makeup case. The three of us never ate together and I chose to think that was my father's possessiveness and not Clara's lack of interest. Iris said that for Clara, we were just duckpins to be bowled over. I said I didn't think Clara was after his fortune.

I was sixteen and I was used to Iris and Reenie, and used to the happy Torellis and now used to my father pretending to be a butler, although watching him bow his head, just an inch, when Mr. Torelli told him to pull the car around, bothered me. Clara Williams was extraordinary to me. I was embarrassed to be so fascinated by her odd, smooth skin and her cool manners and to be so enamored of her voice. My lucky father.

. . .

WE WERE ALL BROKE, but I was more so. I took money, very carefully, from everyone's open purse or wallet. Reenie kept a couple of
quarters in her old black coin purse and Iris always had loose change
now, now that she was back in business. She was Irish Maid, Second Debutante, Silly Shopgirl, appearing nightly near or on Broadway. Iris was working hard, and not just onstage. She told me about
the agents she had to woo, and the stage managers. She told me it
was important to pay for your own drink when the cast went out
after the show and she told me that putting an extra dollar in the
pot made people like you more. She did her exercises every day, she
said, and she was taking dance and she'd gotten into an acting class.
She said her voice was an instrument and her body was an instrument. And my ass is a Stradivarius, she said.

I JUST WANTED TO begin my own life, one that didn't include my
relatives. I showed up at Bea and Carnie's in time for lunch, most
days. They were interested in Clara too. Was she really Negro, what
did she use on her skin, what kind of singer was she, would she ever
let a white person do her hair? I loved that Bea and Carnie thought
that Clara and I sat around, chewing the fat at our kitchen table.
Francisco didn't have time for me. He had a skinny boy with Frank
Sinatra hair sweeping up and shampooing at his shop and he had
two barbers working for him. He didn't need me, he said. He said
that as much as he loved me, I'd be better off working for his sisters.
He trimmed my bangs and the skinny boy watched us and swept up
the tiny snips of hair with a big flourish. I went back to La Bella
Donna.

Bea and Carnie said I'd done so well at the shop, I should come
with them on house calls and pick up some more pin money. You're
not a baby, Bea said. Start planning ahead. House calls meant more

and more careful sweeping up than at the shop. I did notice that the ladies were very happy for me to use the lint brush on their furniture, make tea, and empty the trash, and would you mind, there's a good girl, just take the dog for walkies while I'm drying. I took small things that I thought would not be missed. The house-call ladies were rich but not Torelli rich. Cigarette lighters would be missed. Brooches would be missed. I took a can of peanuts, a pair of navy kneesocks. I found five dollars in a man's raincoat pocket and took it. I thought, I'm planning ahead.

Bea and Carnie spent weeks talking about whether or not to take me to Mrs. Vandor's. Mrs. Vandor was their prize. Her first husband had been a Hungarian nobleman (Bea said) and he died in World War I (or in France, in a car accident, Carnie said). Mrs. Vandor had escaped Hungary and come to this country (with just the clothes on her back, Bea said, or with gold coins sewn into her underwear, Carnie said) and married a White Russian who died of TB. Now she had a beautiful apartment in the nicest building in East Brooklyn and she was their favorite client, ever.

I'd become a good assistant. I thought this was not surprising but Carnie said just the opposite was true. You don't see yourself in ten years, still sweeping up piles of hair and drying the sink with a rag and scrubbing the hair color off someone's face so they don't look spotty, do you? You don't think you'll be doing this forever, do you? I said that I didn't. (My vision of the future was like the paintings I'd seen of the Old West, mysterious, serious, with great beauty at every vista and terrible things happening whenever any people appeared.) There you go, Carnie said. I'm saying, the best kind of assistant is Dora's girl, Kimmy, who wants to be an assistant. Wants to. You see how happy she is when she gets every hair off the floor? I did. I swept for praise, for Francisco's hooded look of approval when he dropped by, for lunch and a dollar and a place at the table. I did not sweep for the pleasure of a job well done.

Kimmy was our mascot. She had a lazy eye and she was a little slow. I never saw anyone be unkind to her. When Kimmy was in the shop, Carnie made a point of saying good things about the nuns, about convents, and how much fun the sisters had. Bea said that a nunnery sounded like a great place to live. In the end, even with the lazy eye, Kimmy married well, a much older man, with his own business and no children, and they moved to Astoria. When her mother got heart trouble, she moved in with Kimmy and her husband and Carnie said to me, See? No one knows anything.

They were not bringing the likes of Kimmy to Mrs. Vandor's. Neither of them wanted to do the cleanup. They liked spending the afternoon with Mrs. Vandor. I think she was the only woman they considered more worldly, more truly cosmopolitan than they were. They looked at the newspaper pictures of socialites and their Greek playboys, of women in tiaras in front of summer houses in Italy and estates in Rhode Island, of men with three last names resting their hands on their horses and sports cars and I never heard a bitter, envious word from them. They mused about famous people's errors in judgment, the same way they did about their neighbors, about my family and theirs. They frequently said, as I do now, Too bad money and taste don't live together. They said, as I could say every day of my adult life, God doesn't give with both hands, honey.

Mrs. Vandor's apartment was to all the homes I'd seen, as Jackie Kennedy would be to all the previous first ladies. It was fresh and chic but soft and so assured that as soon as you walked in, you understood that not only did you live with the wrong furnishings, in whatever unfortunate place you came from, you also had chosen the exact wrong outfit just that morning. You would have had a very hard time persuading me that Mrs. Vandor was not an exceptionally lovely human being, even if she'd walked in dragging a bleeding body and proceeded to kick the living Jesus out of it. Which she didn't. She was tall, fair, and regal, rather than thin (if I hadn't been star struck, I would have said that she looked like a very pale camel), wearing long gray silk pajamas, the top unbuttoned over a long white satin shirt. (Which I couldn't get over—I thought about it for days. Was it underwear, even though it was satin, where else did she wear it, was it something that she wore only at home, the way my mother had, on some Sunday mornings, worn a cotton house-dress while she got ready for my father?)

Bea and Carnie introduced me as their niece and Mrs. Vandor said, Don't be ridiculous—she's not a relative of yours. Some Scotch-Irish and Russian mix. Bea and Carnie looked at me and I shrugged. Mrs. Vandor made us all tea poured into cups I was afraid to hold and afraid to sip from. I tried to keep my lips over my teeth, so that I wouldn't bite the china by accident. Carnie looked at me hard. I put down my cup, rattling it in the saucer, and I held on to a ginger cookie (with lemon cream filling) like it was a life pre-server.

Carnie colored Mrs. Vandor's gray hair ash-blond and then Bea did her hands and feet. Mrs. Vandor closed her eyes until they were finished. I offered to wash the cups and empty the wastebasket and Mrs. Vandor said, with her eyes closed, I wouldn't make that kind of thing a habit. One wishes to be useful, but not indispensably so. She gave me two dollars and a Bonwit's bag with books in it.

"Books make a room," she said. She gave Bea and Carnie each a heavy silk French scarf, red for Bea, emerald green for Carnie, and then she said, at the door, "I'm taking a little trip, my dears. We'll see each other before Christmas." (We would not.)

Bea and Carnie talked about where she was going and why and with whom, all the way home. I took *BUtterfield 8* out of the bag and read it on the train to Great Neck, and on the bus to Pond Road.

THAT NIGHT, I WALKED into the Torelli kitchen for a snack, and almost tripped over my father, drinking a cup of coffee. My father and I were hardly ever alone together. Reenie and Iris were a cou-ple. My father and Clara were a couple. I was, to everyone, includ-ing me, odd man out.

"Hello, stranger," he said.

He asked me what I thought about Iris and her friend Reenie and I said, Not much.

They seem very fond of each other, he said.

I said they certainly did and I might have rolled my eyes a little, disloyally, just to show my father that I wasn't such a fool as Iris to be losing my marbles over other people, other girls, all the time. My father smiled. He said, You know what Oscar Wilde said—women are meant to be loved, not understood. Applies to both of them, darling. And I nodded, although it seemed to me that I was going to be a woman too and I would like it if someone thought they should understand me.

What's in the bag? he asked. I showed him the books. He whistled when he saw *BUtterfield 8* and he asked me if I found it racy. I said I found it sad, and I could see that he liked my answer, and I hoped he'd ask me about the other books and that I'd come up with deep, interesting answers.

"You know what I like to read," he said. "Those Little Blue Books we read on the great trek east. There are thousands of them. As Phineas T. Barnum said, something for everyone."

My father washed and dried his cup and we walked back to the carriage house in the dark. He put his hand out to keep the forsythia branches from smacking me in the face.

When I need to call up my father, when I want to feel loved by him, I remember him dancing with me in my bedroom back in Abingdon, before my mother left me on his porch. I think of him guiding me through the forsythia bushes, his fingers brushing the moths away from my face at the carriage-house front door.

There was nothing wrong with our carriage house. It was not as nice as my father's house in Windsor but it was nice enough in its practical, un-showy way. Everything in it was useful, a little worn, mostly brown. Nothing matched. Nothing was lacy or embroidered. My father and I sat in our living room while he hung up his jacket and put on his slippers. He took all of the books out of Mrs. Vandor's bag: Robert Benchley, Dorothy Parker, S. J. Perelman, more John O'Hara, and *O Pioneers!* by Willa Cather. At the bottom of the bag was an old deck of cards, with green plaid on the back and all kinds of pictures.

"Tarot," my father said, biting off both *t*'s. "The secrets of the universe. God help us." I was not averse to knowing the secrets of the universe. My father threw the top two cards on the table: the Queen of Cups, a grim blonde in a long white dress, on a granite throne. The Lovers, Adam and Eve holding hands under a winged god with flaming hair. He threw down another three, a man weeping in his bed under a stack of nine swords, a dwarf standing on big, star-stamped coins, a rainbow of ten gold cups. My father snorted. "Not the woman her library would have led me to believe," he said. "Appalling."

IN THE MORNING, I found a box of thirty Little Blue Books outside my door. His note said, "Educate yourself."

History of Evolution; Poems of John Keats; Auto-Suggestion—How It Works; French Self-Taught (heavily penciled); *What Every Married Man Should Know; What Every Married Woman Should Know; How to Make All Kinds of Candy; Psycho-Analysis—The Key to Human Behavior; Proverbs of Japan; Proverbs of China; Proverbs of Italy; Proverbs of Russia; Proverbs of Arabia; Chekhov's Short Stories.* And underneath a dozen more: *An Introduction to the Reading of Tarot.*

THE SEVENTY-EIGHT CARDS CAME with a small, stained instruction booklet. Every picture told a story and the stories suited me. Occasionally, the pictures were cheerful: a juggler skipped along holding big coins, the naked lady dipped her pitcher into a starry pond (the Star) but more often, Death rode in on a big white horse, dogs bayed at a frowning moon, lightning struck a forbidding tower and it burst into flames.

I came to love the Tower. Unlike the other seventy-seven cards, whose meanings can be reversed, or at least muted when the card is turned upside down, the Tower is always the Tower. Right side up, catastrophe. Upside down, damn near catastrophe. It scared the bejesus out of my clients, when I got them, and led to extra readings, until I'd choose to tuck it away. Major and minor arcana. Instead of clubs, spades, hearts, and diamonds, the suits were wands, cups, pentacles (the big coins), and swords. You could use them to represent the four seasons, the four elements, the soul, the body, the mind, and the heart. You could use them to represent just about any four things that anyone might want to hear about.

I brought the cards and the booklet to the beauty parlor and I asked Bea and Carnie if I could set up in their shop. Bea and Carnie were great respecters of enterprise, and since—as Bea said—I didn't seem like the kind of girl who was going to land a successful husband or a rich beau anytime soon, they gave me a card table in the waiting area. Neither of them knew anything about tarot but they both flipped through the cards (Bea crossed herself, quickly) and by the time they'd finished checking the cards for anything that would not be in keeping with the high tone of La Bella Donna, they'd already made rules for me. Ten-minute readings, because we had to keep traffic flowing, unless there was a slowdown in the shop, in which case I could expand. (This was fine with me. I didn't think I had more than ten minutes of hocus-pocus in me.) One dollar a reading. (Bea thought maybe fifty cents but Carnie said, What, now she's gotta make change?) And they agreed that sometimes people didn't tip for this kind of thing.

Are you going to tell them bad news? Carnie said. I said that I thought a little bad news was probably part of it. Carnie said it'd be better for business if I didn't give out with imminent death or something really bad happening to a client's child, right there in the salon. (None of us thought for a minute that I had psychic powers.) I wore a skirt and blouse and Carnie did my hair and makeup. (You don't have to be a beauty queen," she said. You just have to look normal attractive because you're in our shop. You represent us. But you need to look like you know something special, Bea said. She dotted a beauty mark near my mouth.)

They steered me to Mrs. Russo. Mrs. Russo's husband had left her six years ago and she'd never gotten over it. She thought she saw him everywhere. She called the police once a month and on their last two anniversaries she had tried to kill herself. Bea thought that if anyone would give me a dollar, it'd be Mrs. Russo.

Mrs. Russo and I faced each other over the little table. I'd wrapped the cards in one of Iris's silk scarves. I made a big show of unwrapping them and I asked Mrs. Russo to hold the cards. She squeezed them like they were Mr. Russo. I flipped over nine cards, for past, present, and future. I said I saw Mr. Russo, lured away by evil companions. I said that he had been in a car accident and lost his memory. I described the present as filled with strength (the woman with a chain of flowers, holding a lion) and said that the future held peace for Mrs. Russo and no pain for Mr. Russo. Mrs. Russo thought this was the best thing she'd heard. She told her sister, who gave me another twenty-five cents, just to say thank you. Mrs. Russo's cousin Sylvia by marriage, with the reputation, watched while I laid down the cards for her cousin. Nice, she said. After my henna, you can do me. I gave Sylvia Russo a man madly in love with her, who wanted to marry her. She looked very pleased. I said that she should not marry this man because he wasn't good enough for her. He was not telling her the whole truth, I said. Mrs. Russo and her sister stood over their cousin's chair. I told Sylvia that within a year, after she turned down the current no-good liar, another man would come along. A good man. That man she should marry. The Russos dabbed at their eyes. I was launched.

The ladies liked that I was an innocent vessel. I described whatever salacious goings-on seemed called for, as if I barely understood what the cards were showing me. The ladies liked that the cards and I seemed to be on their side. After a week of the Russos, and more Russo cousins, I had clients every day. I advised that a miserable, no-good bitch of a daughter (about whom I'd been hearing for six months, from her aunt) should not be given a loan, according to the Justice card, and might come to no good end, according to the Six of Swords, which had a sad woman and child in a canoe, floating away from a dock. Mrs. Sorita should not go to Atlantic City with an old beau from high school, not even just for fun (Three of Pentacles, faintly disapproving). Mrs. Benjamin should let her daughter take night classes and Jeannie could start out local, before she applied to Brooklyn College (Ace of Wands, heigh-ho for education). No one who sat at my table was encouraged to have a fling, to leave the country, to go in or go out of this world like gangbusters.

Suddenly, I had money. I opened a bank account across the street from the shop. I hadn't had a dime of my own that I hadn't stolen, since we'd left Ohio. My father paid for his own immaculate self and for evenings out with Clara. Iris paid for herself and helped Reenie, who'd never been paid much, now that Reenie was single. I'd been wearing Iris's hand-me-downs for four years, badly, and had hardly noticed. Now I bought college-girl clothes and did my hair the way college girls did and I stuffed my bra. I had two pairs of new shoes. The pain in my chest, which I had had since the day I was left on the front porch, eased up. It wasn't grief. It was being broke and badly dressed, and now I wasn't.

10

Bei Mir Bist Du Schoen

Letter from Iris

Upper Richmond Road
Putney, London
April 1947

Dear Eva,

Pride of Israel orphanage. You knew your way around that place like you lived there. You were my tour guide. You must have timed our visit for the baseball game and the boy you had a crush on. (You kept your glasses off and your chest out until the baseball players were called inside.) Then the little ones came out. We stood there like people at a museum, admiring, assessing the different children. There weren't that many different kinds, were there? Skinny, dark-haired, dark-eyed, beaky boys, the occasional little blimp with fat wrists and knees and a wary look, a few blondes. I had said that I would like a baby, but there were clearly no babies to be had, or if the orphanage did have babies, they kept them properly stored inside.

I know you understood that I needed a child for Reenie. I must have told you a million times how much she wanted a baby, how sad it was for her that now that Gus was gone, she'd probably never have one. She told me, and I told you. She looked into adoption and discovered that the adoption agencies would give a pair of married monsters triplets before they'd give one baby to a single woman. You ventured once that Reenie might meet someone else, a man that she could have a baby with, but I squelched that. I'm sorry. I had no business making you snatch that little boy (I can see it now, that awful pile of bricks and Stars of David discreetly carved into the cornices—proudly Jewish but not too Jewish, just in case).

I don't have much confidence in what people remember. It seems to me, I remember some things at a gallop, some moments from Ohio bearing down upon me in huge detail, and other things are no more than small leaves floating on a stream. Memory seems as faulty, as misunderstood and misguided, as every other thought or spasm that passes through us. I know I wasn't so much younger then that I can use youth as an excuse; let's just say that I still thought I was made to triumph. That I was, in fact, *owed* a triumph. I planned to give Reenie a little boy, the way a rich man buys his wife a Cadillac. I thought she would love me even more for my unexpected, staggering generosity. And because Danny was a child, and *not* a car, we'd be like the Nelson family, except we would be Harriet and Harriet and Danny, and Danny would be exceptionally well behaved.

How was I to know? I was raised by a completely normal, lovely mother, with hot breakfasts and sudsy baths and walks to the library, and she died just as I was turning awful, shrieking about my spots and my hair and getting my monthlies—I remember you getting yours. You were fourteen. It was just before everything went bad in Hollywood. You, being you, had read up on menstruation in my

Margaret Sanger book. You just sat on the toilet until I got home and then you gave me your list of sundries, on the back of an envelope. You must have been sitting there for hours. When I got back with the goods, both your legs had fallen asleep and I had to hold you up. I strapped in that enormous pink slab of a sanitary napkin, I assured you that you could get pregnant but that did not mean you had to have anything to do with boys if you didn't want to, and I threw your soiled pants into the trash can behind the apartments.

What I want you to remember is that I cared for you. I want you to see that between my nice mother, who had a maid and two sets of china and a life history of ease and no consequence, and our blithe, inscrutable, crooked father—I had no way of knowing what was required.

You saw Danny before I did. I don't know what caught your eye. I should have had stronger feelings, I suppose. My heart should have filled with love, knowing that this was the exact little boy (you said he was four or five, I had no idea) we were meant to have, but it didn't. I felt the way one might if one were asked to choose among pearl bracelets of rather poor quality, when one has no interest in pearls and never has. We visited three more times and every time, we looked for Danny and smiled and waved and we pulled a bit more at the hole in the wire fence, until a child could crawl through it. You found some scrap lumber that we laid up against the hole, so no one would see. I don't know why we thought anyone would stop him, or us—those children were all at the orphanage because no one wanted them.

Do you remember what Danny said when he started talking to us? He told us that his mother had fallen off a roof and his father was so sad, he had to bring Danny and his brother to the home. We did look at the other boys, but you had your heart set on Danny. You said he seemed nice and smart. You were right, but I certainly saw no evidence of that at the time. What he seemed to me was undersize, possibly nearsighted, and pitiful. When we got his attention and I finally put out my hand to him at the hole in the fence, he just stared at his shoes. I have to tell you, I worried that he was slow and that we should have found a smarter child, but you put the candies right in my hand to encourage him and he toddled over, like a badger coming for his snack. There's a hotel in the north I've been to a couple of times (married lady, Scots, and very keen . . . for about two months) and at teatime, they put out a huge dish of milk and chunks of bread around it and the badgers come around and dip, like matrons at the Connaught. I watched them every day.

Had we gotten a car? Did we bring him home on the subway? That seems impossible but I know we didn't have a car (our father was so strict about not borrowing the Torellis' car for our personal business; that must have been the only ethical fence he wouldn't jump). I think I carried Danny in, wrapped in a red-and-white blanket. (No one can say we didn't plan ahead. Why, we had a sack of candy *and* a blanket.) Danny hadn't cried at all when we pulled him through the opening. He just looked behind him, wiped his dirty little nose, and took my hand. He did look a little the worse for wear in our bathroom, eyes rolling around and his heart beating so fast in his chest that I could see it. Reenie washed his face and hands with a warm cloth (she was afraid that he'd never had a bath and all that water would scare him) and made him a cup of milky tea and we put him in our bed. The sight of Reenie, with the little boy's head on her breast, her hand smoothing his hair, holding the cup for him and singing some Italian lullaby, was all that I wanted. That, and her beautiful smile when he fell asleep. She did ask me where we had found him and I told her the thinnest lie, that a neighbor of the Diegos had abandoned their child to return to Mexico and no one knew what to do with him. Reenie seemed a little surprised that he was Mexican; he didn't look Mexican, she said, but in the end, she saw only his sweet face and big eyes and his stubby hand gripping her skirt, and if I had told her he was Robert of Scotland, she'd have believed that too. I must have thought that Reenie's Catholic heart would seize up at the thought of his being stolen and she'd make us take him back. I had told her once that she could have a baby with Francisco and we'd raise it, but she wouldn't hear of it.

Edgar came in and took off his shoes and watched Reenie rocking this little person he'd never seen. I told him our story about the Diegos and he lit a cigarette. "How extraordinary," he said. "Mexican? Is there any coffee left?" I got him coffee and put a few shortbread cookies around the cup, which I hoped he understood to mean, Don't say a word, please. He drank his coffee and he patted Reenie's shoulder. "I'm sure someone will tell me all about it in the morning," he said. "What's our little fellow's name?" Reenie picked "Dante" and we Americanized it to "Danny" and I suggested "Lombardo" was less troublesome than something Mexican, and Reenie agreed.

In the morning, you and I shopped for clothes at Woolworth's and Reenie practiced the story of Danny Lombardo to the Torellis, making the nonexistent Diegos into Reenie's nonexistent Italian cousins, just to be on the safe side. Mrs. Torelli asked to meet Danny. Reenie steam-cleaned him. At five, we presented him, and whatever Mrs. Torelli was looking for, Danny passed muster. He looked straight into her eyes and smiled shyly. Mrs. Torelli was devastated that any Italian mother could be so cruel. She apologized that she had nothing but dresses for hand-me-downs, because Joey was only three. Danny didn't show his awful orphan teeth and she didn't have to hear his pure and appalling Brooklyn accent. I worked harder on that child's accent than I did on my own. Do you remember? In first grade, he got top marks for diction, elocution, and public speaking, thank you very much.

I assume I never hear from you because of Danny. If you were me (well, there we are, aren't we?), I know you would have pulled up your cotton socks, bound your burned hands, and gotten on with the business of taking care of poor Danny. As I'm sure you have.

I'm enclosing a couple of favorable notices. I have been on the BBC pretty much nonstop since leaving the hospital. The

wisecracking American gold digger, the hand-wringing, fragile
American secretary, the deluded Southern belle. I play older (the
camera doesn't love me the way it would you, and I have the
permanent air—*quelle surprise*—of the older sister). I have saved the
BBC a fortune in airfare. And now I'm on a soap, as the conniving
American sister-in-law who our genteel and plucky heroine can't get
rid of. (Our entire country is, apparently, grasping but resolute, too
coarse to be insulted and too stupid to go home when we're not
wanted. I don't know who these people think saved their skinny
spotty asses just the other day, but I guess it wasn't us.) Nothing
makes you love America like winter in England.

Your sister,
Iris

———————

I DID HAVE MY HEART SET ON DANNY. HE SEEMED TO HAVE NO one, and maybe worse than no one, and I could tell from the way he tilted forward that he needed glasses. I would give him to Reenie and Iris and stand by, wings fluttering, in the background. For the first two days, Danny didn't say a word. He didn't say, Who are you, where are you taking me, who are all these people, when can I go home? He stared at each of us when we spoke to him and Iris was afraid that he was deaf and dumb. She snapped her fingers next to his ear and he flinched but he didn't speak. He woke up when Reenie did and dressed himself and followed her to the Torellis' kitchen. While she cooked and washed up, he pressed up against her. While she served, he sat at the kitchen table and laid his head on it. Reenie carried him back to the carriage house when she was done for the day and put him into bed. She kissed him goodnight and Iris kissed him goodnight and my father and I called out, Good night, from the living room and then Danny spoke.

"I got a brother," he whispered to Reenie. "Bobby."

Reenie got the truth out of Iris and insisted she go back to the orphanage. I wouldn't go. I'd done what Iris wanted me to do and offered up my rescue of Danny to the universe. I wanted to get on with my tarot cards (I had seven clients now) and my makeup and my daily reading about the war, and, above all, my limitless fascination with my body, which was changing every minute. I balanced on the edge of the tub to study myself in the steamy bathroom mirror: pinup girl, mystery woman, farmer's daughter. I could spend an hour examining my underarms and elbows and another hour on my eyebrows.

Iris said nothing had changed at the orphanage. Older boys tossed a tattered baseball. Little boys jumped over piles of trash, throwing rocks at tin cans. Iris went up to the wire fence and scanned the boys. She saw Bobby right away. He was Danny, four years older, and still beautiful. He stood on a stack of bricks, posing confidently, and a much older boy sketched him. Iris said he was a little junkyard Salomé and she didn't want him anywhere near us.

The other boys saw Bobby being sketched by the artist and they muttered, but they didn't speak. The artist was a tall, well-built boy with a heavy brow, and Iris said if she'd been a little kid, she wouldn't have wanted to cross him either. He noticed Iris.

"Hey, miss," the artist said. Bobby hitched up his trousers and twisted slightly toward Iris. The turn in his ivory torso, the neat little fold above his hipbone, was as beautiful as the rest of him.

"Are you Bobby?" she asked.

Bobby stared back. Iris said she could see it all unfolding. She'd chat with Bobby. She'd tell him that Danny was with us. Bobby'd walk out of the orphanage in nothing more than his filthy T-shirt and his loose khakis and he'd come back to Pond Road, with expectations. He'd share a bedroom with Danny and break his toys. Bobby'd become the arbiter of what was right and normal and male, and what Reenie and Iris thought wouldn't count. Bobby had a blackmailer's cool look. He reminded Iris of Rose Sawyer.

"I heard the boys calling him Bobby," Iris said to the artist. "I was just in the neighborhood, visiting friends." She used her Gracious Guest voice. Bobby's eyes lingered on the big vermeil pin on Iris's collar and she knew she was right.

"I must be going," Iris said. "Good luck with your art."

"'Good luck with your art'? You said that?" I asked.

"I did."

"Did Bobby look sad? Did he look disappointed?"

"He looked like a cheap little monkey," Iris said. "I'm telling Reenie I never saw him."

11

You Made Me Love You

BEING FAIRY GODMOTHER DIDN'T WORK OUT FOR ME. REENIE loved Danny the way I never saw anyone love anyone, and it made me sick. She teared up when she washed his pasty little face. She grabbed his hand in the middle of breakfast and pressed it to her lips, right over the scrambled eggs. It was a festival of maternal love, all day, every day. And if Danny didn't flourish, he certainly recovered. He got less pasty. He talked. He followed Reenie like a cheerful little tugboat and he didn't flinch when people spoke to him. I avoided them both.

Before Iris's downfall, I'd had crushes on whichever movie star the magazines were pushing. (Why hold back? Grant, Gable, Flynn, and Randolph Scott.) Now I refused to have a crush on anyone. Women were fools. Men were lucky fools. In my rewrite, Mrs. Torelli would be my mother, Francisco my father, and Mrs. Gruber the beloved, eccentric aunt. Danny, that watered-down, crybaby, weak-kneed version of me, would not even be an extra.

Iris used to say I was a born stagehand. I had attached myself to the Torelli show, like a limpet. I basted the chicken when Reenie let me. I shelled peas. I tied the girls' hair bows and cleaned Joey's face. I removed the morning newspaper (and Mr. Torelli's racing forms, and Mrs. Torelli's hairpins) from the breakfast table, to get the house ready for company. I watched out the window for Mrs. Torelli's hairdresser (her French hairdresser came out from the city on Fridays and Mondays, just for Mrs. Torelli). I watched for handsome Father Dom, who came once a week, to take a walk with Mrs. Torelli and praise the children. On the first Sunday in October, the most beautifully windblown day that month, we had about thirty Torellis in the living room, waiting for Father Dom. Mrs. Torelli told me, in the kitchen, that Father Dom had been crushed by his rejection from the army, turned down as a soldier, and as a medic, and even as a chaplain. In wartime, before a dangerous maneuver, army priests can absolve the Catholic soldiers of all past and future sins, including whatever ones they might commit in combat. Father Dom decided that, because there was a war going on, he could offer field absolution to the Torellis. He accepted all confessions in the solarium, with a bow of his glossy head, and all future transgressions were forgiven, as the Torellis, of all ages, from all boroughs, took a knee in the living room, ate a huge dinner, and marched onto the field of life. I watched from the kitchen and contemplated conversion (Mrs. Torelli would be so pleased, I thought, and all my lies and future lies forgiven), and I helped serve eggplant parm after. Reenie's head was killing her, so I said I'd take over.

BY EIGHT O'CLOCK, EVERYONE was absolved and fed. The big kids were asleep. Mr. Torelli went out to a special meeting with the greengrocers. Reenie was lying down. Danny was in bed and Iris was at the theater, playing someone's saucy Irish maid. Baby Paulie was so fussy, he was twisting out of Mrs. Torelli's arms, arching like a pink fish. Paulie was miserable, coughing and sniffing, in and out of his million-dollar crib. Mrs. Torelli gave him baby aspirin crushed into applesauce, which he threw up three times. The fourth time, I helped her ladle it into him and he slept. I got the girls quieted down and I told Joey the story of Cowboy Joe, which was basically Puss in Boots comes to Wyoming. Mrs. Torelli said I was a godsend and I went to make us both tea. I looked for mothers the way drunks look for bars. Big ones, little ones, Italian ones, Negro ones. All I wanted was some soft, firm shoulder to lean against, a capable hand setting me right and making me breakfast.

I fell asleep on the divan in the Torellis' bedroom and I woke up to Paulie barking like a seal. I ran to Paulie's bedroom. He wasn't hot. He wasn't crying. He was shiny along all his creases and sweating, a little, with the effort of breathing. If every cough sounded like a circus seal, every inhale was a thin train whistle. Mrs. Torelli took us into her bathroom. She hung up her cashmere robe with the silk piping.

"Turn on the shower," she said. "Very warm. Not hot."

She handed Paulie to me and shut the bathroom door. She took off her nightgown and his diaper and stepped naked into the shower with Paulie. "Take off your socks and your shoes," Mrs. Torelli called to me. "You might as well take off your skirt." I did. I counted to one hundred, Mrs. Torelli sang "A-tisket, A-tasket." She sang opera, and then Paulie stopped coughing. There was a soft wheeze and then the sound of his baby laugh. Mrs. Torelli stepped out of the shower and wrapped a towel around warm, pink Paulie and put him in my arms. He laid his head on my shoulder and I pushed his wet brown curls off his face. I saw Mrs. Torelli before she pulled the bath towel around her, a series of ivory ovals, dashes of pink, and splashes of black. I wanted to never leave that room.

PAULIE WAS ASLEEP AND Mrs. Torelli and I were dry and wide awake. I asked her to sing opera again. She looked away, like a shy girl, and sang what she sang to Paulie, *"Come per me sereno."* She told me that her mother had wanted to be an opera singer. Who lives by hope, dies by hunger, Mrs. Torelli said, and I said that I hoped that wasn't true. She said, See, hope.

I offered to read her cards. I laid out a Celtic Cross. I gave Mrs. Torelli the reading of all time. I gave her healthy children (And one more, she asked, and I said, Absolutely, if you really, really want one, because I thought that probably, in the end, she wouldn't) and success for all of them. I gave her more Torelli Markets (because that seemed likely). I gave her good health for her and Mr. T., and better luck for her sister, who had multiple sclerosis (and I didn't say what better luck would entail). I gave her the Lovers and the Sun and the High Priestess, in a neat pile. I gave Mrs. Torelli deathless love, which she deserved.

Letter from Gus

Fort Lincoln, North Dakota
January 1944

Dear Evie,

I fixed the roof in the dining hall, so dirt and shit and snow don't fly in all day. We made a baseball diamond, so people can play. Mostly the real Americans play. I don't know what Germans play in Germany and the Japs don't play with us. After dinner, a German guy will get up, sharpen his mustache, and sing a little Wagner. The older men pound the tables like it's a Munich beer hall. The Japs do not sing Japanese songs after dinner. We are all potential or actual traitors here at Fort Lincoln, but some of us are white.

The guy I fixed the roof with showed me the letter he sent to the INS. He wanted me to tell him that the INS would read it and say, This is a huge mistake, Mr. Hauser. No way that you—fat, dumb, and happy as you were—could be a German spy. Even though you worked for New Jersey Nickel, and were a member of the German American Social Club of Elizabeth, even though you do tend to talk people to death about Germany's past glories—no way you are a spy.

Here's what Karl Hauser wrote to the INS: "I have been in this great country for fifteen years. I have been a hardworking businessman and I have paid taxes. I went to night high school in Bayonne to further myself. My wife, Greta Mazur Hauser, was born in Garden City, New York, and she is an American citizen. My two children, Anna and Carolyn, are American citizens. They were both born at Elizabeth General Hospital. I am not a member of the Nazi party. I do not sympathize with the goals of the Nazi party. To my knowledge, I have no relatives who are members of the Nazi party. We have been in this camp at Fort Lincoln, North Dakota, for one year. Please review my case. Sincerely and patriotically, Karl M. Hauser."

I told him it was a good letter and not likely to get him anywhere. He told me that back in New Jersey, two FBI agents visited his house five different times and took him to some shithole in Maryland the day before Christmas. They asked his wife if their radio was transmitting messages to and from Germany. They asked the little girls if they loved Germany more than America. On New Year's Day, two armed guards took Greta and the kids to Fort Lincoln by train and kept the three of them in the rear car, alone.

I'd been reading about Germany since '37 and I know I said to you, more than once, that I thought most of what I read was a load of bull. I said that I didn't think the German people would stand for that. So, now I know that not only will the German people stand for it, so will the Americans. It turns out we'll stand for any goddamn thing the government will do on our behalf, and if that includes a boot in the kidneys or taking everything a man has and throwing it on his front lawn for the neighbors to pick through, we're okay with that. We're better than they are, I hear, because we're not exterminating a whole people. Future generations will admire our restraint.

It's ten acres here at Fort Lincoln, with ten-foot-high wire fences and another three feet of barbed wire and dogs. We've got two sets of guards, Surveillance for the towers and fences and Internal, who are like beat cops. There is a long list of rules in every building. Right after how to make your bed, it says anyone trying to escape will be shot.

Karl's the good-soldier type. No doubt his German nature. He's volunteering to work on the Northern Pacific Railroad, which a bunch of guys do to get out of the camp. There's a rumor that the guys who help will be freed first. I would go, but I have eyes for his wife, Greta. I figure Karl can go on the railroad and I'll keep the home fires burning.

February 26, 1944

We got an outbreak of TB. The men working the railroad brought it back from hanging around with the Lakota Indian women. I guess misery loves company. So Karl's got it, but not Greta. I've told her to stay the hell away from him and keep her girls, Anna and Carolyn, on the other side of the camp.

March 3, 1944

Karl died last night. Ice is still hanging off the roofs. We've got icicles in the dining hall. This morning, they brought in some more families and single men, about a hundred enemy aliens. In the hustle and bustle, I say to Greta, Let's just have Karl slip away and I take his place. No one wants to breathe near the dead people, so I volunteer to help the hospital people move bodies. We all have towels over our faces and gloves on, and I fall right into line. I say to Greta, Call me Karl. Some broad. She waves to me and calls me Karl. She gets the girls waving to me too, grinning like monkeys.

So, I'm a married man, once more and now, with kids. Don't tell Reenie. Call me Karl Hauser. Throw some rice my way, kiddo.

12

I'm Beginning to See the Light

EDGAR WAS IN A BAD WAY. HE HAD TO TURN SIDEWAYS TO SEE out of his right eye and his balance was off. He was having trouble with all the words he loved. The right, necessary words had come to him his whole life. *Les mots justes.* In the worst weather, in the worst possible circumstance, he'd always known what to say, and now those glamorous, undulating multisyllabic beauties he'd built his life on were failing him, wandering away as soon as they appeared. He drove Joe Torelli off to the hinterlands of the Bronx and spent three hours in the Mott Haven public library, looking up his symptoms. The Little Blue Books hadn't been any real help, although they were reassuring; he didn't have venereal disease or polio.

HE DIDN'T EXPECT CLARA to stop taking care of herself just because he wasn't right. She did her vocal exercises before she went to work, she did her hair, and every day she rubbed the ointment into her skin: hairline, forehead, eyebrows, nose, cheeks, around her lips, onto her lips. Edgar knew she didn't bother anymore with her stomach and thighs. The ointment was like gritty Vaseline, green sludge in a milk-glass jar as big as a box of salt. When he looked in on her, gripping the doorway to keep upright, Clara was working it into her wrist, rubbing the thin lines of white, of worse than white, of nothing.

"*Concordia.*"

Clara smiled and kept rubbing at her wrists. He had said to her that it wasn't worth it to hide the vitiligo from him. He said it was a divine mark of something, a tattoo, a lasso of love. "Lasso of love" had made her smile.

"Yes sir, that's my baby, Concordia with the vitiligo. A Fats Waller number, if only he'd known you."

However, I'm convinced, completely, fully, firmly convinced,
You're the only one for me!

"Rest a little," Clara said. "You oyster, you."

EVERY TIME EDGAR CLOSED his eyes, he dreamed about the past. He dreamed about his life with Charlotte in Windsor, Ohio. He dreamed about his childhood in Chicago. He dreamed about Shorty George at the Savoy. He dreamed about Chez Paree and the Chez Paree Adorables. Jeanette, Gracie, and Harriet. They used to let him into the dressing room at intermission. Gracie threw her black gloves and short black skirt at him and he collapsed in the corner, struck down by red-hot desire and embarrassment. He dreamed about dancing with Clara, the way people had danced when he was a boy, like Vernon and Irene Castle. Sophie Tucker was singing "A Little Bit of Bad in Every Good Girl."

. . .

"Did I ever tell you about my first wife?" Edgar said, poking at the tapioca pudding Clara'd made. He pushed it around the bowl, coating the sides, to make her think he'd eaten some. Nursery food. He had to laugh at himself. He was going to keep up his Englishness, all childhood rose gardens and Tennyson, and keep quiet about his true self, until he dropped dead from whatever was making him so dizzy, dim, and half blind.

"Go ahead," Clara said. "Tell me about your first wife."

She washed out the bowl and cleared the table. She never asked him about his childhood. Clara was a smart woman and a suspicious one. Edgar wondered if she really believed that he was an English aristocrat, fallen on hard times and then harder ones. Charlotte had believed it, but Charlotte believed everything any strong-minded person ever told her. Edgar had made a killing in the early days of Prohibition and left Chicago right on time. He'd managed to lose his Maxwell Street accent and hoist himself up to the better kind of people, with the help of a good suit and the Lobb shoes and gold watch he bought at a pawnshop. He found a man who taught at Windsor College, who drank too much and needed a friend. Edgar became that friend and then he became a visiting professor in elocution and rhetoric and then he married Charlotte. Just as his mother had said, "*Is gut tsu zain klug, is besser tsu zain masidich.* It's good to be smart, it's better to be lucky."

Some nights, when he was lying very still, so there was no vertigo and no nausea, and in the dark he didn't worry that the blindness was getting worse (which it was), Edgar wanted to say to Clara, We've met. When you were a little girl, your brother Smoke used to bring you on his rounds, and sometimes we crossed paths. I worked for Jake Solomon, fifty cents a day, and your brother worked for whoever the Negro gangster was. I can see Smoke now, rolling an oak barrel of hooch through Bronzeville, his skinny arms working like pistons and you sitting on the top step of the nightclub stairs, watching Smoke come along. You swung on the brass railing, the tip of your little tongue sticking through that gap in your front teeth, where I can stick my tongue now and feel the tiny bite of your teeth on either side. I used to take a handful of mints from the maître d's stand—that was just about my whole lunch some days—and I'd give you a mint every time I saw you and you'd smile but you never said a word. Clara Williams, Smoke Williams's baby sister, from Armour Square in Chicago. I knew you then and I know you now. At night, this was the most comforting thought he had.

"MY WIFE CAME FROM a very good family. The Reardons of Ohio. I had gotten quite a good position at Windsor College, elocution and rhetoric. Charlotte's father was the president. That man sat at the same grand old desk, in the same grand old wing of South Hall, for forty years. I thought he'd outlive me. Charlotte graduated from Windsor the year I arrived. Her mother had passed several years before, so her father needed Charlotte to play . . ." The word "hostess" had just dropped out of his verbal lineup.

It was tempting to say that Charlotte was beautiful. It'd be good for Clara to hear that, that someone young and beautiful had loved him. Charlotte had been crazy about Shakespeare and sweet as a kitten, and just twenty-one, and perfect, the way youth is. She had wavy brown hair that she pinned up most of the time, and when girls were going to barbers and getting bobbed, Edgar and her father forbade it, and that was the only thing they ever agreed on.

Clara, at two or twenty, would never let him tell her how to wear her hair.

He can't remember the exact color of Charlotte's eyes anymore but she had a nice, old-fashioned figure, with soft, large pale-pink breasts and a tiny waist, small even after Iris was born. She had the most beautiful arms, slim, smooth, perfectly rounded. He did everything he could to keep her in white sleeveless evening dresses.

"She was just a lovely woman. No one admires this anymore but she was very feminine, very . . . a woman."

Clara struck a match on the stove and lit an Old Gold. He should stop now, but he kept going.

"I didn't bring much, I'm afraid. I was an assistant professor and she had the Reardon name, which was not insignificant in Ohio. Lots of family money, and an inheritance to come, and, I think I may have said, my family was nothing but an old English name. The very picture of genteel poverty, and of course I had no people in America at all." He knows that this is what he has meant to say, that it sounds slick and smooth inside of him, and even elegant, after a fashion, but he has had to simplify it, in order to say it and all that's left is, I married a rich girl.

Clara slipped off her loafers and stretched. She did her exercises and vocalized for about a half hour. She bent over and touched the floor with her flat palms. Edgar, in the old days, even just a few months ago, would have hugged her from behind, pulling her to him, while she laid her forearms against the floor. Stop bothering me, she'd say, but she always laughed and went limp in his arms.

"I was brokenhearted when Charlotte died."

"And poor Iris," Clara said.

At the wake, his father-in-law pulled Edgar onto the back porch and told him to behave himself. He said that if Edgar couldn't look after his own daughter, Iris could live with him at the president's house until she'd finished college or married. Edgar went back into the parlor and recited Browning until every woman in the room cried. Brigid, the Irish maid he'd paid in full before Charlotte died and never again, passed sandwiches and the monogrammed linen napkins Charlotte had had in her trousseau. Ecru with brown embroidery. Haute Ohio. (He used to say things like that to Charlotte, jokes about Ohio, even about the solid, stolid wealthy Reardons and her disapproving father, and sometimes Charlotte laughed, briefly, but after Iris was born, she'd leave the room, carrying the baby, and he knew now that only a fool mocks his wife's people.) Everything in her trousseau was watered silk or Scottish cashmere or heavy linen, stiff as whipped cream, some distant relatives of Brigid's having gone blind with the stitchery, which was carefully only brown and tan, so no one would think they were overreaching. He'd told Brigid to use every scrap of monogrammed linen in the house. Coasters curled under drinks, guest towels lay over the racks, and little linen squares rested under plates.

Iris sat by her grandfather and held his hand. She repeated what the guests were saying to him or improved on their remarks in her husky, penetrating voice. Edgar took on the professors and their wives' sympathy until the sun set in the parlor. His father-in-law left, sad and angry that it was Charlotte, not Edgar, in the casket. Brigid lit all the lamps and cried in the kitchen. Edgar gave her a basket of leftovers and he looked in on Iris, who was asleep on a couch, in her clothes. He has no memories at all of the next six months. He's a little hazy on the arrival and departure of Hazel and on life with Iris and Eva, except that it was bloody hectic and the girls either fought or Eva sulked or they conspired like thieves. Which they turned out to be, making off with everything but the Reardon family silver, which he'd had to sell by the time he left Ohio. And then there was that great trip east, with the girls running their lines and singing with Francisco, whom he will always love like a brother, his large Mexican homosexual brother. Even if work and life keep them apart, they have a drink every year on Zapata's birthday and they know there is more if they need it. And now, Great Neck and the Torellis, whose innocence and kindly self-absorption are a gift from God. And, now that odd little boy, a good kid, whoever he is, and his girls, and Iris's Italian girl, and Clara. Everything else falls like shuffled cards, but the details of each day of his life with Clara stay with him.

13

Never a Day Goes By

Letter from Gus

May 1944

Dear Evie,

They're offering one-way tickets to Germany again. I talked to Col. Lennart the night we set up for our talent show and he told me he'd seen official papers telling the camps to prepare to keep some of us here after the war ends, just to be on the safe side. When the war is over, they'll let the Japs go, the idea being that they won't be hard to find. But Krauts, white and English-speaking, we might be Hitler's henchmen in waiting, so they'll be keeping an eye on us as long as possible.

Greta, who has some of that quality of your sister, Iris—that is, she can be a bossy bitch—says, "I have family in Pforzheim." Since I came to this country when I was a baby, and none of the Heitmanns ever saw fit to take a vacation in Rhineland, I have no idea where Pforzheim is.

"It's beautiful. It has a big medieval town center. It's called Die Goldstadt," she says, "the Golden City. We make watches, we make jewelry, and my aunt and uncle are still there." I go right back to the colonel and say, with a straight face, that we are volunteering to be repatriated.

We leave tomorrow.

I'll be seeing you.

Karl Hauser a.k.a. Gus

U.S.A.
October 8, 1944

Dear Evie (and Uncle Sam),

Ellis Island, home of Lady Liberty. We've been packed in, like enemy sardines, for two weeks. The other sardines are South American Germans, people with names like Carlos and Juanita Heinzfelt. I have no idea what we are doing with them, or how they got kidnapped by their own governments and delivered to us, but there are hundreds of them, red-faced men in white suits, women in bright silk dresses. We may be enemy aliens but, by God, these people are really foreigners. Most of them don't even speak English. You hear them screaming in Spanish or crying their hearts out at their end of the hall. Our girls are tired and bored, playing tag all day with a few of the other American kids. No Japs are being sent to Japan and I don't know if that means that we have something worse in store for them or if it's just too fucking far. There was talk that the Irish were making common cause with the Germans but I don't see any freckle-faced people being sent back to Dublin.

They found an old Swedish ship for eight hundred of us, the *Gripsholm*. It's bright white and lit up like Christmas. Maybe they hope we'll be strafed *before* we get to Germany. It's the first ocean crossing for us, but some of the older people have been through this before, going the other way, and the South Americans just got off a boat a few weeks before. When we see the Statue of Liberty getting smaller, a lot of people cry and I take the girls to the other side of the ship.

When you and I met, I wasn't exactly father material. Reenie and I had tried—or we hadn't tried to avoid having kids—but nothing came of it. I hope it was my fault, that I was shooting blanks. I hope Reenie moves on and I hope she pops out a dozen kids if that's what she wants.

I'm in love with these two little girls: fat, funny Anna with the biggest blue eyes you ever saw, and Carolyn, with the freckles, already a serious woman. She's Eleanor Roosevelt at six, but prettier. These are *my* kids. I can't imagine how but I hope you meet them.

November 19, 1944

They had a train waiting for us right at the harbor, and down we went, a Noah's Ark of enemy aliens: miserable Germans, baffled Brazilians, and ten American guards.

Montreux is colder than a witch's tit. The Swiss are just like the weather. They put the food down on the table and they look away until we leave the dining room. Some of the old people are not so steady on their pins and the Swiss just watch. Fall down, piss yourself, choke on a turnip, it's all the same to them. Greta's asked the real Germans for help in making a map to get us to Pforzheim. The South Americans wrap themselves in blankets when they come to meals. They stare at the snow like it's shit coming down.

The Swiss are not happy to have us here. I bet the Germans will be thrilled.

November 30, 1944

We get to Bregenz. We talk about having a little Thanksgiving celebration but the people born in Germany are not inclined to celebrate and the rest of us feel more like Indians. The South Americans are freezing their asses off and have no idea what's going on. Greta and I say, "Happy Thanksgiving," to the kids. Greta asks the kitchen to make an apple pie for the kids. No dice.

December 6, 1944

Friedrichshafen

They swapped the German POWs for American POWs today. The Americans cheered and hugged one another. Then they handed us over to the Germans, like putting out the cat after a long day. The Germans weren't glad to see us, the Americans didn't give a damn if we dropped dead, and those South Americans were whisked away so fast I have no idea what became of them.

We walked a couple of miles over torn-up track, with four suitcases, the gold dollars sewn into my shorts, and two cold and weepy girls. We got to a boardinghouse. Greta made herself understood and she got on the phone to her aunt and uncle.

Here's what her uncle said: Why are you here?

How long are you staying?

What will you eat?

I wasn't even offended. Who in the name of Christ would leave America to come to Germany?

Karl Hauser, formerly your Gus

14

Let's Fly Away

My father's illness became a long, bumpy, terrible road to a place we didn't want to go, except that the road itself was so awful, we couldn't wait to get there. Clara told me that she'd missed her mother's death and had only heard about her brother's, and that these long days must be Someone's way of making up for that.

Sometimes my father thought Clara was his third daughter. The three of us were having dinner around his bed one night, balancing our plates on our knees, and he said, I don't know what I would do without my girls. I am the happy version of King Lear, a lucky man with three lovely daughters. Iris and I looked at each other and Clara waited until my father fell back asleep and said, You think it's nice for me? Being the third daughter, and the dusky one, the one who gets to brush his teeth and wash his wienie? I don't remember that scene from *King Lear*.

Iris had other fish to fry. She got bigger parts on Broadway, and came home at two in the morning, running up the stairs to Reenie.

Iris and Reenie both felt there was no reason for Danny to spend time in a sickroom with a man he'd hardly known before, who didn't know him now. In the daytime, Reenie cooked, and in the evenings, she watched Danny, leaving a lot of days to me and Clara, talking our way through the washing and the drying and the slow misery of feeding my father.

Clara said, "The first time I saw your father, I was walking out of the Silver Star Diner."

I said I loved their French toast.

"He raised his hat to me, like I was white," she said. "I liked that. I haven't always been in the company of gentlemen."

I nodded.

"Your father doesn't mind appearing foolish. That's a good thing."

I never saw my father as foolish. When I was a little girl, I saw him as a god, generous with the Hershey bars, and now I saw him as clever and shallow. Thin silver plate over nickel, is what I thought, and the thought must have showed on my face.

"You think this was nothing for him? You think your father lived in his own nice house, with an Irish maid and his own pretty family and taught English poetry three days a week and now he is a symbol of Joe Torelli's success, Joe Torelli's Rochester? You think this is what your father was hoping for? To open the front door for Joe Torelli and leave around the back?"

She put her hands in front of her, like she was praying for the strength not to hit me in the face.

My father opened his good eye and looked at Clara. He pressed his left hand over his heart, which was what he did now when he had strong feelings he couldn't express.

"Here now," Clara said. "It's okay. It's just me. It's just Clara. And Eva."

He put his left hand on hers. "I've forgotten some things."

"It doesn't matter," Clara said and she lay down next to him.

She put her head on his chest and pulled his hand down to her shoulder. I picked up the leftovers from breakfast.

"My dear," he said to her. "My love."

Then he said, *"Mamele."* And Clara lifted her head.

"Oh, boy," she said to me.

"Darling girl," he said. "I know you."

"I know you too," she said, still looking at me.

"No. I know you. Your brother took you everywhere. I never saw a guy so crazy about his little sister. Smoke Williams. I know you."

My father turned his head and fell into one of his quick, restless sleeps.

He didn't make much sense anymore. He talked about the green river Wye and the stately homes of England and sometimes about me and Iris, when we were very little girls together, which never was. Sometimes he would get very sentimental about my mother, which I found unbearable, but I didn't know how to tell my dying father to please shut up.

Clara said, "I did have a brother called Smoke. His name was Henry. I loved him. I'd go on his rounds with him, delivering liquor to different clubs. Everywhere we went, he made sure someone gave me a glass of milk, or a cookie or a little sandwich. I don't remember your being there."

"We played pool," my father said, with his eyes closed. "The Green Mill. Smoke ran the table. Who could forget?"

Clara said to me, "Honey, I have to get ready for tonight. Can I leave him with you?"

My father persisted. "No? *Nu?* Izzy Vogel, the Jewish boy at Chez Paree? You don't remember me? See the ears, see the big blue eyes? What happened to your brother?"

"He died in the riots," Clara said. "I'll take that stuff down," she said, and left the room.

"Yisgadal yis . . ." my father said, raising his hands to the sky.

. . .

ALMOST EVERYTHING HE SAID after that was in another language. Clara said it was Yiddish. He sang to us in Yiddish. He sat up in the bed, frowning, and said, "*Ich voyn bei* Grand Avenue, Chicago."

One afternoon, my father put his hands on Clara's shoulder and stood up. He gestured for his slippers, and I couldn't get his swollen feet into them. He shrugged. He took Clara's hand for a few steps and, barefoot, led her onto a dance floor, somewhere.

"Oh, the turkey trot," Clara said, over his shoulder. "Years ago. My aunt and uncle used to do all these crazy dances. Turkey trot. The camel. The grizzly bear."

My father danced another few steps and stood still, in the middle of the room.

"Oh, I wish I could shimmy like my sister Kate," he said and fell, bone by bone, to the floor.

THE DOCTOR CAME TO the house in April, when the tulips and forsythia were everywhere. Where there weren't enough flowers, the Torellis nestled small pink and white plastic chicks. They placed a pair of three-foot-tall porcelain bunnies and bouquets of giant pink and yellow ribbons at both ends of the driveway, and the doctor drove over the ribbons. Every time someone rang the bell at the carriage house, Clara would sit down in whatever room she was in and say, Doorbell.

"I'm not the maid," she said.

Clara and I had both read the article in the *Great Neck* magazine, written by an anonymous maid, complaining about no privacy, shitty leftovers, and notable stinginess in vacation and salary. Clara told me that one evening at the Nite Cap, a regular customer, a big woman from Alabama, read the entire article aloud from the stage.

"She says, 'And I say to you, ladies and gentlemen, next white woman ask me do I mind watching the kids for them on Thursday night is gonna get "I sho'nuff do and here's my foot on your fat white ass."' And you know who bought her a drink?" Clara said. "That nice Ozzie Patterson. Patterson's Cleaning Company. Patterson's Livery. And you know what else he did? He bought me a Manhattan. He bought me two and he drove me home. In his Oldsmobile."

"That was nice," I said, as if Ozzie Patterson, with his two businesses and his famously kind disposition and his obvious good health, were of no concern to me.

THE TORELLIS SENT A priest to sit with my father. It was a very Torelli thing to do: kind, well intentioned, a little tone-deaf. Not a single person in our extended family was religious, except Danny, who did actually pray on his knees every night, asking for miracles (bicycle, train set, hang glider). Danny was devoted to Saint Joseph of Cupertino, the patron saint of aviators, which he must have picked up from Reenie. When the Torellis told Reenie that Father Dom was coming over, Reenie walked out of the kitchen and into the garden to cool off. She came back in and told Danny to go play outside. She walked over to the carriage house and started setting the table, in the middle of the day.

"You want to give me a hand, here, missy?" she said.

Reenie threw down the plates. She said she'd given up on the Church. She said she wasn't one of those cafeteria Catholics, picking and choosing. She knew women who used diaphragms and took communion and men who committed adultery every week and never even bothered with acts of contrition. They opened their filthy, sinful mouths wide for the body and the blood of Christ and Reenie did not believe in that. She said she understood that the Church wasn't open to her, any more than her mother would have been. Most Italian men were like her father, she said, may he rest in peace. Their attitude toward the priest is You mind your business, I'll mind mine. Reenie said she didn't care for Pope Pius XII, who never said a word about the murder of the Polish Catholics, never mind the Jews. She said that she thought there were two possibilities, that Jesus was as the Bible described him, and her soul was in good and blessed hands, or Jesus was a cardboard figure pasted together by a bunch of smug priests and cowed nuns, and her soul, if she had one, was on its own. And so is yours, she said.

If Reenie didn't send Father Dom home, I thought Clara would. Clara leaned in the doorway, watching Reenie assault the table. Clara said she didn't like to talk to priests. She didn't like to talk to Baptist ministers either, but she certainly knew how. She told Reenie she didn't understand a thing about Catholics. It's all praise Mary, she said, women doing all the hard work and letting men run the church and calling the shots for everyone. When she was growing up, she said, her minister was a good-looking man, shiny black hair curling down to his snowy white collar. The ladies quoted him when it suited them, fussed over him, and carried on but didn't they manage to spin the churchly world on their strong brown fingers. The doorbell rang and Reenie poured us each a glass of wine. After five minutes, Father Dom, who clearly knew when a confession was coming and when that ship had sailed, came back downstairs and left. Reenie went back to the house, looking like a woman who'd wrestled and won.

If our paths had crossed earlier, Clara said, if someone had brought you when you were a baby to the Pilgrim's Hope Baptist Church in Chicago, you would have heard me sing when I was fourteen. I had a vibrato like a hummingbird. You could hear me almost every Wednesday at midnight, she said, and people I didn't even know talked about me and my sweet voice. Do you believe in Jesus? she said.

I said that I didn't. I said that I hadn't been raised that way.

Good, Clara said. She said it was bad enough when white people believed in Jesus but it was insane for black people to believe in Jesus, although she didn't go around saying that. She didn't believe, ever, that Jesus was going to deliver her to anything, anywhere. She said she absolutely did not believe that after two thousand years a white man was going to come back from his own lynching to help out Clara Williams or take her hand or be her friend.

When I had started having trouble with my skin, she said, I went out and got the names of doctors and I lay under special lights and bought jars of gray powder and a bottle of blue paste that burned so bad, I cried just opening the jar. You know what I didn't do? she said. Pray. I know your momma left you, she said. I left my mother. I had a pretty voice and ugly skin and I thought my best bet was a world of pink lights and heavy makeup. You know what my mother did when I told her I was going? She gave me five dollars and a ham sandwich and she went to church. What'd your mother give you, she said.

My mother left me a suitcase, I said. That was all I'd ever said, and "a suitcase" was always enough to get me a kind look from whoever I was telling. Francisco had practically burst into tears when I told him.

What was in the suitcase, Clara said.

I described my two white blouses, my cardigan, the two sets of underwear, and two pairs of socks. There was my brush-and-comb set and my nicest hair ribbons. I said that she hadn't left me a photograph of herself or of the two of us.

That's right, Clara said. She was saying to you, Look ahead, not behind.

THE DOORBELL RANG AGAIN.

"Oligodendroglioma" is what the doctor said. Iris sat with us for that and listened while we told the doctor everything: the new language and his all-day headaches and now the vomiting and his bowels and his right side entirely paralyzed and sleeping most of the day. The doctor said, Yes, that's what this tumor is like. And he said, He didn't learn a new language, you know. Whatever that is, it's the tongue of his childhood.

Mamaloshen is the word he was looking for.

15

Harbor Lights

I SMELLED SMOKE. I RAN INTO MY SISTER'S EMPTY ROOM AND heard Iris screaming outside, on the patch of lawn near the kitchen door. I should have gone to Danny, or to my helpless father, but I ran downstairs. There were no flames anywhere. Smoky threads rose from Reenie and Iris, rolling on the grass as one person. Iris rose up on one knee and Reenie lay on the grass, crying out weakly. I ran into the house and called the ambulance. Then I carried Danny to my father's room and lay him in bed next to Edgar.

"*Vos?*" he said. "*Vu?*"

I wrapped Edgar's arms around Danny.

"Just keep him here," I said. "We're fine."

"Of course," he said. He shifted over. "Looks like a nice kid."

I heard the sirens and ran back downstairs. In the red and blue flashing lights, three big men in white jackets put Reenie on a stretcher. I wanted to say, Save my sister, but Iris wasn't dying. She was calling Reenie's name.

I'm here, I kept saying. Iris was weeping and panting as they put Reenie into the ambulance. Two of the big men came beside us.

"Now, you, miss," the biggest man said to Iris. "Easy does it."

I touched her warm hair.

"Let me die," Iris said.

The big man nodded gently and the other two put her on the stretcher and shut the ambulance door behind her.

"You can follow," the man said to me. "Lenox Hill Hospital."

"I can't," I said. "I can't drive."

MR. AND MRS. TORELLI came down the gravel drive, in their thick bathrobes and velvet slippers. Mrs. Torelli put her arm around me and asked me what had happened. I said there was a fire but it didn't spread and she said, Thank God. Mr. Torelli asked me where they were taking them and he said that Lenox Hill Hospital was a good hospital, with good doctors. My cousin's a doctor, he said. I'll give him a call tomorrow. Mrs. Torelli pushed back my hair. You're gonna want a shower, she said. I could see the soot on her hands.

I looked in on my father and Danny, heads together on my father's big pillow. The kitchen had black streaks above the stove and toward the door and a pot of sauce splashed over the floor. I cleaned the floor and washed the pot. I shut the door to the kitchen. Mrs. Torelli would pay someone to fix it. I threw my smoky pajamas in the garbage. I took a shower and watched the gray water pool around my dirty feet. I used Iris's special chestnut shampoo and her rosewater face cream and I wrapped myself in her pretty blue robe. This is the Tower, I thought.

Letter from Iris

7 Queensberry Place
South Ken, London
April 1947

Dear Eva,

One of Carnie's ladies has caught up with me in London. She knows that you and I are sisters and that I am on the stage, which she finds thrilling. She is no longer a smart young lady from East Brooklyn (talk about your jumbo shrimp!) but is now a VIL—Very Important Lesbian—around town. She called on me to give a little hometown news and to get some Hollywood stories from me. I sang for my supper with stories of Mr. Thalberg getting frisky with his cigar and Garbo not wearing underpants and being a complete cow—all true. So, Diana Lapidus, as was, tells me that you're well and happy and still reading palms. She said, with much wink, wink, nudge, nudge that she hears you have a son, and I assume this is Danny. It must be Danny; you wouldn't have gotten rid of him—although you might have wanted to. He was not going to be the handsomest or easiest child. I could be mistaken, of course.

. . .

Let me start again. I was thinking about the two big trips we took, Ohio to Hollywood, Hollywood to Brooklyn. On my way up, on my way down.

I know I am leaving out the big middle.

I have this dream about once a week. I take Nembutal sometimes and then I have just the remains of the dream, the watery marks it leaves on me and the bed.

In the dream, you and I are dancing to "We're in the Money." Do you remember this? When you first came to live with us (and wasn't that a pip? I don't think there was another man in the world who would have said to his sixteen-year-old, recently bereaved daughter, "Yes, dammit, stop bothering me. Obviously, she's your sister. Now you have someone to play duets with." Didn't he just take the cake?), from time to time, you'd do a whole routine from *Gold Diggers of 1933*. I don't know what possessed you, but you were much better than the eyeglasses and cut-in-the kitchen hair had led me to expect. You had done the routine with your mother, I think. Or for her. I never got the feeling that your mother was an artiste.

First you did the parade from "Remember My Forgotten Man," which was hilarious. You marched across the living room, changing hats, helmet to newsie to baseball cap, and then you froze for a second, eyes down, hands in pockets, to demonstrate the plight of homelessness. Suddenly, you lifted your chin like a mad chorine and did the tap dance that the girls in the gold-coin hats had done. We did that number together, once, right before we left Ohio. The Rotarians' annual talent show, first prize, one-hundred-dollar bond. I made us gold hats, and Mrs. Drysdale (that fat widow next door, who always had her eye on Edgar?) gave me yards of gold braid and we sewed it onto the lapels and cuffs of our blazers. I put pancake on your legs and mine and I wouldn't let you wear socks with the tap shoes because it wasn't sophisticated. You had blisters like grapes

after, and I'm sorry. I couldn't figure out how to make those
gold-coin bottoms, so we wore short skirts with gold-ball fringe, also
courtesy of Mrs. Drysdale, who would have done anything for
Edgar's approval. Poor old thing, I never said a word to Edgar. Of
course, we didn't tell him about the show, and two days later we were
on the bus with every bond and dollar bill I'd hidden away.

In the dream, we're tap-dancing to "We're in the Money" and we
are too, too marvelous. "We're in the money, come on my honey,
look up, the skies are sunny . . ." We are *shimmering,* from our gold
caps and gold capelets to the gold lamé halter tops down to the
giant paillettes of our short shorts and our gold tap shoes. We are
Ginger Rogers vulgar and cheerful. We are like white-girl Nicholas
Brothers—sharp and sexy, fearless and exuberant. We are not trying
to please, we are the Gods of Pleasure, and lucky them who get to
see us. We leap from tabletops onto piano tops and then back
downstage, light bouncing off our gold coins, gold sweat flying. We
come down two long gold staircases, on opposite sides, and dance
downstage once more. I give you a twirl, you give me one, and we
hold it—I hear myself whispering to you, One, Two, Three, Four,
and the camera—I now see we're in a movie and this is the final
shot, a long shot of our bodies, behind a fountain of gold coins, filling the screen.

   It would be great if the dream ended here.

In the dream, I'm in a restaurant, just like real life that night when I
met Mr. Fox and Mr. Fletcher at Sardi's after the show. They said I
had star potential and they wanted to offer me something big. That's
what hooked me. Directors may be complicated and intellectual (you
couldn't prove it by me) but actors are so simple. Give us the good
stuff and we'll follow you anywhere. Genuine praise (not the "Darling, how do you do it?"), sincere gushing from someone important
and not on our payroll and not in our bed and we do whatever you
want us to, sucking in that reefer, fucking that donkey. Sorry.

In the dream, Fox and Fletcher are in green suits and I am sitting between them. The table is covered with food, which is not how it was. I didn't want to seem, one, impressed, two, unladylike, three, presumptuous, so I ordered a small steak, a green salad, and a glass of red wine. They kept saying, Have the shrimp, how about lobster thermidor, and I thought, Not yet, I won't. In the dream, just like in real life, I am thrilled and suspicious. I had this kind of dinner in Hollywood, and look how that turned out. In the dream, it's like Rome before the fall: small birds stuffed with glazed, glimmering things. Everything surrounded by frosted grapes and vegetables carved into flowers, a jeroboam of Champagne in a giant bucket (finally saw one this past year, at New Year's—huge), and two rings of enormous shrimp hanging off a crystal bowl and all facing right, like the Esther Williams swimmers.

In the dream, I drive home with the crystal bowl of shrimp on the passenger seat. This is what I really did want to do. There was a big bowl of shrimp on the table, and I wanted to bring some home to Reenie. She would have made scampi for us, or we would have just sat up and devoured them at the kitchen table. In real life, I didn't say much to Mr. Fletcher and Mr. Fox that evening, Thanks for the swell meal and the compliments and the expression of serious interest. In the dream, I say thank you and I keep looking at the truly enormous shrimp, thinking about how pleased Reenie will be with them, and me.

In the dream, just like it was in real life, Reenie is waiting up for me, in her pink kimono, with her hair piled up on her head. In the dream, she's happy to see me, her eyes are sparkling. In real life, she was steaming. It was the way it always was when I came back late. She yelled that she didn't leave Gus (which is not how I would describe it but . . .) so she could be my mistress. She didn't turn her back on her church and her family so she could be my dirty little secret. Once she threw a plate at the wall and once she broke my tortoiseshell sunglasses. I go toward her, to say I'm sorry—and I am sorry but I did think that a little discretion wouldn't kill us and I was not prepared to have Messers. Fletcher and Fox over for a home-cooked meal in the carriage house with Danny yelling for Mama, and you and Edgar playing dominoes in the front room.

The dream is no different from real life, at this point. Reenie did have a pot of sauce on the stove. She did say, I wasn't gonna start cooking till you walked in the door. I'm not sitting down to cold food anymore. I did say, Honey, I ate. She lit a cigarette off the stove, and I won't ever know what she was about to say. A rope of flame leaped from the burner to the end of her hand and wrapped around her chest and shoulders like a blue-and-orange curtain, like a bit of stagecraft pulling her up to the fly loft. Fire ran down the back of her robe. I started screaming and pulled Reenie out of the kitchen, rolling her around and around on the damp grass, until my hands were too burned to be of any use and Reenie had stopped screaming.

In the dream, just like in real life, the yard is dark, no light except for the porch lamp. I can hear Reenie breathing. Her whole body was black and red and ash, a deep shadow on the dark grass in the black night. I'm glad that I can't see her clearly, although I feel her hair on my arm. I can't feel my hands. They hang like red, blackened meat from my wrists. My fingers flutter like thick ribbons.

In the dream, the light from the porch fades until I can't see a thing. Edgar sleeps through everything. You come running downstairs in my fancy green silk nightgown, crying, reaching for me. There's no Danny. He's not missing. It's like he never was.

In real life, the last thing I saw was you beside me in your pink pajamas, fumbling with your glasses. You told me later that Edgar and Danny slept through the whole thing.

I don't think I was at Reenie's funeral. I hope it was lovely. I hope someone sang "Night and Day," because that was our song. I imagine the funeral was while I was in the hospital. Lucky us, that there were Torellis who specialized in things other than perfect fruits and vegetables. Dr. Andrew Torelli, taller and presumably smarter than Joe Torelli, was on his way to being a big man in burns and trauma at Columbia Presbyterian. Did you meet him? In my recollection, I was alone in the hospital most of the time. Dr. Torelli checked my hands where the burns were worst and he said the best person for this kind of damage was Dr. Arthur Litton, who practiced in England, where they saw a lot of this during the war. Dr. Torelli had studied under Litton at Columbia. The Torellis had a driver take me to the airport and to the gate. My hands were essentially useless and everyone did everything for me on the plane, although I could turn pages with the outside edge of my left palm and I could hold a cup between my forearms. I drank cups of gin for eight hours and someone took me to Queen Victoria Hospital, and there, in short, I recovered use of my hands. In not so short, eight months of exfoliating and grafts that didn't take and physical therapy the likes of which you have only seen in reenactments of Mary, Queen of Scots's imprisonment. The nurses were thoroughly bovine or as tough as the pilots they cared for (and I knew, and they told me, that they were there to take care of the airmen. I told everyone that I'd been burned while trying to save my sister, who died, and that did get me some sympathy). At night, I wept over Reenie and my hands. A nurse gave me hot milk with a little codeine for the first two months and then she saw I liked it and cut me off, saying, Enough, meaning enough codeine, enough grieving, and probably, that she'd had enough of me.

Dr. Litton was young and smart and second in command. Dr. McIndoe was the great man, and the savior of the RAF and other burned pilots. I met Dr. McIndoe once, and when he saw I was not a pilot, had my whole face, use of my legs and at least eight distinct fingers (as opposed to the slabs of pink patty so many of the men had), he lost interest. "'Not my cup of tea,' as the chorus girl said to the vicar." He let me stay at the hospital, anyway.

The airmen gave me hope. I doubt that most of them had started out as exceptional. They started out young and patriotic and full of that masculine excitement over testing themselves and, generally, full of themselves. They had a Guinea Pig Club (named for Dr. McIndoe's endless, often successful, experimenting on their limbs and faces) and they got used to me. Boys with half-faces, skin like red fungus from neck to hip or legless and rolling their wheelchairs to bring me a beer because the Guinea Pig Club was celebrating something. We celebrated Fridays. We celebrated that no one had died this week. That William Best had been offered a job in the office of British Airways. That Tom Marshall's glass eye fit like a charm, after three bad ones. I loved being their girl, and I sang my heart out for the Guinea Pig Club on every occasion. I gave them Noël Coward like they'd never had before, and I gave them the last of the red-hot mamas, complete with patter, and I cannot tell you how much I wish that everything I learned there stayed with me. You know, the crisis passes, the crucible cools, and there we are, slightly improved, not much altered. I expressed gratitude every day and I tried to be charming, as we'd had enough money only to cover the first month of my treatments.

How are you? How is Danny?

Peace in our time.

Iris, the Singing Guinea Pig of Queen Victoria Hospital

16

After You've Gone

IN THE DAYS AFTER REENIE DIED, I MOVED AS FAST AS I COULD. My plan was to help everyone, but sorrow made me deaf and blind and awkward. I poked Danny in the ear with a comb when I tried to fix his hair. I dropped scrambled eggs on my father's bare chest, because Clara wasn't around to feed him. I tripped getting the mail and skinned both my knees. Danny ducked when he saw me coming. I didn't understand why I kept falling over. It was much worse, and more awkward, than my worrying. Worrying was my nature. My father had been a beaker of etiquette and big ideas, Iris was a vase of glamour, and I was the little brown jug of worry. I worried about my father, almost immobile except for the tiny tremors and startling, meaningless gestures. I worried about Iris, because the last time I saw her she was being shoved screaming into an ambulance, smelling like charred meat. I worried about Danny, because I had no choice. Clara, who could have shared the worrying and helped with Danny, was on tour for another three weeks. By the time she came back, I planned to have nothing to say to her. She would beg me to tell her about this difficult time; she'd put both of her hands over mine and I'd turn my back on her. Oh, it's over now, I'd say.

Telling Danny that Reenie was dead, that Iris was in for a long recovery in a hospital somewhere, and that the person taking care of him for now and the indefinite future, was me, was the worst day of my life. I would rather have been left on that porch, sick to my stomach, watching my mother motor down an endless road, for every day of my life than ever relive, or even recall, telling Danny his mother was dead.

His mouth opened and closed a couple of times and he looked up at the ceiling. He smiled, as if this were one of our odd, grown-up jokes, the kind he didn't get but always wanted to. His face stretched and reddened around his wide, painful smile and then he turned his face away from me and cried, pressing himself into the back of the couch. Oh, how could we, I thought.

I am so sorry, I said. I am so sorry. I am so sorry we let this happen. I know I'm not at all the person you want taking care of you. I don't blame you. I know I am no kind of mother at all but I will try. Danny, I swear to God, I will not leave you and I will try.

Try, he said and we lay down on the floor, crying over what we didn't have.

REENIE'S FUNERAL WAS JUST four days later and short and small. I let Father Dom preside because who was there to object but me, and I didn't have the energy. Mrs. Torelli made the arrangements. Francisco came, to represent, and the five of us sat in the smaller chapel of the Torellis' church on Middle Neck Road and Father Dom spoke kindly, and even warmly, about Reenie and her loveliness and her devotion to the Torellis (leaving out Iris and glossing over Gus, the German spy). He focused on Danny, which I appreciated, and on God's will, which was appalling, as my father would have said. He wrapped it all up in a half hour. I thanked the Torellis and Francisco and I took Danny out for ice cream.

The next day, the Torellis had brought over a basket of fruit for me to deliver to Iris, for when she got out of her coma at Columbia Presbyterian Hospital. All the Diegos came to take me there. If I'd been left alone, making sure Danny caught the bus and that my father didn't fall out of bed, I might have been so busy, I wouldn't have gone to see Iris at all. Carnie banged on the door at 7 A.M. I told her I couldn't really drop everything to drive over to the hospital. She picked up the Torelli basket and handed me my loafers. Danny stood in the doorway of his room, pulling on his lip, which drove me crazy.

Let's put on our shoes, I said. I found his Raggedy Andy doll and most of his bagel and we all went to the hospital, Danny on my arm like a barnacle.

Bea kept Danny in the hospital cafeteria. ("What can you do?" she said. "Reenie's dead. Iris is a mess. Who needs to see that? You have to, he doesn't.") Carnie and Francisco stepped back to let me go into Iris's room first, to find a way to hug my sister gently, but with great feeling. My great feeling was that this was all a bad dream, that it was impossible that Reenie, adored by Danny and Iris, was dead and gone. I hadn't loved her but I had liked her and she had taken care of Danny and made my sister happy and that was, pretty much, good enough for me.

Iris opened her left eye (the right side of her face and neck was layered with gauze and tape), and even that did not look like my sister's eye. That bright, sometimes acid, leaf-green light had gone out of it. Francisco kissed Iris's forehead, and I did the same. Carnie sat at the foot of the bed. She told Iris a few stories about hijinks at La Bella Donna. I sorted everything in the basket and made a tower of the chocolates. I peeled a tangerine. Francisco said that I was taking care of everything at home, not that it was all on my shoulders, but I was doing a great job and Iris didn't have to worry about

a thing. Iris closed her eye. Carnie went to relieve Bea and Francisco said, You need to rest. I'll leave you girls alone. He took the
tangerine and went into the hall. He didn't come back.

I walked around the room. You know, I said, I thought it was
better Danny didn't come in and see you like this. Iris nodded and
the tubes taped to her chest and the cocoons on her arms and shoulders moved slightly. I said, We probably have a month at the Torellis. They need a butler and a cook and a governess. And I don't
think Danny and I can cover those bases. Iris closed her eye.

We sat for a few moments and she opened her eye again.

She mouthed the word *Reenie.*

"Can I touch you here?" I said, and I rested my hand on her left
leg. She nodded. "I thought someone would have told you."

Iris held my eye, furiously.

"I'm so sorry," I said. "They did everything they could for her.
She was . . . she wasn't . . . she was not alive by the time she got to
the hospital."

She mouthed the words *I know.*

"You know? You mean you already knew?"

Iris nodded.

"Does it help to have me tell you?" I said.

"No," she said.

ON THE WAY HOME, Francisco let Bea drive and he sat in the back
with me, with Danny sprawled across us, half asleep. Francisco told
me that when Iris's hands were healed, he had some tricks to help
her, to make her hands look pretty. In the backseat shadow, he
traced designs and contouring on my hand. (You shade the tips of
the fingers in pearl, he said, so they catch the light. The burned
areas, if there are any, you layer with a sheer foundation and then a
peach one and then you use just a little brown to slim the fingers.
Plus, she has to wear nail polish, always, to make her hands look
finished.)

Iris was in the special burn unit for another two weeks. The Torellis sent more fruit baskets, to her, and to me. Danny and I ate fancy pears and ginger cookies and Golden Delicious apples, and I have to say that he never asked for a decent meal. I figured that when he lay in bed, praying in his mysterious way, he asked God: What kind of people steal you from your life, however miserable, and give you a better life, however peculiar, and then take it away, just when you've just gotten a tiny bit comfortable?

Every morning, I fed my father poached eggs and jam from the little jars tucked into the fruit baskets and then I took Danny to school. I quit going to La Bella Donna, even though I knew that wasn't the smart thing to do, and looked after my father, who didn't really need anything except a milk shake and a bedpan. I didn't have it in me to tell women what might happen to them.

I'd walk to Danny's school and sit outside his classroom until the bell rang. We'd take the bus into town and go shopping for things we liked. I stole nail polish for me and Captain Marvel comics for him. We bought ice cream cones at Kriegel's and walked over to Grace Avenue Park to do my nails and read. We watched the kids play. When it got a little cooler and darker the kids went home and Danny and I put our goods in my bag and we played on every piece of equipment, and perfected a standing double on the slide and then we took the bus home, for our fruit and cheese and cookie dinner.

I don't know who visited Iris. Even though I think that I am, really, in the red cul-de-sac at the bottom of my heart, a better person than Iris, I know that if it'd been me in that hospital, she would have slept in the chair beside my bed.

17

Hitler Has Only Got One Ball

Letter from Gus

Pforzheim
January 2, 1945

Heil Hitler! Just kidding. People here salute all different ways.

Fick dich and the horse you rode in on. Or, *Mein Gott,* when will this war be over? Or, You can have my sister if we can have your chicken. Or, What are you looking at, *Hurensohn?* (SOB, to you.) Or, I'm doing my best here—don't shoot me or steal from me or turn me in. (I'm working on that last one. I hope it will keep us alive.)

The little girls *Sieg Heil!* like you wouldn't believe. If this country weren't being strafed, shit on, and starved, we'd have to take them downtown and buy them little Bund Deutscher Mädel outfits. BDM is like the Girl Scouts—if the Girl Scouts gave badges for Jew-killing and world domination. The girls goose-step around the little square of dirt in front of the house all morning. I don't discourage them. I'm hoping their enthusiasm makes us look good. Greta just flaps her hand up at the wrist and looks away.

Her aunt and uncle are decent people, what we think people in the old country should be. Salt of the earth. We've got no butter, no chickens, and no gas. The old man tinkers with this and that, sharpens knives, and does a little black market in cigarettes when he can. The aunt cleans the kitchen twice a day and makes potatoes sixteen ways. Occasionally, there's a mashed turnip that we could use to patch tires, if we had tires. These people wish we'd never come. The old lady hisses when I come into the kitchen. We make the girls play outside until their lips are blue. But the aunt and uncle share their dinner with us every night and twice, the old man and I have hitched out to a farm so I could fix some prehistoric tractor. Most mornings, we just keep walking until someone with a few eggs needs a knife sharpened.

They lost two sons on the Russian front. They don't know where their third boy is. I haven't seen another man in Pforzheim with all his limbs, and under forty. There's a young guy up the road and he gets around with a cart on four wheels, like a kid's wagon but big enough to accommodate a grown man. He must have been six-two when he had legs. We're friendly, and sometimes, after a few shots, Hans asks me to tell him the story of our coming to Germany. He laughs until he cries and sometimes I do too.

There's no work for me in town. There were watchmakers and jewelers on every corner and now there's nothing.

January 28, 1945

We got bombed for the first time last night. Greta was throwing dishwater in the yard because the drain was backed up and I was pulling the curtains. The girls stood on the porch, calling the cat. The bombs started falling and the girls looked up. I don't think they knew what they were seeing or hearing. The alarm screamed out and we hustled down to the cellar. I carried Carolyn, Greta took Anna and the old people, and the cat hurried down behind us. The lights went out. We slept in the cellar, in the smoke. In the morning, Uncle Horst and I pulled down the back door and what was left of the kitchen. We are all fine.

Your pal, Gus

GUS AND HANS LISTENED to the radio address of Marshal Harris, from London. The marshal said, "It should be emphasized the destruction of houses, public utilities, transport and lives, the creation of a refugee problem on an unprecedented scale . . . are accepted and intended aims of our bombing policy. They are not by-products of attempts to hit factories."

The man was as good as his word, Gus thought.

DRESDEN HAPPENED TEN DAYS before Pforzheim. Herr Altmann's brother drove his old truck three hundred miles from the outskirts of Dresden, where there were still some roads, to Pforzheim. Gus helped him out of the truck and he made the girls play in the yard while Greta changed the dirty bandages around the old man's neck and ear. He talked for an hour, and Greta translated for Gus. The center of Dresden was destroyed. He'd driven past piles of rubble taller than the people who came out from the cellars. He said the rubble was brick, stone, bicycle frames, burning tires, wood framing, people's coats and hats and shoes, and underneath and in between that, people. He said he passed dead people without a mark on them; they'd died from asphyxiation. Gus asked Greta if she was sure that's what the man was saying. Greta said, I'm sure. His name is Klaus, Greta said, and Gus shook his hand.

. . .

GUS HERDED THE THREE elderly Altmanns and Greta and Carolyn and Anna in and out of the cellars six times in two days, with small bombs falling and small planes flying low overhead. Gus asked Greta to ask Klaus if this was how Dresden had started. Klaus said no—Dresden had started with a bang, and Gus and Klaus laughed in the cellar.

After the first round of bombs, Gus and Klaus and Herr Altmann drove the old truck around parts of Pforzheim to view the damage and see if there was anything they could do. They saw half-buildings, walls with window spaces, transoms without doors beneath them. A church spire lay in the street, leaning up against the library, closing off the road. A nurse ran under it. At one house, flames were still running up and down the house like imps, having blown out the windows and opened the roof.

They drove home, and the bombs fell as they got out of the truck. Girls, into the cellar, Gus yelled. Greta, *mach hinne*! He felt the fire roll down the steps, old wood or dirt steps, into the cellar, right behind him and the girls. Jars of cherry preserves exploded. The cellar lights blinked and flared up and then snapped into darkness. The bombs stopped and Anna stood up and stamped her feet, to get out. Klaus said, Sometimes when people run to get out of the cellar, they burn their hands and arms on the metal hasps. Gus wrapped his hand in his coat and pushed the door open, just two inches. He found the world on fire. Light rained down. It lit up the sky like the town had done on New Year's and the light pooled, still bright and burning, on the cold ground. Blood-orange flames spread through their yard and through their iron fence.

For three days, ashes fell like snow. Gus kept the girls in and they watched the flakes coming down and drifting up. All the German women Gus knew collected something; his mother and his grandmother collected snowbabies, Schneebabies. His mother had loved the ones with a prickly white bisque all over them, only their

pink, smooth china cheeks and dark eyes visible. *Schneeflocken.*
Snow-covered. Everything around what was left of the house was
schneeflocken. There was one last series of bombs, for most of a day.
His family lay in the cellar for hours, on the dirt, their coats on top
of the broken glass, as the sky thundered and the rest of the house
blew apart and the floor above them rolled up, like an old rug.
When Gus came to, all three of the Altmanns lay dead, side by side,
near the cellar steps. Anna and Carolyn had died next to Gus, arms
and legs out wide, like starfish. He couldn't find Greta's body.

Afterward, people said more died in Dresden than in Pforzheim.
More died in Tokyo than in Dresden, Gus said, and who cares.
Before he left Pforzheim, Gus walked to his friend Hans's house.
Hans's body was still in his yard, his arms around his mother. The
four wagon wheels lay on them like wreaths.

Part Three

1945-1949

18

Going Home, Going Home

I HAD BEEN GONE FROM THE SALON FOR WEEKS. I WAS BROKE again and couldn't borrow from anyone. As my father would have said, if he could talk, One should only take advantage of those who can afford it. I told Danny he had to start taking the bus home, and I went back to work. When I finished reading the cards for Mrs. Russo and her never-returning husband and made contact with Mrs. Rubio's son, lost at sea, Bea said, Stay for a drink. Francisco came into the salon with a box of cookies. Bea said, Looky here. We love you. That Danny is a nice little boy. He's funny, Carnie said. Guess what, she said. Bea, here, got married last week. She and that Artie eloped, like a couple of kids.

I said that was a wonderful surprise, and then Carnie said, You could say that—she's got a miracle bun in the oven. Oh, I'll look like a beached whale by Thanksgiving, Bea said. And did Carnie tell you? She's being chased all over East Brooklyn by a dentist with a little girl. Dead wife, not divorced. He's nice, Carnie said. Rabinowitz.

I said I was glad for both of them. I said they'd done plenty for us and no one could have done more. That card table, I said. You set me up in business. You and Mrs. Vandor. We still don't know what had happened to Mrs. Vandor, Carnie said. Life's a mystery. I think she ran off with her piano teacher, Mr. Shmottlach. Bea nodded. That's what we think. Good-looking guy. Foreign.

Can I keep reading cards here? I said. They looked embarrassed. Of course, Carnie said. No one's throwing you out. We're just saying things have changed, so we can't take the two of you in and we wish we could.

Francisco would—he loves you like a daughter (You know what she means, Carnie said) and he really likes Danny—but he has his hands full. I understand, I said. Bea and Carnie made big eyes and they looked over at Francisco and shook their heads. He has his hands full, they both said, with setting up a new barbershop in Penn Station, with a manicurist and a shoeshine stand. (Inside the shop, Bea said. You know he's smart.)

I said that was great and Francisco said his sisters had been generous in backing him and they both thanked him for thanking them and then everyone looked around and we all had some cookies.

This is where you want someone, a Mrs. Vandor or a Charlotte Acton, to grab the plate of cookies and say, Aren't these marvelous?

Also, Bea said, Francisco's got his hands full at home too. Carnie looked like she wanted to cry. I have a boy staying with me, Francisco said. He's straight from Mexico, he's a hard worker, and he's staying with me until he gets on his feet. Your little *taco de ojo*, Carnie said, and they were off and running in Mexican but quietly, until Francisco slammed his hand on the table and the sisters shut up. It's just for a while, Francisco said. Believe me, I know what you know, he said to his sisters. I'm teaching him English. Carnie said, You're cooking for him. I am, Francisco said. I cook for him and I play conquian with him. Yes, Encarnación, we do play cards. It's shocking, I know. He sleeps on the couch. Jorge is a beautiful boy, Francisco said. He's beautiful and I'm not a fool. He starts night school in two weeks.

Carnie rolled her eyes and said, We'll see. And we did see. Jorge went to night school and he met an Anglo girl named Gracie Shreve from Long Island City and he brought her to Francisco for his blessing. They married and Francisco went to the wedding and hung pictures of Gracie and Jorge slicing the cake, of Francisco and the Shreves lifting their glasses, of Francisco waltzing with the bride. Gracie sent a card every Christmas, with a picture of her and Jorge and their two little boys, all looking very well, and Francisco put them up on the mirrors of the barbershop, near the framed photographs of Francisco and Mayors La Guardia and O'Dwyer.

Francisco sighed and put his hand on my shoulder. I've got something for you in my car, he said. Before you go. In the car, he rummaged around and found a brush-and-comb set with fire trucks on it for Danny and some rhinestone combs for his sisters. We went back into the salon, and Bea and Carnie were sitting still, arms flung on my tarot table like they'd been shot in the back.

"It's the president," Carnie said. "He's dead."

"In Warm Springs," Bea said. "Ah, he's dead. Who killed him? Our president."

Francisco pulled me onto the dirty velvet couch. I cried in his arms and Bea and Carnie cried in each other's arms and we all sat around the table and wept and listened to the radio, which reported every detail of the president's aneurism and his collapse and the moment he said, "I'm afraid I have a terrific headache." We could all imagine him saying it, that plummy, patrician voice that managed to be the voice of people who never spoke that way, never dressed that way, never went to a single place Franklin Delano Roosevelt had ever been, and he spoke for the three of us.

"I have to get Danny," I said. "Do you think the school told the kids?"

Francisco said, "You tell Danny the president was a great man. You make sure, no matter what some lying, Republican schoolteacher *pendejo* tells him, that your little boy knows we won't see another like that man. You tell him."

"We all have to go home," Bea said, and she turned out the lights.

People were driving all over the road, and on the shoulders. I passed men driving toward the city with tears streaming down their faces. I could see the people on the buses above me, white handkerchiefs pressed against dark faces. I picked Danny up and he was shaking. I told him what Francisco told me to say and when we got home, the two of us got into my bed and listened to the radio all night. I missed my sister, then.

OUR OWN FUTURE, BY which I mean mine and Danny's, was not so clear and, where clear, not so rosy. We'd moved. The Torellis were as good to us as anyone could ask. I certainly hope that if I found myself with a lot of money, four children, and a big house on the water and my butler fell ill and my cook died and my kids' governess hightailed it to England, that I would be as generous and patient with the survivors as the Torellis were. But I doubt it. Mrs. Torelli said we could take the living room couch and the hutch and the pots and pans and she handed me an envelope with two months' rent for a small house on Old Tree Lane. She'd found it through the new maid's sister and put a deposit down before I ever saw it, which was reasonable. I was eighteen and taking care of a sick old man and an eight- or nine-year-old boy I hardly knew, making my living as a fortune-teller in East Brooklyn, and I wasn't likely to say, No, thank you, not quite, let's keep looking. Mrs. Torelli said good-bye to us pretty much the way she'd said hello—kind and a little surprised to find herself in our company. Mr. Torelli had had plenty of experience with damaged goods and the wishes and hopes of all his scheming cousins, and my guess is that he knew us by the end. He stood in the fork of the driveway and watched Ozzie Patterson carry my father like a pile of firewood and plant him head up and feet down in the back of his car. I carried down carton after carton, like an ox on a muddy hill, and when I was about to go upstairs for a final sweep, Mr. Torelli gave me a fifty-dollar bill.

"My mother died when I was eight," he said. "Good luck to you."

I packed Danny into the car with his Tinkertoys and Raggedy Andy and the pilot's jacket Reenie had given him for his last birthday. I stood in the big, curving driveway and wished what I always wished, that I could turn left and go to the Torellis', instead of taking a quick right to the carriage house. Clara waited for us at the new house, sipping a cold drink at the kitchen table and supervising Ozzie's idiot cousin (her words, not mine) in unloading our beds from the Sears truck, a gift from Ozzie Patterson. The Sears driver was Negro. Our next-door neighbors on both sides were Negro too. The old man across the street was white and sat on his porch, smoking and watching. Little Ruthie Post, Danny's dearest friend, who lived only a couple of blocks away, sauntered past (always as if she'd been touring her estate and just happened to pass our cottage) and invited Danny to walk her to the park, so he missed the tearful shifting and unloading of my father, of our few furnishings, of Reenie's clothes, which were too big for me, and of Iris's clothes, which I refused to send her.

OZZIE CARRIED EDGAR TO the attic and tucked him in, and when he came down, he washed up and offered Clara his arm. They left. I cleaned hard for the rest of the day and then gave up for a good, long time. I made pancakes for me and Danny and soft scrambled eggs for my father. I sat with Danny while he prayed to Saint Joseph of Cupertino and he let me kiss him goodnight, in his new bedroom, with the new bed and airplane-shaped rug, courtesy of Ozzie Patterson and his devotion to Clara.

I went back to the attic to sit by my father. His brain tumor was killing him. He wouldn't get better and he wouldn't die. People say that even if the dying seem not to hear you, they do. After a few nights at the new house, while changing a bedpan, I told him, "It's all right—you can let go." My father must have heard this as a call to arms. He rallied. He started opening his eyes for a few hours every day and muttering in Yiddish. Clara said we (meaning I) should get someone who spoke Yiddish to encourage Edgar, and I did. I found Bernie Smedresman of Bernard's Fine Dry Cleaning. Mr. Smedresman was short, round, unstoppably kind. He was a bowling ball of good will. He brought the bagels and accoutrements, and sometimes Clara and Ozzie stopped by for bagels and lox. Mr. Smedresman brought herring in cream sauce, but only Ozzie tried that.

Falling in love with Ozzie Patterson didn't stop Clara from directing my father's care. She supervised what I cooked for him and when I fed him and she made it clear that I would now be giving him his sponge baths, not her. And I thanked her every day, just for showing up. Twenty minutes after my father died, she'd be gone, in a puff of smoke and a shimmer of silk, and I didn't blame her. She came most mornings to make herself a cup of coffee, kiss my father on the forehead, sing a few songs to him, and come downstairs to smoke a couple of cigarettes and laugh at me. What a mess, she'd say. A baby with a baby. She'd poke Danny in the back, telling him to stand up straight and be polite, telling him no girl wanted a mealy-mouthed, hunchbacked boyfriend. She'd hand him a comic book and me her red lipstick. Fix yourself up and eat a decent meal, she said. God knows, the way you look now, you got to get up twice to cast a shadow.

THE WAR ENDED. THE blackout drills were over and the streetlights came on. We hadn't ever kept the garden hose, metal buckets, and long-handled shovel we were supposed to have at our house. I didn't have anything more than a broom, a sponge, and a box of borax. We didn't even have a ladder, and when Danny threw a ball on the roof, I had to climb past my father, out the attic window, and get it while Danny told me to be careful. The Victory parade went up Middle Neck Road, from All Saints' Church to the green, on January 12, just like the big one in the city. We had two drum majors leading the band from the Merchant Marine Academy, and high school girls handing out flowers and flags, and a jeep covered in red roses, carrying three soldiers, waving stoically. The ministers and a priest and a rabbi stood in the gazebo on the lawn behind the library and read the names of our dead. Danny and I cheered for the living and cried for the dead, like everyone else. I hoped that Gus was in the first category, but I doubted it.

If you'd asked me what I understood about fortune-telling, I would have told you that no one came to see someone like me because they were happy. I would have said, People come because they are so frightened, they wake up in a sweat. They look into the well of their true selves, and the consequences of being who they are, and they're horrified. They run to my little table to have me say that what they see is not what will happen.

The end of the war turned everything upside down. (Maybe not for the Germans and the Japanese, but they weren't coming to my little table.) People were getting married and having babies and buying houses, going to school and getting divorced, all double-time. Aside from the two grieving Gold Star Mothers who came every week, to see if I could give them a reason to live, the women at La Bella Donna came to ask me about the future, not the past, and they were not taking no for an answer. A friend of Mrs. Russo's came by to say that she was thinking of moving back to Pennsylvania without her husband. I've got a farmhouse there, she said. And friends. What do the cards say about that? One woman came to me, a new bride. All she wanted to hear was how many boys, how many girls, and would she be pregnant by Christmas. Two of each, I said, and absolutely.

When the soldiers came back, business boomed for the car dealers and the beauty parlors and for me.

Francisco and I had found a pair of rooms for my little business on Danny's first day of school. Francisco kept muttering, High traffic, low rent, easy parking, and he found what he was looking for. He'd negotiated my low rent with a man his age and size and when they finished, they smoked their cigars on the back step. Who'd you say I was, I asked. You're my youngest daughter, he said. Plus, you have a gift, just like my late wife, may she rest in peace. You won't charge him for a reading, if he ever wants one and you lock up by eight o'clock. No funny business.

We carried up my shepherdess lamp and two small chairs and the folding table I brought back from La Bella Donna. (Take the chairs, Carnie said. Take the tablecloth too, Bea said. Good luck, honey, they cried out from the steps of La Bella Donna.) We bought four fat safety candles from the hardware store and covered the furniture with pieces of Iris's old dresses (lace over black silk for the table and green velveteen stapled to the chairs). Francisco painted every piece of glass black. He got a bolt of chicken wire for the windows and layered old scarves and sheets over them until every view was of a cloudy night sky.

Psychics, like dress designers and psychoanalysts and madams, have to pay attention to their place of business. If I'd had money, I would have gone for opulent fabric and Oriental rugs and maybe a little samovar whistling in the corner. Malachite objects would dot the shelves, along with a mysterious, large mahogany box and a faded photograph of a sad-eyed little girl with long curls and a floppy satin bow. Depending on the customer, she could be a relative, a murdered Romanov, my young self (And who's to say that you yourself are not an escaped Romanov, is what my father would have said), or my spiritual guide. (You'd be amazed. Every kind of child, every kind of medieval healer, every kind of dear departed auntie, serves as someone's guide to the spirit world. I have noticed that no one uses foreigners, unless they can master the accent. You don't see Italian psychics, for example, with Norwegian guides. Or vice versa. The afterlife is worse than East Brooklyn.)

Francisco liked my setup. He liked that the women could pick up cookies from Stricoff's and a roast chicken from Arrandale Rotisserie and finish their reading with me before the kids came home from school. He said he wasn't sure that men would appreciate all that. But, he said, a man who has to go to a psychic is in such deep shit, he doesn't care where he is.

I hung a small sign in the window, ASSOCIATION FOR META-PHYSICAL RESEARCH. Like the Star of David at Danny's orphanage, meaningful to those in the know. I offered free readings to the ladies at Stricoff's bakery, in exchange for day-old everything. I offered a two-for-one for sisters and I offered packages of five, for those who expected to need it. The whole world was bursting with things for women to buy, and I was one of them.

19

Spring Will Be a Little Late This Year

Letter from Gus

Trutzhain, Germany
August 1945

Dear Evie,

A tree is measured best when it's down. That's what they said about Lincoln and that's what they'll say about Roosevelt. I hear that in Tel Aviv, they trimmed all the flags in black and flew them at half-mast. I hear a Negro man played Haydn on the accordion as the funeral procession passed through Warm Springs, Georgia. The women here are weeping like they're all Eleanor. Maybe all Jewish women *are* Eleanor Roosevelt—better-looking, not as good a writer, but the good heart, the sharp mind, the endless mixing into other people's business. We have four rabbis now, so we had a lively service. No one here says, He didn't do enough. One man here, his brother was on the *St. Louis* when it got turned around and the relief people got him to Israel, where he's now eating oranges. So, no harm, no foul. The people here loved that fucking jaunty cigarette holder, the stiff upper lip, the expensive overcoat. Our goy. I remember the Republican bankers and the fat cats who accused him of being secretly Jewish. The Jew Deal. President Rosenfeld. Clearly, there was no other explanation for the man's decency and concern for the poor. Flattering, I guess.

The Jews say there were three worlds, *Drei velten:*

Die velt (this world),
yene velt (the next world)
Roosevelt.

I can make a joke in Yiddish, which brings me to—

I'm Jewish now, which I wasn't when we knew each other. (I don't think it'll bother you but the anti-Semitism of decent people keeps surprising me.) With four rabbis hanging around, we steamrolled the conversion process.

I worry that when we next see each other, I'll be looking at a grown woman, smart as a whip, funny and straight as a die, and you'll see a dried-up piece of salami, with a bum leg and a missing incisor. Did you go to college yet? Did some smart guy propose?

I have to tell you, I'm not exactly making a living. I got myself to a DP camp in Trutzhain, not the best, not the worst. The Trutzhainians, the Trutzhainiks, got rid of all the Nazi criminals. (Except the ones they didn't get rid of, who are back in their old offices, pretending they were fucking monarchists. I prefer the honest bastards, spit-shining their boots in prison and greeting each morning with *"Heil Hitler!"*) Then the camp had to make room for the Poles.

(Forgive me, but the most anti-Semitic people on earth, with the possible exception of the Ukrainians, who are *butchers*. I'm hoping none of your people are either one.) We've got Polish Jews, some nuns, some whores, and some German Quakers. The lice are unstoppable. You shave your head on Monday and find the little bastards back on Friday. There's not enough food, and some people are still wearing their uniforms from the camps, prayer shawls wrapped around their feet, tucked inside the boots they've been given. God help them. Once a week, we count off to see who's died.

I came the way most of us came, limping and bare-ass, the soles of our shoes tied on with string, or wood slabs held to our feet with half a shirt. We had learned to leave everything behind, except food and weapons. I had some rabbit meat and a knife tucked into my belt. The man next to me, a Gypsy who'd lost his way, had black rolls in every pocket and a crowbar down his pants leg. We carried the others, dragged the dying, and dropped the corpses at the feet of the nurses. Some of these people are goodness itself. The rest are the usual mix: liars, cheats, lazy bastards, sadists who couldn't beat a man in a fair fight but will hold back a bar of soap from forty kids with running sores.

I'm teaching English—what do you think of that? We call it Rudimentary Conversational English. I give everyone a name Americans will be able to pronounce. When a lot of Jews named Bob wash up in New York with heavy accents, don't be surprised. I'm teaching them all to say, "Gus sent me."

I have a pal, Lev, from Moscow. He told the Americans that he'd be tortured and murdered if he went home. He recited our Declaration of Independence—phonetically. He doesn't speak English yet. He said, The Poles won't budge and neither will I.

In July, they sent a couple of hundred Polish Jews home, in patched pants and jackets, wearing borrowed shoes, carrying one loaf of bread each. They were murdered in Kraków, in Sosnowiec, and in Lublin. In Kielce, they were beaten to death by eight hundred Polish

Worker party heroes, who came at them with crowbars and clubs. When some decent people carried the Jews to the hospital, Polish soldiers robbed them. They stole the shoes off the unconscious. Jews ran to the train station and got on trains going anywhere. Passengers threw the Jews off the moving trains. Our Polish correspondent reported that Cardinal August Hlond said that violence in Kielce was unfortunate and probably caused by the concerns of Poles for the safety of their children. Cardinal Adam Stefan Sapieha said that the Jews had brought it on themselves. So, in the last year, a hundred thousand Jews—don't say we can't take a hint—left Poland. Here in Trutzhain, we're not going anywhere. Obviously, I'm a special case. The International Red Cross workers can't believe I'm even here. They refer to it as the "misunderstanding." I agree that there seems to have been a misunderstanding.

 Grusse und Kusse, kiddo.

Gus

January 1946

Zei gesundt, Evie!

 This means Be in good health. The Yiddish is coming along. I am now the senior lecturer in English at the Free University of Trutzhain (there's no junior lecturer). I make up job application forms and have people practice filling them out. I've explained that Americans are as punctual as Germans but more casual in their speech. I tell them someone will give them a nickname and they should accept it. I don't tell them that even in America, they can round you up and keep you in with barbed wire. Why rain on their westward-ho parade? Everyone here will settle in the Bronx, Brooklyn, or Queens, places where I know the street addresses. My dead parents are now sponsoring twenty-seven people. Also, I've given everyone here an advanced degree from 1932, when that could have happened. I gave myself a certificate from Bonn (engineering) and an advanced degree from the University of Pforzheim (mathematics).

(Do you remember Pforzheim? Did those letters reach you? Do these? Exactly once, we've had mail. A woman got a letter from New Jersey. Everyone in the camp touched it, for luck.)

Six weddings and four babies in the last three months. Lev changed his name to Lew Stern. For a few days, he was Louis Smith, but since he couldn't pronounce his own goddamn name (Louise Smeet, he kept saying), we decided to aim a little lower.

Two starving Jews, Mr. Cohen and Mr. Ellenbogen, are sitting on a park bench, sharing their last piece of bread.

They look across the park and a priest's putting up a big sign in front of his church: CONVERT NOW AND WE'LL GIVE YOU $1,000!

"Oh, boy," says Cohen. "I'll do it!"

An hour later, he comes out, looking happy.

Ellenbogen says to him, "Did they give you the money?"

Cohen spits in his direction. "Is that all you people ever think about?"

Your Gus

February 1946

Dear Evie,

We have six soccer clubs. We've got one made up entirely of orphans, Die Yesomim, and another, A Schanda und a Charpeh (A Scandal and a Disgrace), for cripples. They are some tough, toothless SOBs and to watch a pair of them on crutches, scrambling down the field is to believe in . . . something. You tell me.

Yesterday, Mr. Schwartzwald, six blue numbers tattooed on his left arm, called Mr. Warburg, also with six blue numbers tattooed on his left arm, a Nazi. They were in Auschwitz together. They lay in a

ditch next to the crematorium chimney and watched their wives and
children go up in smoke. They crawled here, lame and sick with grief.
They've recovered, so they can fight over our infirmary supplies. After
Mr. Schwartzwald called Mr. Warburg a Nazi, Mr. Warburg called
him an anti-Semitic SOB. I'm sure there is a phrase in Yiddish for
this kind of thing, but I don't know what it is.

Your Gus

20

To Each His Own

Ruthie Post was our savior. She had loved Danny since the beginning of third grade (or whatever it was she felt for him—she dragged him around town like a pull toy). Her friendship and Mrs. Post's introductions to the small grocery store and the smaller candy store (making sure that Mr. Herman and Mr. Davis knew that although it seemed unlikely, I could and would pay my bills) made our new life on Old Tree Lane manageable. Ruthie was our guide to all aspects of Arrandale School's fourth grade. What Ruthie said, went. She told Danny what kind of Buster Browns to wear, to keep his ears clean (Billy Moore did not and no one would sit with him, ever), and that it was important to start out with a lunch ticket in fourth grade. Apparently, everyone knew who had a card and would experience the satisfying exchange with the lunch-room monitor and the sharp sound of the paper punch, and who would not. According to Ruthie, if you established your high status in September, no one held it against you if you were brought low and forced to carry a lunch from home in November.

Ruthie Post had told Danny that the school bus came to our corner at 8:18. She told him that he'd be standing with three skinny little white girls (and she didn't say white trash, because Mrs. Post would not have let her, but her eyelids drooped and we knew) and a Negro boy with thick glasses. Ruthie felt that the three girls were not the troublesome kind and that Danny'd have no trouble with Roger, the Negro boy (son of the idiot cousin). Ruthie told Danny to be nice, but not too nice. She said he should say hello to her cousin Roger but not sit with him on the bus. Ruthie told Danny that that would be bad for both of them. Danny asked Ruthie if she would be on the bus both ways and walk him home. Ruthie said, as I wanted to, and never did, "You're big. You walk yourself home." I was so grateful to have such a brutally plainspoken girl around, I promised Danny I'd wait for him with milk and cookies on his first day.

Francisco had promised to come help me with the finishing touches at the shop and I lay on the couch and stared at our blotchy, blooming ceiling until he came. I put the milk back in the refrigerator because I couldn't buy any more milk if it went bad. I left the cereal bowls and Danny's crusts and my own socks and shoes and old newspapers and Danny's toys scattered around, like flares at an automobile accident. I was trying to put a shape to my life with Danny and I don't know which one of us was more surprised and distressed at my failure. Every morning, I yanked the covers off him and said, Good morning, like I meant it, and watched him wash his face and brush his teeth and cheered him and hustled him through breakfast and out the door. Our day of crying on the couch in the carriage house was behind us. We were like the soldiers in Stalingrad, moving forward only because backward wasn't possible.

21

Not in the Day and Not at Night

RUTHIE POST LIKED DANNY ACTON BETTER THAN HER GIRL-friends and she liked his strange little family. Her own family was nothing special. Danny sat right next to her in Mr. Hoerger's class and he was the only other person reading at the Bluebird level. Danny lived three blocks from Ruthie on Old Tree Lane. He had his own room, like Ruthie, and his grandfather lived there, and Danny's aunt, who was raising him, and the Negro lady, who was like a visiting nurse. Ruthie's mother had expressed a lot of interest in the Negro lady.

"I'm just asking you, Ruthie, is she a member of the family?"

Ruthie said she didn't think so. She said that Clara Williams sang at the Nite Cap, which was *the* jazz club on the Island (and Ruthie said it the way the lady did, stretching out "the"). Ruthie didn't say that she couldn't say what color Clara Williams was, although Ruthie was sure that the lady was a Negro. She had Negro hair. Her hair looked and smelled like it had Glossine in it, which

Ruthie's mother used on all her ladies. Her skin was no color—it was the color of fat on a pork chop, the frizzled edge of a bug bite after your bath. One time, when Clara Williams was visiting, she didn't close the bathroom door and Ruthie and Danny watched from the hall as she did her makeup. She patted her face all over with foundation, on a sponge. ("You wipe it off when you use your fingers," Danny said. "Francisco said you shouldn't even bother putting it on without a sponge, you're just coloring your hands.") She did her eyelids with a tiny brush and a bigger brush for her sparkly plum powder and she spat into a little black box to do her mascara. Danny started to explain and Ruthie punched him in the ribs. She knew. She watched her mother do it every morning. She did not need some fat little white boy telling her about eyelashes. Then Clara Williams did her rouge and they both watched.

Clara Williams unbuttoned her blouse and Ruthie got goose bumps.

When she was a grown woman and had learned to look through white people like they weren't there, had learned to close her ears to the murmurs of black men sitting on stoops and white men passing on the street, their brows lowered over pale, hot eyes, long after she'd memorized the poetry of Nikki Giovanni and could quote Angela Davis on freedom like she'd sat at the sister's right hand in a previous life, when someone referred to "people of color," she would think of Clara Williams stroking foundation down her rounded, colorless arms until they turned a pinkish tan, pulling a compact from her emerald-green purse and powdering her now-pink arms, from armpit to fingertip, paying extra attention to the crooks of her arms, pushing the powder into her skin.

Ruthie and Danny watched Clara Williams come out of the bathroom. She put on her red lipstick and smoothed her eyebrows and snapped her compact closed. She twisted the gold clasp on her purse, and Ruthie and Danny threw themselves back on the rug in Danny's room. Ruthie thought that Clara Williams might check up on them, and she glued her eyes to Betty and Veronica in the comics, joyriding.

22

Step We Grandly

CLARA WASN'T ENTIRELY READY FOR GOOD-BYE. SHE'D COME UP the walk with a bouquet of flowers Edgar wouldn't see and a Dutch oven of soup he wouldn't eat, and Danny watched her struggle and went to find his baseball under the hedges. She forgave him for not helping her. He would miss her, and she would miss him in a different way, and his way was worse. She handed Eva the flowers and the soup and went upstairs.

She shook her head until her neck was loose, and when she composed herself, she looked toward Edgar. It wasn't really Edgar anymore. It was just a shell, but it was terrible to leave even his shell. One evening at the Nite Cap, when Edgar was still well and had just got paid and it seemed to everyone there that Clara was, that night, about to knock Ella Fitzgerald right off her high horse, Edgar had put a milk-glass vase of white roses on the piano.

"Marry me," he'd said that night.

. . .

SHE'D SAT AT THE foot of his bed, grateful and sorry that she'd let Ozzie drop her off. She should have kept Ozzie out of it. It was shaming to Edgar, not that he knew. It was shaming to both men. She didn't want to stay. She felt for Danny and Eva and she hoped things would get better for both of them, and she had no wish to be part of what happened next. She was almost middle-aged and had been loved by an interesting man and was now loved by a better one, a man who would be around for a long while and love her until they were old people, rocking on the porch. Clara couldn't picture rocking on any porch, anywhere, with Edgar. Ozzie might not make her laugh the way Edgar did, but she could do without. She could amuse herself.

Bei mir bist du schoen, *it's such an old refrain,*
And yet I should explain . . .

———

EDGAR ACTON, NÉ ISADOR VOGEL, DIED ON TUESDAY. THEY BUR-
ied him on Thursday. Clara left on Sunday.

During the funeral, Clara thought about the packing she had to
do. It was relaxing to have the bits of Hebrew, which meant nothing to anyone, making an odd, old music of their own, and it was
good to have the rabbi for comic relief. He was like no rabbi Clara
had ever seen, thin, American, eager to please. Mrs. Torelli was
there, in dark-gray silk, for all the Torellis. Danny was a drooping
pile of clothes, and she saw Eva pull him up gently a few times and
he sank as soon as Eva'd turned back to face the pulpit. Neither of
them cried. After the funeral, Eva hid the Torellis' giant ham in her
room so as not to offend Mr. Smedresman, who'd brought the bagels and lox and four kinds of herring, and that's what people ate.
The big Mexican makeup man they all loved brought a tower of
Italian cookies and took Danny for a walk. When they got back,
Danny's little Ruthie had come by with her impeccable mother, and
the woman eyed Clara until she'd moved under Ozzie's big arm,
protecting herself. Mrs. Post left a casserole of macaroni and cheese
on the table, hugged Danny, patted Eva on the shoulder, and pushed
Ruthie out the door.

The day after Edgar's funeral, Clara helped Eva pack up his
clothes and belongings. She had two more days before she and
Ozzie would jump into his big, clean car and drive west to Detroit.
She and Eva walked Edgar's worn clothes and worse underwear to
the bin behind the AME Zion Church. Eva asked if she'd thought
Danny would recover. Clara said that she thought that depended
on Danny's nature, that some people bounced back from a train
wreck and some people couldn't get over a bee sting. They dumped
the clothes and Clara offered Eva a cigarette.

"Ozzie wants to marry me," she said. "In Detroit."

"Absolutely," Eva said, and she ground the cigarette out on the brick wall behind them.

OZZIE DROVE SLOWLY THROUGH Great Neck and then faster and with purpose, the summer dust flying behind them, a little of it settling like brown talc on her dress and in Ozzie's hair. Clara touched his thigh, like a steel spring under her hand. They drove to Detroit in three days. Ozzie listened to the radio, Clara thought her thoughts. Edgar would lie like a white field of bits and bone just beneath the green layers of her life, for the rest of her life. She'd hear a deep English baritone on the radio or a white man holding forth somewhere, the way men do, or see a picture of John Barrymore, who Edgar must have copied, right down to the white wings at the edge of the dark, glossy hair, and Edgar would pop up right beside her.

Now all she wanted was to put some serious distance between her and his funeral. She made Ozzie stop for pie at the first farm stand they came to.

IN HER OLD AGE, her color was almost all gone. The only brown left was a thin ribbon of it around her neck, but she kept up with the ultraviolet light because she felt good afterward; she didn't feel hopeful, the way she had when she was a girl, but she liked the doctor. She had a black dermatologist and she told everyone about him.

It was hard to go from relaxed (if you call hot acid relaxing) hair to natural, and the first haircut left her feeling naked, but from the first time she saw those beautiful Negro girls on television, their hair explosions of self, big, beautiful treetops above their bright faces, she'd been thinking, Let me have a little of that. She found herself a young woman to do her hair and she liked the beauty parlor. They loved her enthusiasm and she loved their acceptance. On Sunday mornings, she did a little gardening and she thought about writing to Danny, and even to Iris and Eva, but it'd been too long. She pictured Danny with no trouble. She saw young men like him all the time at the library, sometimes at the movies. He'd have longish hair and those crazy bell-bottom pants and a bright-yellow shirt, blue aviator glasses, and maybe a leather peace sign around his skinny neck. In her imagination, Danny was slim and smooth, bouncing in his Beatle boots, but things might not have worked out so well. He might be pudgy, with thick glasses and facial hair that looked like something from between your legs. One time, she'd taken Danny into town on her errands and a good-looking Negro man stopped to say that she looked like Miss Lena Horne. Danny pulled himself up to the man's rib cage, adjusted his glasses, and said, Oh, mister, I don't think Lena Horne can hold a candle to Miss Clara Williams. Danny had been her little man, and she should have made more of him.

On Sunday afternoons, in good weather, she took a drive through the countryside. She'd found a radio station that played oldies and she took one Kool, only one, from her glove compartment, drove with her window rolled down and her elbow on the door, like a cool cat, and when she found the radio station, drove for hours. She missed Edgar and Ozzie, she spoke to them both all the time, although not at the same time, and at bedtime, she pictured their graves beneath a willow tree, with a space for herself in between. When the state trooper came upon her wrecked and twisted car, with not an inch between the guardrail and the steering wheel, she heard his footsteps. He spoke softly and Clara heard him say, Ma'am.

Letter from Danny

220 Old Tree Lane
Great Neck, New York
The United States of America,
The World,
The Solar System
May 11, 1946

Dear Iris,

I found an envelope with your address on it in Eva's nightstand. The Torellis wrote FORWARD on it. My teacher Mr. Hoerger says that I am a good reader and a good writer. I am way ahead of most of the other kids in fourth grade reading. I wrote some poems that are sort of like Langston Hughes, except not about the Negro people.

I hope when you go to bed at night, you think about us. I hope you think, Boy, that was pretty bad, what I did. Here are the people who were in my life and now are not: my brother, Bobby. My mother, who died making dinner for you. Clara. Ozzie Patterson. Poppa. You.

Poppa died. I'm sure Evie wrote to you but you didn't come to the funeral. It was me and Evie and the Diegos and Ozzie and Clara and Mrs. Torelli but not their kids. And Mr. Smedresman, who used to bring the bagels. Knowing Mrs. Torelli, she wanted to show respect but she was scared to have her kids in a synagogue. The rabbi was not like a regular rabbi. I have Jewish friends who go to Temple Beth El. Rabbi Waxman looks like he should be vice president or governor. This rabbi looked like Bugs Bunny. Evie sat down with me before and told me she thought that Poppa was really Jewish. I don't remember him doing anything Jewish. When we lived at the Torellis', I used to sit in the Torellis' back room, off the kitchen, and help Poppa sort the mail. I hardly saw him after he got sick. Mom said he got confused and thought I was his own little brother, who he hadn't seen in a really long time. And then Mom died in the fire and you left, and Poppa got worse and then—did you hear about this?— Evie and I had to move, with Poppa, because, since he couldn't be a butler and Mom was dead, the Torellis needed the carriage house for a new butler and cook. Evie said that I'd have my own room, which I do. We never see the Torellis. Cathy, Mary, and Joey go to Catholic school. I don't miss them. I have a best friend, Ruthie Post. We are the best readers in fourth grade.

After Poppa's funeral, the Torellis left a big ham for us and we ate ham sandwiches and split-pea-and-ham soup for a week. Jews don't eat ham.

A lot of nights, before Poppa died, Ozzie and I played catch. Ozzie is a very big man. He was a three-sport captain in his high school. He played football at Alabama State University, which is a good school for football. Ozzie was the one who helped us move Poppa. I sat in the front with Clara and Ozzie and Ozzie's idiot cousin drove the pickup behind us, with all of our stuff. Mrs. Torelli gave us some old furniture so that when we got to our new house it wasn't empty. Clara visited us but she didn't live with us anymore. Ozzie said that growing up in a house of women and a sick old man wasn't good for me. Sometimes Ozzie threw the baseball right at my head. He said that a boy like me should know when to duck. We worked on my spitball. When it got dark, Clara would come out to get us. She was always dressed up, in her sparkly stole and her dark-blue dress and her silk high heels, so she waited in the driveway—she didn't come onto the grass. Ozzie and Clara would get in his Oldsmobile and go out for dinner or to the Nite Cap. Ozzie said, Hi-de-ho, and I said that back. Then I'd sit on the steps until Evie made me come in.

I don't know what you took me from that orphanage for. (Evie told me I wasn't left on the steps, in a basket, like you said. She said you saw me and you liked my looks and tricked me into coming with you and then you and Mom kept me.) My friend Ruthie Post is a Negro girl, and she says that the Negro people have suffered a lot in America. And Ruthie says that she feels sorry for me.

You don't have to write back. Evie and I are in a nice house, on Old Tree Lane.

I asked Evie if you were dead. She said that she didn't think so. She asked me if I wanted to write to you or send you a photograph. I said no, but I did want to write you this one letter.

Danny Lombardo Acton

23

They Can't Take That Away from Me

Clara's leaving was so hard to bear, it made me say and do things I was sorry for. On Monday, Danny dropped a bottle of milk and we watched it break and flow to every corner of our little kitchen. She left us flat, Danny said. He kicked the wet glass against the wall. She left us flat as a pancake and never looked back, he said. She never loved us. I slapped him, and shame on me. Danny went to his room. I stared at the milk on the linoleum until it began to set and then I got a sponge and cleaned it up and piled the milky glass in the garbage can. I sat on the picnic table in the back and smoked and thought, and not for the first time, that it was hard to believe that Reenie was dead and my sister had flown the coop and all the rest was going to hell in a handbasket, leaving just me and Danny. Whatever the opposite of miraculous is, that's the word I was looking for.

If it had been up to Reenie and my sister, Danny'd be back at an orphanage and I'd be in some crap apartment, with a Murphy bed and a bathroom down the hall, trying to forge a college diploma. Sometimes, Danny and I took a walk to the far end of Old Tree Lane, where the nicer houses were. We passed window boxes and stone planters full of geraniums. Danny's eyes got big and he'd breathe in deeply. Every time, as we'd head back home, Danny'd exhale and say, "This street smells like my mother." He had dreamed up a version of Reenie, half actual Reenie and some bits and pieces of radio shows and a little Eleanor Roosevelt and his faint memory of a woman leaning over his crib, smelling of geranium powder. He must have been sleeping in a crib until the day we took him. When he got to the carriage house, he fell out of bed four nights in a row and Reenie put pillows all over the floor. Every morning, I'd walk past his room and see him lying on the floor, waiting for Reenie. He made a small waving gesture if I looked in on him, and it meant Hello and Move along.

I DIDN'T ARGUE WITH Danny. When I made him do things he didn't like, he threw Reenie at me. My mother was beautiful, he said. My mother never made me eat eggs, he said. My mother was the greatest cook in the world. My mother and I were going to move out of that stupid house and far away from you and stupid Iris, he said. My mother sat by my bed until I fell asleep, every night. I agreed with everything he said about Reenie and sometimes I said that I was sorry for both of us, not to have her around. One night, after we'd fought over meat loaf (I won't eat it, he said. Don't, I said.) and he'd taken himself to his room and gotten into bed with his clothes and holster on, I sat at the foot of his bed. He made sure that no part of him, even under the covers, was touching me.

You should complain, I said. This is pretty bad. Sometimes, I said, I am so angry and miserable, it makes me want to cry and scream right in people's faces. It makes me want to kill people. Who? Danny said. Well, considering, I said, I'd like to kill Iris.

Danny nodded. I stretched out next to him, but not touching. Before I went back to my own room, I put his toys in tableaux I thought would make him laugh in the morning: Raggedy Andy on the brown pony, his old blue rabbit stuffed into a truck.

"It's just us," Danny said. I turned out his light.

He did not then list the people who were gone, and neither did I. He never said that of all the people to wind up with, I was undoubtedly the least equipped and, overall, the worst. I thought it was too bad that he had to be so tactful, so young.

THE NEXT DAY, I washed the kitchen floor, which I had managed to do not once in my short lifetime, set the table, and made dinner, and afterward, I washed the dinner dishes and made Danny dry. I took out some cookies and chocolate milk, to bribe him through the cleanup, and he watched me as if I had some bad news I was going to share.

"Everything's fine," I said. "I just thought a chicken dinner might be nice."

"It's nice," Danny said.

"I thought I could tell you a story," I said. "Not a bedtime story. You're too old. But, still. I could tell you a story."

Danny said, "Can I go outside?"

I listened for the *whapada-whap* of the tetherball and watched the clock for five minutes. I went outside and grabbed the ball.

"My serve," I said, and I hit the ball hard, but a little low.

We were remarkably evenly matched. I had some height; he was determined.

"ONCE UPON A TIME," I said, afterward, "there was a little boy named . . . Harry."

Danny smiled and stretched out on the couch.

"Or Roland De Rapscallion," I said, rolling my *r*'s. "Maybe his name was Fat-Fingered Louie."

Danny flipped around, so his head was near mine.

"No," he said.

"All right," I said. "You got me. His name was Danny. Danny was an amazing boy. He had light-brown hair, which was, amazingly, just the right color for a boy with brown eyes, and when he got to be big, he wore amazing eyeglasses, which was especially good because it helped him see, and he saw a lot. A lot. He needed to be good at seeing and thinking because Danny's life had not gotten off to an easy start. When Danny was born . . ." I stopped.

All I knew about Danny's past was what Reenie told me—that he'd said his mother had died and his father had put him and his brother in the Pride of Israel. I didn't know if he remembered more and didn't say or if the door had shut firmly on all that and there was no reason for me to poke my nose in. On the other hand, I was a lot older and had forgotten very little and forgiven less, and it might be the same for him. I wiggled my hand, for Danny to take over.

"Danny was born to his mother and father and his brother. When Danny was very little"—he made his voice squeak, to show how little—"his mother died. He was too little to know what happened but Danny had a brother, Bobby, and Bobby said that their mother fell off a roof and their father was so sad and so messed up, he had to take Danny and Bobby to the orphanage, to take care of them. Which wasn't so bad, but Danny didn't like it. He wanted to go home. His brother, Bobby, said they didn't have a home anymore, that Pride of Israel was their home, and Mr. Greenberg was like their father."

"After a while," I said, "he sort of got used to the place. And Mr. Greenberg was . . ."

"Okay," Danny said. "Danny was one of the little kids. Everyone was okay."

"So, then a crazy thing happened. These two women came along—out of nowhere . . ."

"Out of the blue," Danny said.

"That's right—out of the blue. And they wanted a little boy. They wanted an amazing little boy with brown hair and brown eyes. They wanted a little boy to join their family. And most of all, at home, there was Reenie Lombardo, who was waiting for her friends to find her the perfect little boy."

"Why didn't she go herself?"

"That's an excellent question," I said. "Why didn't she?"

"Because she was cooking," he said. "She was a really good cook and she made dinner for the Torellis every night."

"That's right. She was a great cook. So, these two women, Itsy and Bitsy, saw this one little boy. 'Holy cannoli,' Itsy said to Bitsy. 'That's the one.'"

"Who was Itsy?" Danny said.

"Who do you think?"

"You're Itsy," he said.

"So Itsy said, 'There's something about him.' 'You're right,' Bitsy said. So they asked the little boy to come home with them. He said okay, even though he had to leave Bobby. They took him home and after a long trip—"

"And a bath," Danny said. "Reenie gave me the longest bath ever. I never had a bath like that."

"That's right. He had a very long bath and he was amazingly clean and when the steam cleared, he looked at Reenie and she looked at him, and I know she felt that she had found the amazing little boy she was looking for."

Danny turned his face toward the cushion. I put my hand on his back.

"Come on, hero," I said. "Maybe that's it for tonight."

We put our arms around each other and I tucked him in.

"It's a good story," he said. "But kinda sad."

. . .

WE TOLD EACH OTHER the story every night for weeks, and we managed to get in some unkind remarks about Iris's disappearance and a few jokes about the rabbi at Edgar's funeral. I said that Edgar had saved Danny's life during the fire and we both liked that. We didn't dwell on the fire but Danny told me he could see the smoke, even from Edgar's window, and I knew that meant that he had heard the sounds as well. We told the story of our move from the Torellis' and the happy landing on the shores of Old Tree Lane. (So long, Torellis! Hello, Old Tree Lane and crazy Mr. Mason across the street, with the overalls and no underwear!)

I made myself drive back to the Pride of Israel orphanage to find Danny's brother, the awful and adorable Bobby, but I failed. Narrow mattresses were stacked on the lawn. Window screens were propped against the railings. I walked across the playground and through the front door, propped open with a rock. They had found a permanent home for every American child, the social worker said. The end of the war was a good time for that. They were closing their doors at the end of the month. I saw boxes and crates and bed frames behind her. I was glad to go home and go on with the story of Amazing Danny, whose original last name was lost to him, and to me.

24

Prisoner of Love

RUTHIE POST USED TO TELL DANNY THAT THE HOUSE OF THE Lord had gold plates and sparkling fountains and beautiful fruit piled on silver platters. Dorothy Berman's house was just like that.

"Pure gold basins. Wicker trimmers. Gold spoons and hinges of gold, for all the doors and inside and outside. Everywhere. That's what it says in the Bible. Kings seven fifty." Ruthie whispered to Danny while an old lady in a gray dress with a white lacy apron led them to Dorothy's room. "Everywhere."

They didn't even like Dorothy. No one liked Dorothy. Ruthie's brother told them that in junior high, some people got made fun of and sometimes it was really bad. But in fifth grade, most everyone was in a big pool, moving from year to year. Dorothy Berman stuck out already, and she liked Ruthie and she liked Danny.

Dorothy took them downstairs to the finished basement, set up like a soda shop, with a counter and spinning stools and big pink neon sign that said BERMAN'S. Dorothy leaned against the soda fountain, like it was a baby grand piano. She stretched out an arm, bent her elbow, and rested her brown curly hair on her hand, looking right at Danny. She sang, "Don't know why there's no sun up in the sky, stormy weather . . ." She showed her dimples.

It was worse than embarrassing. It was scary.

Dorothy pulled Coca-Cola bottles out of a red chest and they all drank their sodas, silently. Danny thought the visit seemed so likely to go bad. The gold hinges. The frosty bottles of Coca-Cola. The privacy. In Ruthie's house, which was more like a normal house, there was always a mother or an aunt swinging by purposefully to see that there was no nonsense and no scuffing of the floor and no eating of things meant for dinner. It was like the Berman house was empty.

Dorothy cleared her throat and went back to the soda fountain. She indicated with her chin and Ruthie and Danny sat down at their bistro table, with the red-and-white leather seats. Dorothy put her hand to her heart.

"Good morning, heartache, what's new? . . . I've got those Monday blues, straight through Sunday blues . . . ," she sang. "Sit down."

It was worse than before. It was beautiful and breathtaking, the kind of performance Clara Williams talked about sometimes. It was giving voice to the heartache of being Dorothy Berman, which Danny thought was a lot. Dorothy was the apple of no one's eye. Her mother drove her to school every day in a clean dark-blue Caddy, and dressed her as if she were a fairy-tale princess, in wide pink skirts with a petticoat and party shoes, and it only made her look worse.

Danny leaned toward Ruthie, so they'd be in it together, and Ruthie, who usually pulled away, leaned toward him. Dorothy threw her head back, showing her fat little neck, and the pink neon letters behind the soda fountain lit up the tiny hairs on her jaw and her gold locket and she sang blue and low and slow. She sang like Billie Holiday. Clara said that Billie Holiday woke up crying. Clara said that if you sing the blues, you know that if you can't make friends with grief, you've got to at least make way for it.

Dorothy curtsied and joined them at their table.

"I'm pretty good," she said, and she was so pleased with herself, Danny felt better. "How about a game?"

Danny and Ruthie knew dodgeball. Ruthie was good at double Dutch and Danny was very good at shooting marbles. He relaxed. He knew how to play games.

"Let's go over here," Dorothy said.

"Over here" was the storeroom, beyond the soda fountain (Dorothy called it the lounge). It was stocked with cases of soda, boxes of crackers, tins of sardines, plastic boxes of drink stirrers and frilled toothpicks, little glass jars of curled anchovies.

"Each one of us will go in and then come out and do something . . . surprising. Danny, you come out and surprise me and Ruthie first."

Ruthie and Danny looked at each other. Ruthie liked to scare Danny because he was easy to scare, and once she fried his hair flat and steaming with a hot comb and once Danny picked a handful of honeysuckles and stuck the bunch under Ruthie's nose, which did surprise her. This wasn't that.

Dorothy turned on the light and pushed Danny in and shut the door. Danny rested his forehead on a case of crackers, sweating, until Dorothy finally opened the door. She looked disappointed. Ruthie looked at Danny and said, "Dorothy, you go. You're the one who knows how to do this. We're just guests." She said "guests" like it was code for idiots and Dorothy smiled and pushed them both out.

Danny and Ruthie sat with their empty Coca-Cola bottles. Dorothy came out in her underpants, with a serious look, holding a big blue box of matches.

Danny put his hand on top of Ruthie's. Ruthie said, "Thankyou-forhavingus." Danny said, "SeeyouMonday." They ran past the old lady who had let them in and past the little black dogs with the bows on their heads, past the gold clocks in the front hall and the gold faucets in the front hall bathroom, and they walked, very quickly, to the corner.

The corner was no help. The corner was a thick green carpet of lawn and another big house with columns set far back from the lawn. You could see water past the house.

Ruthie said, "I'll sit over there and you ring the doorbell and you ask can you call home for someone to come get us now." Ruthie was very careful to say someone and Danny appreciated it. Ruthie didn't say a thing when his mother died, because it was too terrible to even talk about and when he and his aunt Eva moved from the Torellis' to Old Tree Lane, just three blocks from Ruthie's, surrounded by other small houses, with nothing but a picnic table and their rusty tetherball set instead of the Torelli pool, all Ruthie said was, "It's nice."

Eva would be at work, telling people's fortunes. Eva would say, Oh, big guy, is there any way you can take the bus?

Danny said, "You ring the doorbell and call your mother. I'll sit here."

They had been secret best friends for a long time. Danny knew that Ruthie would be better at bell-ringing because she had a way about her, but he knew that this was not a neighborhood with Negro girls in it. Danny knew that he should offer to go to the door, because he was white, but he was almost pissing himself already and when the lady of the house asked him why he was standing on her doorstep, he knew he would throw up on her black pumps. They walked back to Dorothy Berman's house, where Dorothy sat on a stone bench, in the middle of her vast front lawn, fully dressed, her bare feet on a granite tortoise, sipping a Coke.

"You guys," she said fondly. "Where'd ya go?"

DOROTHY TOOK THEM UPSTAIRS. They trooped past the old lady, who opened and closed her mouth while she slept in the library. Dorothy Berman's room was the most beautiful thing Danny had

ever seen. It gleamed. It shimmered. The silver centers of the embroidered pink daisies on her bedspread shone. She had her own
pink velveteen couch, which Ruthie was edging toward, and she
had a pink-and-white desk, with a white wood desk chair. The
cushion on the chair matched the pink and silver and white pillows
on her bed. There were eight pillows for nothing but decoration,
two of them shaped like stars.

Danny wanted to sprawl out on the bed. He would take his
shoes off and his belt, and then he would stretch his arms under the
covers and feel the silk all over him. He would roll off his socks,
where the girls couldn't see him. It was very hard to just stand there
and not touch any of the pretty, pointless, expensive things. He
wanted to chase Dorothy Berman out of the house and tear through
the rooms, ripping and running, and then set it all on fire. Fire
trucks would roar up, Dorothy Berman and her stupid dogs would
sit on the big front lawn and eight firemen in their black-and-
yellow coats would pull out their hoses and there'd be nothing left
of the Bermans' house but black wood and wet grass. It was good
luck, Danny thought, that Joey Torelli hadn't had a room like this.
Joey had a nice room, with a carved headboard and curtains with
sailboats on them and fancy lights with sailboats painted on them,
but he didn't have anything like this, so Danny had never wanted to
kill Joey.

DOROTHY OPENED HER TOY chest. She had Monopoly and Sorry!
and Chutes and Ladders. Ruthie said, Let's play Sorry. Monopoly
can take all day, she said.

They played through a game of Chutes and Ladders. "Some
people call it 'Snakes and Ladders,'" Dorothy said, and Ruthie and
Danny nodded. With another girl, Ruthie might have rolled her
eyes and Danny would have shrugged, but the image of cheerful,
saucy Dorothy in her blue-sprigged underpants and the big blue
box of matches, Dorothy's smooth white chest, her two chubby

little mounds and her rosy nipples, and all of these very disturbing things together rose up in front of him when Dorothy spoke. Danny saw her sailing down a chute, brown curls gleaming in the sun. She climbed the ladder and Danny could see her bottom in her underpants. Dorothy smiled when Ruthie beat her and when Ruthie eyed the four gold lockets lying on Dorothy's pink dresser, Dorothy put one in Ruthie's hand. "'Til butter flies," Dorothy said. "I can give you one too," Dorothy said, and Danny put his hands in his pockets.

WHEN DANNY IS A teenager, and Ruthie has moved hundreds of miles away, he will find himself, with new friends in darkened movie theaters, watching horror movies in which some idiot feels the need to explore the dark, menace-filled basement. The entire movie audience shouts, "Don't go in the basement!" but Danny never shouts. He grips the armrests and thinks, in the last row of the Playhouse Theater of Great Neck, he thinks, *Dorothy Berman.*

Letter from Gus

Trutzhain, Germany
April 1947

Dear Evie,

Spring is busting out here. More goddamn babies, more homely girls marrying schlemiels like there's a white sale at Macy's. We're breeding. We got green grass. We got flowers. A small blue flower the little girls go crazy for. They make a game of weaving grass baskets and filling them with the flowers. They leave the baskets on people's pillows. Not mine, but other people's.

Hey, there, I'm now Gersh Hoffman, Jewish schoolteacher. Hey, you'll say, where are the records of your life, Gersh Hoffman? I say I don't know why no one can find my records. I say I was interned at Stringtown and Camp Forrest. The government people here are a little embarrassed about my deportation, so no one checks too carefully. As everyone here now knows, I'm here "through a shameful miscarriage of justice." I'm quoting a visiting Brit who was glad to throw a little shit on the Americans.

(Meanwhile, the Brits are practically chaining Jews to their bedposts to keep them from going to Palestine.) People want to get me home before another bad thing happens to me. They better fucking hurry.

Your Gus

25

On the Sunny Side of the Street

LUCKY JEWS. GUS THOUGHT THIS EVERY TIME HE STOOD IN THE steam of Stricoff's bakery waiting for his rye bread, every time he caught a hot doughnut from the cart near the high school, every time he ate brisket at the railroad station luncheonette, watching the bookie in the corner booth go about his business. And lucky Gersh Hoffman, he thought. Just when the school board had decided that since they were going to have all these smart Jewish kids tumbling in, it might be good to have a few Jewish teachers of the right kind (preferably veterans, and truly American, preferably teaching math or Latin, the kinds of subjects troublemakers were not drawn to), Gersh Hoffman showed up, a limping, accentless, hawk-eyed Jewish teacher of math and engineering. Instantly hired at a decent salary after only one quick round with the Loyalty Oath ("I further swear that I do not advise, advocate or teach, and have not within the period beginning five years prior to the effective date of the ordinance requiring the making of this oath, advised, advo-

cated or taught, the overthrowing by force, violence or other unlaw-
ful means, of the Government of the United States of America or
of the State of New York . . ."), which he swallowed like cold coffee.

He was happiest in the stores. He shopped almost every day.
Just the sight of food made him happy, and he loved the food of
Great Neck. Six whole roast chickens, turning on a spit in the front
window. Tuna fish decorated with a tomato rose, and a bowl of egg
salad with the day of the week spelled out in olive slices. Sandwiches the size of lunch boxes. The German deli was run by a distant cousin of Kaiser Wilhelm and the Great Neck Jews loved the
place; they flocked to Kuch's. They said to one another, What a
character he is, Otto, strictly old country, I'm telling you. Gus didn't
think that Negroes would rush to shop in a store run by some retired slave owner, eager to share memories of fun times on the plan-
tation, praising Massa's old-fashioned Mississippi charm. Jews were
still chasing that absurd, wishful feather. Eventually, Jews would
become like everybody else. They'd elevate smaller grievances; they'd
cherish hurt feelings and ill treatment like they were signs of virtue.

In fifty years, Gus will read about Jewish young men and women
writing long essays, even whole books, about their experiences as
the grandchildren, or the grandnieces and -nephews, of Holocaust
survivors, as if that entitled them to anything, and some of them
will choose to tattoo the string of numbers on their forearms, and
none of it surprises him.

We tried, he thought, watching the nice families drive to the
synagogue, religious but not fanatic, the father parking about a
block away, giving the wife a hand getting out of the Olds, then
Sylvia, Rachel, and David climbing out and following, like duck-
lings in blue wool. All of us, the DPs, the soldiers who liberated the
camps, even the survivors who came here—we tried to keep it from
you. We protected America from what happened, like a man takes
care of his wife. The man doesn't mind when she closes her eyes at
the scary part of the ride, of the movie. He loves her for that sweet,
willful ignorance. She gives him something to protect, a nice world

in which bad things don't happen. It's a pleasure, and a relief, to keep that ignorance intact, even as it comes between them.

As much as Gus loved the food and the bustle of Middle Neck Road's sidewalks (a dozen different pairs of high heels, all staccato, a big-assed drum line), Gus loved the Chase National Bank even more, and he read everything he could about the bank and the Rockefellers; when Chase merged with the Manhattan Company, he followed the purchase like he had skin in the game. The Chase Bank was the archway through which Gus's new and lucky life was running.

When all the real estate moguls and movie stars and orchestra leaders lost their shirts, their houses, their ridiculous racing yachts, and their unpaid-for Rolls-Royces, the sensible men at Chase foreclosed. George Dodge and Walter Chrysler and their friends moved out of Great Neck or moved on or died. The bank took back their half-timbered Tudors with carriage house, pool house, and pool, their Bauhaus-on-the-Sound, their Nantucket-style seventeen-acre estates with the white gravel circular driveways and Moorish lawn decorations, divided them into three and four and even six lots, and said, Someone's got to buy them. And the Jews said, Please, let it be us. And the sensible men at Chase, who did not themselves live in Great Neck, said, Fine, we haven't had a Jew since 1891, when that rich Irishman got a house for his own tailor, to always have him nearby, but, let it be Jews. Eventually, they would let African Americans buy too, but not in the 1950s. (Ralph Bunche, no. Joe Jones, a little later, yes, because every town needs a good taxi service, and eventually, East Asians, yes, with their very smart kids who frankly made the Jewish kids look like slackers, and when the Iranian Jews come in the 1970s, it's the Ashkenazic version of Katie-bar-the-door, as far as Gus can see, but too late. Gus knew his history; unless you actually kill the people you have let move into your town, there is no getting them out. Their children will mix with your children. Sooner or later, their children will marry your children. Sooner or later, they will be jumping the broom and smashing a lightbulb in the same joyful, fierce move. Their children will be more beautiful than any child ever produced in your otherwise monochromatic family tree.)

The Jews came in, from Brooklyn and Queens. They came to houses near the railroad station and on Baker Hill, with cheap suitcases. They came in on the G.I. Bill, and the lucky veterans, who held the top tickets in the lottery, put their five hundred dollars in cash in an envelope and drove their in-laws' cars from Flatbush Avenue to Ramsey Road. The *Great Neck News* carried prim editorials, complaining of dirty-faced city children dashing out of overcrowded moving vans, trailing firecrackers and bad habits from the outer boroughs. (Eventually, the rich men building Long Island Jewish Hospital, with their Jewish partners, told the editors to shut up and confine themselves to writing about the lovely rhododendrons of Kenilworth and the prompt service of the Fire Department, which they did. Five years later, the *Great Neck News* carried ads for Fein Furniture and the Cohen Brothers' Steem-Cleaning.) The Jewish veterans moved their pregnant wives into three-bedroom houses, which looked a lot like the three-bedroom houses to the right and left of them. On summer nights, twenty-five noisy Jewish kids—and the occasional Castellano and O'Brien—poured into the wide streets, playing running bases or monkey in the middle or flipping baseball cards until someone's little brother was left empty-handed and started to cry. They ran from one end of the block to the other, through six narrow backyards, chasing fireflies and one another and hurrying to watch Bobby Feldman throw himself out of the willow tree again. Gus had introduced himself to the two Mrs. Schwartzes, at either end of Ramsey Road, who made iced tea and lemonade and put plastic pitchers on a card table on the front lawn, and he'd met the fathers, accountants and shoe salesmen and furriers, called out "Hey, Koufax," "Hey, Helen Keller, heads up!" and took turns throwing and catching for the kids until it was too dark.

Gus walked down the streets where the families were and slowed down to listen and look, to see if Eva was among them.

Letter from Iris

Queensberry Place,
South Kensington, London
January 2, 1948

Dear Eva,

God is Milton Berle.

Diana left me. Or I threw her out. One says—at least I do; who knows what you say. Perhaps this has never happened to you—"It isn't that you are leaving me; it's the way you're doing it." This is complete horseshit. She's leaving me pretty much the way I expected, which is to say, she's leaving me the way I would have left her, if I'd been quicker off the mark. She piled all her clothes into a friend's car while I was working and I came home to a great, gobby violet-scented (and misspelled) letter of self-justification.

What I should find is a bearable, bendable producer of the older male variety. We would look good in the papers and at opening nights and he would go his merry way with boys or girls and I would have a very, very pleasant suite of rooms somewhere in Mayfair. I actually picture my suite sometimes. Terra-cotta walls with cream trim, a charming watered-silk living room, with mohair throws, warm and light, with a few moth holes, to show that we are just plain folks, *au fond.* My bedroom would be grand, the size of Mrs. Torelli's with no Mr. Torelli to mar the picture, suspenders slipped off those thick, furry shoulders and a face full of shaving cream.

I know what I should do and I certainly understand how to do it. Only an idiot could be Edgar's daughter and not know how to size up and seize opportunity. Apparently, I'm that idiot. I hope you're not. I hope you're married by now and have a nice Jewish husband to help you with Danny. All of my friends tell me that Jewish husbands are the best kind but the only one I know here drinks like a fish and has a chorus girl on every limb. When I was in Hollywood, people talked all the time about who was Jewish and who was not. Eleanor Roosevelt, although this seems unlikely to me. Walter Winchell, Danny Kaye, Jack Benny, the Gabor sisters, and Lauren Bacall, which is fabulous. If I were the prime minister of Israel, I'd put her face on all the stamps. I don't know why Jewish people find this all so interesting.

I got to see Diana and the lovely earrings I gave her, twinkling like starry nights on the earlobes of some knock-kneed writer last night. And I thought of Mrs. Gruber, who would at this moment tell me it's time I faced facts. *Azoy gait es,* don't you know?

I'm giving up on love entirely. The soap opera pays the bills right now, and the rest of the time, I'm fund-raising for my favorite plastic surgeons, Drs. McIndoe and Litton. We want to start a clinic in London. I am known more widely, and with great affection, as the Singing Guinea Pig. Could be worse.

I hope to hear from you.

Iris

26

Find Out What They Like

I THOUGHT I WOULDN'T TRY TO FIND MY MOTHER UNTIL I WAS forty. I thought that by then, I wouldn't be angry. I thought, I hoped, that by then, she'd be near the end of her wretched, empty life and I'd be in the happy middle of mine, understanding that her leaving me, dumping me and that cheap brown suitcase on the porch of my father's house, had not doomed me. *Au contraire,* is what I hoped. By forty, I'd be a more forgiving person. I might, by forty, have a nice apartment with a beautiful black poodle. Instead, twenty-one and Danny and I could not stop thinking that if I could do it, surely she could have too.

I couldn't wait. I needed to tell Hazel a few things.

It wasn't as hard to find her as I thought. She'd become a little bit famous. Not Lana Turner famous, but famous in Chicago, where she'd become the next Aimee Semple McPherson. (Edgar despised evangelists more than the tarot cards. He said that if religion was the opiate of the masses, they should demand a better drug.) There was a condescending article about her in *The New York Times*— "Divine Healing and Hope, Promises Hazelle Logan" (Please note the new spelling). And a nice big picture. I would know her anywhere, in any costume. She's wearing a pleated Grecian-style thing with a wide belt, and her head is thrown back, overcome with something. I showed Francisco the article. He asked if I was going to forgive her or punish her and I said I was pretty sure that I was not going to forgive her. Good, he said. I'll babysit. When I left, he and Danny were playing cards.

DURING THE WAR, I'D seen every newsreel about the Kindertransports in Europe, all those poor Jewish kids sent far and wide to save them from the Nazis. I dreamed about little Jewish children crushed into trains, with their little bags and teddy bears, their weeping, hopeful parents on the platform, tying little notes to their coat buttons and making them sandwiches. I thought about them during the day, sweeping up at the beauty parlor. Your parents are on their knees with grief as you grow smaller and smaller, on your way to a better life. Oh, you lucky little bastards, I used to think.

Maybe my mother hoped I'd have a better life with Edgar. When I was younger, I liked to imagine her driving south from Windsor, tears falling as she drove, maybe pulling onto the shoulder when she was just overcome with shame and loss. Even when I was a kid, I suspected she felt more like a woman who'd dropped off a very bulky package. An easing of soreness and relief. Shake out your wrists and fingers, arch your back, and turn your face toward the sun.

This package arrived in the Chicago station and checked into a decent hotel. I took a shower and left my clothes in the bathroom to steam (thank you, Iris). I pulled my hair back in what I hoped was a chic little bun and I put myself together as Bea and Carnie would have. (And I could hear my sister saying, You let that bitch get a good look at you, Evie. Let her see who you are.) I threw up in the bathroom and I took another shower. I caught a cab to Hazel's temple, the New Jerusalem. The cabbie asked me if he should wait. If I had been a more realistic and reasonable person, if I had not been twenty-one and still fooling myself, I would have said, Wait.

THERE ARE HOUSES LIKE my mother's temple all over Great Neck. The smaller estates, is what the Realtors call them. Doric columns and wide white porches. Maybe a pair of stone lions, or swans or griffins at the beginning of the driveway and a set of very tall, carved front doors, with a golden eagle or a bronze fist, for the knocker. Two acres, not twenty. My father told me not to be impressed by those houses. That's not what people with real money build, he said. He said, Real money is privacy, real money is that if you scream, no one hears but the servants. This is just show. This is vulgar.

Nevertheless, my sister used to say, it beats the hell out of poverty.

A TALL, CORPSEY-LOOKING GUY in a white robe and a silver belt answered the door. He told me to wait for Mother Logan. That about killed me. I sat in the hallway, admiring the bits and pieces of marble. (I was enough Edgar's daughter to notice that although the effect was of marble, it was not actually a marble hallway.) Hazel came gliding down the hall, her arms outstretched. And then she saw it was me and her arms dropped to her side.

"Charles thought you were press," she said.

She stood very still, looking me over.

"All grown up," she said.

"I'd like to talk to you," I said. It wasn't true. I didn't want to talk to her. I wanted to gut her like a fish.

She led me down the hallway and through an auditorium with the predictable burgundy curtains and a two-story gilded organ and some kind of crazy gold elves or babies riding silver swans on either side of the stage. I pretended not to notice. I set my face like I was walking through a New Jersey bus station.

She sat me down in her office. A civilized person would have offered me tea or a cold drink. I could hear my father's voice rocketing through me, sitting with her. She didn't say a thing. She smiled at me, in a new way. My mother, as was, smirked at the world and grinned when I had amused her, and she used to have, for my father, a very soft look. Her smile now was false and pearly, prissy and ecstatic. And frightening.

"I missed having a mother," I said. Go for broke, I thought.

"How old are you?" my mother said.

"I'm twenty-one."

"I was fifteen when I had you."

I have to say, she looked great. She looked better than me. Her hair was blond now, her brows were still dark, and she didn't have a line on her face. The gray silky thing she wore did a good job of showing off her assets and covering what looked like a pretty big caboose.

"How could you leave me on that porch," I said.

"I was twenty-seven. I gave you more than enough years, didn't I, and you know I took good care of you." And she had. "You seem fine. I wasn't cut out for teenagers. Plus, your father and I were going to be finished sooner or later, and my money was on sooner. And when he was done with me, baby, he'd be done with you. I know the type. I did you a favor."

It was hard to concentrate on what she was saying, when she looked the way she did, and she kept her voice low, and soft. There were seraphim painted on the wall behind her.

"Call me impulsive. It worked out," she said.

I couldn't ask her anything. There wasn't a single question to which I'd get the answer I wanted. The wicked people of the world are not supposed to be calm and composed. They are supposed to have hysterics and take poison like Hitler and Göring, or fall on their swords like the Japanese soldiers when they had to surrender. They are not supposed to cross one leg over the other and show off their white stockings and nice ankles.

"How is your father?" she said.

The greatest struggle in my life is between a dignified silence and having my say.

"Dead," I said. "Of heartbreak."

"Not over me," she said.

I stood up. My mother sat for another second, looking at nothing, and then she stood up too. We were, not surprisingly, about the same height. She walked me back through the auditorium and down the fake marble hall. The man in the white robe was waiting for me.

"Are you staying long in Chicago?" she said.

"On my way even now," I said.

"If you want to see a show—"

"See your show?" I said. "I wouldn't piss on you if you were on fire."

That was the only part I felt good about, afterward.

BACK HOME, I GAVE Francisco the highlights, after Danny went to sleep.

"People," he said. "They can't be underestimated."

We drank our beers.

"Carnie called me. She got elected president of the PTA, in Rye," he said.

"That's a good thing to do," I said, and we laughed.

He told me that Bea and Carnie had closed La Bella Donna. He said it'd be a lot harder for us all to get together. Plus, he said, what with the dentist and the little girl, Bea's new husband and their new baby.

"Even if I don't see them for years," I said, "I'm always going to be really happy to see them."

"They ask after you," Francisco said. He raised his beer bottle toward me. "I say you're making money, raising Danny, and living right."

27

Now Is the Hour

THE THIRD THURSDAY OF THE MONTH WAS MRS. RONSON'S DAY. She was twenty-five and looked forty. She dragged herself up my stairs, every month, to talk about her dead baby daughter. Linda had died in her crib a year ago. They tucked her in at night and in the morning, Mrs. Ronson found her blue and still. The doctors had nothing useful to say. Mrs. Ronson paced around my room at every visit. She talked about how angry she was at God, and at the doctors, and at her husband, and she talked about trying to get pregnant.

I flipped over the cards because she expected me to, and as soon as I got to a card with a man on it I said, "You have to forgive your husband. He's grieving too." I turned over the Ace of Wands, up-side down, and said, "You won't get pregnant as long as you're so angry with your husband." Last month, she asked me to contact her daughter. I said Linda couldn't send a message, because she was just a baby. But I threw my head back and gurgled and leaned from side to side, rocking my chair. When I sat up I said Linda was beautiful and happy. I saw her. She wore her little yellow romper with the ducks on it. She was playing with other little children, on a big blanket, in a great green field. I felt worse for Mrs. Ronson than for anyone else I read for, and I wished she wouldn't come.

She was a few minutes late for her third Thursday and she was transformed. She had lipstick on and a pretty shirtwaist and she'd pushed her sunglasses on top of her head, like a movie star. She looked at my cloudy-sky windows and tossed her purse onto a chair.

"Gosh, it's a little gloomy in here."

I shuffled the deck and put it in front of her.

She smiled and held the deck, shaking it like a martini.

Mrs. Ronson told me she was pregnant. She said she owed it all to me. She giggled. She said that, of course, her husband deserved some of the credit. She'd been talking to her husband about me. She said Mr. Ronson worked for the FBI and she said that he was one of the head men for missing persons in New York. It's been nearly ten years since they declared Judge Crater dead, Mrs. Ronson told me, and almost twenty years since the judge disappeared. It was a very big case, she said. I started to shuffle the deck but Mrs. Ronson put her hand on my wrist.

"I told Ted how good you are," she said. "I told him how you've found things for people, you found those diamond earrings for a friend of mine, and how you even found that missing girl."

I'd found Mrs. Cohen's earrings by making her trace her steps from Best & Co., where she'd tried on six suits, to her driver taking her home, where she drank too much, waiting for her husband to get home, and fell asleep on the wicker couch in the sunroom. The earrings were caught under a cushion. I'd found the runaway, a young woman living in the Village, waitressing at Caffe Reggio, and sleeping around, but I did that by thinking about what I would do if I'd had the girl's money, and her awful parents.

"They're doing a big search for Judge Crater. With a psychic from Interpol. Ted said I should ask you if you'd like to come along and assist. He said he'd talk to you and if you were cleared, you could assist. And get paid."

I SHUFFLED THE CARDS as Mr. Ronson came up the stairs. He had questions and questions and forms for me to sign. I would have said no but my whole body lit up with yes at the sight of Mr. Ronson. I wasn't going to sleep with him. I wasn't even going to flirt with him. I was so tired of baloney sandwiches and lost eyeglasses and paying the bills and the greatest pleasure of my life being tetherball with Danny and the occasional neck rub from Francisco. I just wanted to hike along behind big Ted Ronson, and watch the sweat come down his thick neck, watch his hard shoulders press against his suit jacket. I wanted to watch him swagger up the dirt trails in the Catskills as we looked for Judge Joe Crater, Good Time Joe, once of the New York Supreme Court, last seen getting into a cab on an August night in midtown Manhattan in 1930. And that's what I did.

HENK CROISET LOOKED LIKE a psychic. It was a hot summer day and every other man with us wore a black suit. They all had the clipped, sharp FBI haircut, wide circles of clean pink skin over their ears. Monsieur Croiset, as I was told to call him (I was Miss Acton, who is helping us with this inquiry. She's in your line, Croiset, is what Ted Ronson said.), wore a safari suit and had hair like Albert Einstein. He wore a red beret and carried an oak walking stick with the head carved to resemble a fox. M. Croiset lives in France, his interpreter said. M. Croiset's most recent success with Interpol was finding the bodies of two girls who'd been kidnapped from France. He found their corpses in an orchard of cork trees in Portugal. M. Croiset didn't speak English. Ted Ronson and the other men wanted to show that they weren't impressed by him, but they were.

M. Croiset was having a great time. He talked to himself as we

walked along and he hummed. He pulled together some wildflow-
ers and handed them to me. When my hands were full, he put a few
in his buttonhole. He chuckled at the rabbits and squirrels. He
waved his hands at the butterflies. When he spoke, the interpreter
shouted out the translations as we walked. One time, M. Croiset
called out "Sally Lou Ritz," and laughed. Sally Lou Ritz was the
showgirl Judge Crater was dallying with hours before his disappearance. "O-hi-o," M. Croiset said. The FBI men looked at each
other. One of them said he'd interviewed Sally Lou Ritz about six
years ago. She took care of her aging mother in Youngstown now
and she looked like hell, he said. M. Croiset said "Sally Lou Ritz" a
couple of more times, just because he liked the sound of it, and he
pointed toward a stand of trees.

Under the biggest tree was a circle of flat, mossy stones. M.
Croiset told us, through the interpreter, that there were some bones
under the largest stone. While the men took off their jackets to pull
up the stones, the interpreter said that M. Croiset was sorry but the
bones didn't belong to the judge.

The men kept pulling. We all stood around. M. Croiset leaned
against the tree, wiping his face with a handkerchief. *"C'est dom-
mage,"* he said a few times. *"C'est une femme. Ce n'est pas* Sally Lou
Ritz." We both watched the digging with interest. The FBI agents
got excited and the FBI photographer started snapping. There was
a medium-size skeleton under the rocks, and M. Croiset crossed
himself and went over to look. He talked and the interpreter told us
that this was the skeleton of a dead girl from about sixty years ago.
M. Croiset had tears in his eyes. The interpreter said that the girl
was a servant, that she had told her lover that she was pregnant and
he had killed her. Then he went to sea. Ted Ronson told the two
youngest men to stay with the skeleton and the rest of us walked
back to the FBI cars. They dropped me and M. Croiset and the
interpreter at a diner and said they'd be back in an hour.

"We're probably going to stop for the day," Ted Ronson said.
"We have to check out this body."

The diner was dark and sticky, hot air pushing at us from the big fan in the corner. The pies were sweating. I told the interpreter that we might just want to have lemonade and ham-and-cheese sandwiches and potato chips. I said I was sorry about the food, which would probably be awful. He told M. Croiset, who smiled and said, *"Limonade! Parfait."* M. Croiset spoke to the interpreter for a little while and the interpreter said that while we waited, M. Croiset suggested that we could play a game. I said sure. The interpreter told me to picture anything in the world. Anything, he said. From anywhere, even outer space.

I was sweating like a pig. My skirt stuck to my legs and even my feet were sweating in my sneakers. I pictured the window of Holman's toy store in Abingdon, when I was a little girl. My mother and I went every year, a couple of weeks before Christmas. We went to admire the windows, which were always beautifully decorated, and we went to pick out one toy that I really liked. My father would come the day after Christmas or the next day and the toy I wanted would be produced. Mr. Holman and my father and mother came through every year.

I pictured my favorite of all the Christmas windows. Mr. Holman had hung dozens of glittering snowflakes on a fishing line, so they seemed to float in the window. The window was framed in candy canes and there was a little village, all red and black, in front of a lake made out of a mirror. Around the lake, spreading out to the corners, was a miniature countryside of fields and forests, of green, snow-dusted pine trees, old-fashioned villagers, rushing by with packages, a couple of Model T's and at the very edge, a barn, glowing from within, its doors flung open and a cow and calf lying down in the middle. And all of that, including the cow and the calf in the golden light, is what M. Croiset sketched on the back of the place mat. He smiled at me and put down his pen. He took my hand in both of his hands and he nodded to the interpreter. He was so intent and his face was so expressive, I felt I knew what he was saying before the interpreter spoke.

"Vous n'êtes pas fait pour ce travail."

The interpreter spoke very quietly and kindly. "You are not cut out for this kind of work."

"Ne vous inquiétez pas. Votre secret es dans de bonnes mains."

"Don't worry. Your secret's safe with me."

M. Croiset pressed my hand. He handed me a napkin so I could wipe my eyes. M. Croiset spoke again, but this time I didn't know what was coming.

The interpreter said, "M. Croiset feels that you have not found your gift."

M. Croiset spoke again, and this time, he seemed a little annoyed with the interpreter.

"I beg your pardon. You have not yet found your professional calling. M. Croiset sees that you are a mother and a daughter."

M. Croiset spoke.

"Like a mother and a daughter. He sees the little boy and the older man, from Spain. You are loved. He says that soon you will find your calling." The interpreter paused. "He says do not lose your nerve when the time comes."

M. Croiset kissed my hand.

Ted Ronson came through the door, sweating like the rest of us. I didn't look at him twice. They bundled us into separate Oldsmobiles and took M. Croiset and the interpreter back to the city. The two junior G-men drove me home and told me not to talk about what I'd seen or repeat anything that'd been said. I told Danny and Francisco what happened. I included finding the skeleton, not finding the judge, and the amazing place mat. I left out the part about my being a complete fraud. I told them that M. Croiset had mentioned them both, but I didn't say he said I was a mother and a daughter. Danny said that he might become a G-man and Francisco and I nodded, as though we would not strip naked and publicly declare ourselves Communists to keep that from happening.

Francisco slept over the whole week. It was so hot, I let Danny sleep on the living room floor, on top of a sheet. The crickets made a racket every night. We all woke up at dawn every morning because of the heat. On Saturday, at dawn, Francisco said we might as well have breakfast. He squeezed a dozen oranges and made scrambled eggs and sausage. I made cinnamon toast for Danny, who tore the crusts off and ate my sausage.

Francisco stamped his feet. He stood up suddenly. He pointed to his chest and pushed his fork and plate and the eggs and the rest of the sausage onto the floor. His face became deep, dark pink. Danny and I stared at him. I pushed Danny out of my way and dialed the operator. Danny was bouncing up and down in terror.

Oh, God, please, I said, I need a doctor. My father is choking.

The operator was smooth and friendly. Where do you live, she said, and I told her and she said, Well there's nobody right near you—and I thought she meant white and I screamed, I don't care who you get, get me a doctor on the phone, and she did.

This is Dr. Snyder, he said.

Oh, Doctor, oh, Doctor, I said.

Francisco was almost purple.

Oh, he's choking, he's choking. He can't breathe.

The doctor's voice was like silk. That's all right. You take two deep breaths. Now, how old is he? And can you tell me what he was eating?

I said he was old and had been eating sausage.

All right. Hit him hard on the back a couple of times.

I stood behind Francisco and pounded him as hard as I could. He grabbed the back of his chair but nothing changed. Danny was crying in the corner.

It's not helping, I said. Oh, God.

Okay, now, lie him down on his back. I made Danny help me get Francisco on the floor. He was rigid with fear and his face was getting even darker. His hands were fists.

A pillow, I said. Does he need a pillow?

Not right now, the doctor said. Is he lying down?

I said he was.

Here's what we're going to do—it's going to be a little scary but you have to do this, and you have to do this now.

Tell me, I said. Do I have to wash my hands?

We're not going to worry about that now, he said. Get your sharpest knife and get a napkin.

A napkin? A linen napkin?

I waved my arm frantically at Danny—Get a napkin! Hurry!

Now, tell him that you're going to help him.

I'm going to help you, I said to Francisco, and he kept his dark eyes on me. I told the doctor, I told him.

That's good. Get on your knees on your—are you right-handed or left-handed?

Right.

Get on your knees on his right side. Feel his Adam's apple. Do you feel that?

Yes.

Good. Do you feel that there's a smaller bump a little farther down?

I did feel it but I had to press on Francisco's soft skin and his fleshy neck and I apologized to him.

Now, in between, the doctor said, there's a little valley. Use the edge of the knife in that little valley and make a sideways incision. Just a cut, sideways, just through the skin and half an inch across. And then you're going to open up the cut a little bit. You'll see a membrane, a thin, translucent membrane, like frog skin, and you're going to cut through that too. Then you're going to keep that incision open with your thumb and forefinger.

I worried that I would cut his throat.

And you'll need the napkin, to blot the blood that will come out. It won't be a lot of blood. It'll be okay.

Danny, I screamed, Napkin! Danny was standing right next to me and put it into my hand. I gave him the receiver.

You tell me what the doctor says, I said, and you look away.

I pressed the knife into Francisco's neck until blood began to seep. I spread the edges of the cut apart with my thumb and fore-finger.

He says you need a straw, Danny whispered, while staring at the kitchen clock. You need two.

Go get the straws, I said, from the pantry. I kept the knife in. I picked up the receiver with my left hand.

I made the incision. He looks like he's going to die.

He's not going to die. Take the paper straws and put them in the incision.

Do I take the knife out?

He paused.

Yes, take the knife out right now. Put the straws in and blow into them a few times. Four times. Puff into them.

Danny handed me the striped paper straws and I put them into the incision, like into a milkshake. I puffed into them. Francisco turned dark pink, then pale pink. Tears ran down his face.

Yes, yes. Will he be okay?

Well, he can't talk, the doctor said. But he can breathe. Keep the straws there. Do you have any tape?

I turned to Danny. Do we have tape?

He brought me the Scotch tape and held the phone to my ear, because my hands were starting to shake.

Now, wrap the straws with tape and then tape the bottom to the skin. You want to stabilize the straws. I looked at Danny and he gave me the receiver. He wrapped the straws in tape and then pressed the ends to Francisco's throat.

Do you have scissors? the doctor said.

Scissors, I said, and Danny ran to my room and got my sewing scissors and he made two very neat cuts in the tape.

We've taped it, I said.

Good, the doctor said. This is very good. Now, trim off all but two inches of the straws.

I did that.

Now, he said, I'm going to call the operator and get an ambulance.

I gave the doctor our address and phone number and he gave me his phone number and Danny and I sat on either side of Francisco, stroking his hands and watching the straw.

You saved someone's life tonight, Dr. Snyder said.

I washed my face and hands over and over, trembling, until the ambulance came. I told Danny what a wonderful job he'd done. We followed the ambulance, in Francisco's car, with Danny leaning forward the whole time, his chin on the dashboard, peering through the fog. We got to the hospital twenty minutes after they'd checked him in and gotten him settled. There was really nothing for us to do, but we couldn't sit or sleep. We walked around the hospital and ate the stale pastries in the cafeteria. I told Danny that for the purpose of visiting hours, we were going to say that I was Francisco's daughter and Danny was his grandson, and Danny beamed. Who was your mother? he asked. I said that I never knew my mother. He shook his head. I know, I said. What a pair.

We begged the nurse to let us sit in Francisco's room and watch him sleep. Danny slid off my lap to stare at the sleeping man in the next bed, whose leg was held up with pulleys and was the size of an entire mottled human being. Danny asked me what the man had and I told him to ask a nurse. He stood in the hall and waited for a nurse and he whispered his question. She said, Elephantiasis, and Danny reported back and we liked how awful that sounded. Danny said *elephantiasis* about ten more times.

We went to the hospital for the next four days, at dinnertime, and each time, we just missed Bea and Carnie. We brought in some fruit and Francisco said, "Oh, the Torellis of yesteryear." We smuggled in vanilla milk shakes from Kriegel's and shared them. We took turns holding hands. On the last day, I met Dr. Keith.

"You're the little surgeon," he said.

"I am."

The nicest nurse, the one Francisco liked, said, "You'd make a great nurse."

Dr. Keith didn't say anything until the nurse walked away.

"You wouldn't," he said. "You don't have the right temperament. But you are damn good with a knife."

DANNY AND I BROUGHT Francisco home. I thought we might move him into my father's old room but Danny said, "He won't like it up there. It's lonely. If you put him in your room, I'll be right across the hall and I can get him things. Like water, or anything. I can help."

I opened the windows in the attic bedroom to get rid of the smell of urine and old man and menthol. I cleared out every trace of my father, except his glasses and his books and an almost empty bottle of my father's aftershave, Zizanie, which he'd worn since I was a little girl. The scent used to last from Sunday to Tuesday in my mother's house.

I slept on the living room couch for a couple of days, in case. Finally, I looked in on Danny and on Francisco and gathered up my blanket and pillow, my radio, my books, and my pajamas and I went up to the attic room, which was just what I wanted. I put my father's glasses in their alligator case into my nightstand and the Zizanie bottle in my bottom drawer. I set my pile of Little Blue Books and poetry on the bookshelf next to his books. I could hear my father quoting John Cowper Powys on Whitman: "'He restores to us courage and joy even under circumstances of aggravated gloom.'" He would always say "gloom" in his deepest voice, lowering his eyebrows and making me laugh. My father quoted everyone, from Shakespeare to Emerson, on the subject of destiny, and then he'd point out that except for the Greeks, everyone agreed: The stars do fuck-all for us; you must make your own way.

· · ·

I CALLED ON DR. Snyder. There wasn't a nurse out front. I sat in his waiting room with a bottle of Macallan Scotch in my lap, leafing through magazines, until he walked in. I was a little disappointed. He was plain and furrowed, with thinning hair. I had to say my name twice, and my address, before he knew who I was. He brought me into his office, a room just big enough for his desk and chair and my chair. I put the Scotch on his table and told him that Francisco had come home, and he said that was great news. We looked at each other. I told him what Dr. Keith had said about my surgical skills and he laughed. Bob Keith's no fool, he said. I crossed my legs and let my skirt ride up to my garters. Dr. Snyder came out from behind his desk and pulled me up. He pulled at my bra until he held my bare breast and I pressed my hand against him until he was so hard, I thought he'd hurt himself. We necked on his desk, pushing his files and his pens to the floor, until his nurse knocked. I straightened my skirt and my bra. He straightened his tie. I took a quick look in the mirror and reapplied my lipstick, while he watched. He looked over my shoulder and wiped the red off his chin. We looked at each other in the mirror. We were breathing hard and still a little excited and beyond that, deeply pleased with each other and ourselves.

FRANCISCO MADE MEXICAN CHICKEN soup and tortillas and Danny showed us his spelling test, with the big red 100 across the top. Francisco kissed him, and while Danny was setting the table, Francisco showed me a contract for the Penn Station barbershop. He was selling it to Jorge and Gracie, who wanted to expand.

"I'm retiring," he said. "And we got some money in the bank."

"I'm going to be on the spelling team," Danny said. "We're going to have a tournament."

We cheered for ourselves, and ate the soup, and when the ice cream truck came, I gave Danny a dollar. The three of us sat in the back on the picnic table, blissfully eating our Creamsicles. I thought, I'll be a doctor.

28

It's Been a Long, Long Time

I BEGAN TO THINK I SAW GUS HEITMANN EVERYWHERE. His long, foxy jaw. The sharp, pocked cheekbones. His wide shoulders, dipping to the left, driving the car ahead of me. It was ridiculous to think I'd seen Gus in Great Neck, as if he hadn't died or, having not died, had chosen to come back here. I told Francisco, who said, "Yeah, I saw De Gaulle in Nassau Hardware. Right behind me."

IT TURNED OUT, Gus had seen me. He'd been looking for me. He'd called the Torellis three times and he said that each time he'd felt sicker than when he'd reentered Ellis Island and had to claim to be Gersh Hoffman, Nazi victim. He never reached Mrs. Torelli, who I think would have told him where I was. He got a snippy girl with an English accent, who was probably the new governess, and he got a shy Negro maid, who thought he was selling something. Twice, he got Joey, who yelled, HelloHelloHello, into the receiver and hung up. Once, he dialed his old number in Lake Success but the woman didn't know any Reenie Heitmann and a man took the phone from her and told Gus to stop bothering his wife. Gus said that he'd never thought he was a coward until he sat looking at my name and address and phone number in the Great Neck telephone book, and couldn't bring himself to dial.

He didn't want to be Gus Heitmann anymore. He wanted only to be Gersh Hoffman, Jewish math teacher, and he wanted to find me. He never told me what he would have said to Reenie if she'd answered the phone.

DANNY AND I WENT to Stricoff's bakery like other people went to church. We were Sunday regulars, and if it was a bad week, you could find us picking out a chocolate babka on a Wednesday afternoon. That's where Gus saw us. He said we looked like the tall and the small of the same person. He watched me give my ticket to one of the Stricoff sisters and get handed a box and a small white bag and right before we made our way through the throng of Sunday shoppers, the old men with their lists and the other young women with their small children, Gus got into his car and followed us home. He parked his car a block away, like a real spy, he said, and stood on our corner. He watched me and Danny carry in our groceries. Francisco held the door open for us, saying, as he always did, "Hail the conquering heroes."

Gus said when he saw Francisco, he hated him. He said that he couldn't imagine why I had married a man like that, but he saw me hug Francisco and it looked like I loved him and he thought that there was no reason to get in touch, after all. I put on my dungarees and Danny and I played while Francisco put the groceries away and started dinner. Gus watched us, hidden by our hedge, batting the hell out of our tetherball. When Danny wrapped the ball around the top of the pole, I cheered, and we went back into the house for Danny's math and my med school applications. I looked back, at nothing, at the sound of a car starting, and Danny tugged on my sweater.

THAT NIGHT, IT WAS raining like the Flood. Trees bent toward the ground, the sky cracked white every few minutes, and black, oily water ran in the black streets. Thunder woke Danny up twice and I sang to him. On the third verse of "Did You See Jackie Robinson Hit That Ball," he fell back asleep. I tucked him in with his old holster, just in case. Francisco was reviewing the transcript we'd devised before typing it on our state-approved and watermarked paper. I was taking a break from organic chemistry, skimming my Little Blue Book on modern mathematics. Francisco had already aged the parchment for my high school and college diplomas and done the calligraphy. A man he used to shave had a brother-in-law who had the state seals for New Mexico, New York, and New Jersey, and now, so did we. Francisco had amortized all our medical school expenses over the some thirty-five years I could expect to practice and he said I was a good investment. He kept a ledger book of what I owed him. Sometimes he wrote in things like Teaching Danny Spanish: $10,000.00, Eva's Eyebrows: $2,000.00. We graduated me magna cum laude from the University of New Mexico. (Not summa. Do not overreach, my father had said.) I applied to medical schools in New York and I hoped that they felt about New Mexico the way I did, that it was American, and legitimate, but wide open and a little unknowable. My UNM transcript showed that I had aced everything, including classical music and botany (well rounded), and had spent three years as a lab assistant for the recently deceased Dr. Andrew Azores. His reference letter emphasized that he had never recommended a woman before; nevertheless, he believed that without in any way compromising my femininity, I would contribute to the field of medicine. Dr. Azores approved of what he felt was my natural interest in pediatrics. He emphasized my devotion to medicine, my skills, and my modesty.

There was a suggestion that I would never marry. Francisco and I both thought Dr. Azores was a pompous ass but he was, entirely, our pompous ass. We didn't give me Phi Beta Kappa, on the off chance that someone on some admissions committee would give a damn, and thinking to help or hurt my cause, call the Phi Beta Kappa office.

29

How High the Moon

Letter from Iris

Queensberry Place
South Kensington, London
September 3, 1948

Dearest Eva,

I understand why you never wrote. I'm sorry that I stopped writing. It was too hard. It was like etching my awfulness on every mirror. I have tried to be a better person. I even look in the mirror less often.

The clinic is becoming a reality. I continue to be the Singing Guinea Pig, and now I am on the board, which means I beg rich people for money, every single week, on behalf of Dr. McIndoe and the boys, and, in my own mind, on behalf of Reenie. I am usually partnered up with a very handsome, badly maimed RAF major. I don't know that most people see his handsomeness. I imagine they see the ruined remains. That's what we count on—because just as the rich person begins to wince (usually as Teddy is knocking a tray of crab puffs to the floor with his stump, or misjudging the distance from the glass to his twisted mouth), I cut in with my pretty ways and waltz them into another room, so they can write us a check in comfort. We have perfected this. I love Teddy and he loves me. If I was going to sleep with a man, it would be a short Scotsman with one arm and half a face and a taste for morphine.

I've been a guest star on *Café Continental* six times now and it looks like our West End revue will run forever. I am enclosing a check, which I hope will be helpful to you all. I'll send you a check every month that I'm working, from now until I die.

Oh, Eva, please forgive me for every shitty, unspeakable, unforgivable thing I did to you. I know that as lists go, this is one with real depth and real breadth. I have no business staying away— except that I think you are better off without me and at least here, I make myself useful. If you write me and tell me to return, I will.

If you can, forgive me. If you can, let me make amends.

Your sister,
Iris

———————

Gus Heitmann stood at my kitchen door, water dripping off his hat. He looked worn out and he was soaking wet.

"Gus," I said. "My God." I kept my voice down, because of Danny.

He smiled at me, uncertainly.

"Look at you. You're all grown up," he said. "Married, with a little boy."

Francisco snorted.

Gus and Francisco said hello. Francisco was not going to say, I'm not her husband, you moron, so I said so, politely. Francisco settled back in at the kitchen table and picked up his magnifying glass. I wish I'd thrown my arms around Gus's neck and kicked up my back foot or squealed his name or any of the things that a normal woman would do, seeing a man she was fond of, who she thought was dead. I let Gus in and I put his wet hat on top of the refrigerator.

We sat in the living room and Francisco stayed in the kitchen, listening in. Gus told me that he had been living in Great Neck for a few months, and he started teaching at the high school in a month. He was kind of a loner, he said, and everyone knew him now as Gersh Hoffman, that he'd changed his name while he was in Germany. It made no sense to me, changing one German name to another. He talked about his hard times in Germany and looking me up and not calling and then seeing me in the bakery, and I could hardly listen. I was just waiting for him to ask me about Reenie.

"Let me get you a drink," I said. "I guess you're trying to find Reenie."

He said that he had looked for her and he had looked for me, but he'd lost his nerve.

I had to tell him what had happened. I told him the short version, without the details, which, even so, was awful to tell. He put his hands in front of his eyes.

He said, "Oh, Christ. Oh, poor Reenie. I am so sorry." He put his head in his hands, and I apologized too. I said that Reenie was dead by the time they got her to the hospital, and I started to explain that we didn't have a hospital close to us but that would be changing soon, and Gus lifted his head to look at me. I thought it might be now that he asked me what had been going on with Iris and Reenie.

He said, "How'd the fire start?"

I said I didn't know, that no one knew.

"Spontaneous combustion," he said. "How 'bout that. Where's your sister now?"

I told him that she had gone to England for surgery and we weren't in touch.

He said, "Too bad. You didn't have much family."

I said the same was true for him. Gus asked me about my father and I told him that Edgar had been sick for a while and died and he said he was sorry about that too. He asked about my husband and my son and I heard Francisco muttering in the kitchen. I said that I really did not have a husband and that Danny was my adopted son. Gus looked furious, and I thought that the details of Danny's life could wait until another time. Or never. Gus asked me if I had gotten his letters. I said no and he sank down in the couch.

"That's too bad," he said. "If you'd gotten my letters . . ."

Francisco said, "I'm making coffee. Who wants some?"

Gus stood up. "Good to see you," he said. "We should have that drink next time. Maybe we'll play cards," he said.

I said that I'd be glad to do that. I told him that I worked near Stricoff's bakery and that I was usually home by five o'clock. I asked him if he had a day in mind to get together and he said no. He asked me what I did for work and I said that I was a psychic, that I did tarot card readings. I wasn't happy to say this.

"She's worked with the FBI," Francisco said. I knew that he thought I should tell Gus that I was applying to medical school, that I was not planning on spending the rest of my life as Madame Fruitcake, peddling bullshit to decent, unhappy people, as Gus might see it.

"You don't say. You'll have to tell me my future sometime." He walked into the kitchen and got his hat. He shook Francisco's hand on his way out the door.

I sat at the kitchen table and Francisco moved the valuable, watermarked papers that would be my transcript and closed his typewriter case.

"He thought you were my husband," I said.

Francisco smoothed his hair and he arched an eyebrow. "Naturally."

"What was that about?" I asked.

Francisco poured us beers.

"The lightning stopped," he said. "Danny can get a good night's sleep."

"What was he in such a goddamn state about?" I said. "I mean, I understand. About Reenie."

"It was very sad about Reenie. On top of that, the man was disappointed. He thought that when he finally pulled himself together and came to find you, there'd be magic and he would be transformed by your loveliness, which he has, probably, exaggerated over the years, and then the two of you would melt into each other, in an incandescent moment of mutual and perfect understanding. As one. Forever. I think, in his mind, Reenie was already out of the picture. Not that he wished her dead. And here you are, not waiting for him, with the little boy and the fat old man and no incandescence anywhere."

"Christ Almighty," I said.

"I'm going to bed," Francisco said. "Tomorrow, we send in your magnificent transcripts. I gave you an A-minus in organic. Say goodnight, kiddo."

"Good night, kiddo," I said. I sat at the table until I fell asleep. At dawn, I dragged myself to bed. I had gotten used to the idea that people lived and you loved them, or didn't, and then they died and you were bound to miss them, often even if you didn't love them. I was used to Gus being dead and now he was not only alive, but stupid and angry, and he'd trailed all my dead and gone people into my house, right along with that sad, wet hat and his lined, hard face.

I DROVE TO GREAT Neck High School and read *The Fundamentals of Physics* in the parking lot until the three o'clock bell. It was Firenze Gardens all over again. I watched Gus make sure a bunch of boys got on the bus without killing each other or falling under the tires, and when he lit his cigarette and the last bus pulled out, I walked over. I apologized for the other night. I wasn't the one with the problem, but I was certainly sorry. I was surprised when I should have been gracious, and I had given him nothing but very bad news. I was sorry about that and I said so.

Gus pushed his hat back on his head until he looked like a farmer. I'm glad I heard it from you, he said. Maybe we could have dinner. I was a knucklehead, he said. We could start again. I said that I thought that was a good idea and he said, How about my place? I can cook. I thought he needed to be careful with a buck, like I did, and I said yes. I told Francisco where I was going and he told me to wear slacks and my blue sweater and my navy-blue loafers. He said a little lipstick wouldn't kill me. Are we acting like this is a date, Francisco asked. We are not, I said.

Gus's place was neat and clean and close to empty. The couch was a mustard-yellow brocade with one brown pillow on it and there were no pictures on the walls. There was a rocking chair with no cushion, an old rag rug in the living room, and another small rug

in front of his kitchen sink. I was seized with love for my house at
Old Tree Lane and Danny's trucks and racing cars and his grimy
socks and Francisco's three pairs of reading glasses and the path my
stockings took every Friday night, from the tub, to the stairs, to my
room, each of us helping my stockings get back to where they be-
longed.

The place smelled like spaghetti sauce, and not the kind that
Francisco made. Gus asked me what I liked to drink and I said a
whiskey sour. I don't have that, he said. I said whatever you have is
fine, and he poured me a glass of red wine that tasted like a saddle.
I sat down on the couch and thought how much I should never
have come. Gus sat down next to me, dropping an arm over my
shoulder.

"Oh, my," I said. "Like kids at the movies?"

"I've missed you. I thought about you a lot. If you'd gotten my
letters . . ."

"I didn't," I said. "I thought you were dead, somewhere. Or not
dead, but not coming back. I didn't think you were a German spy.
None of us did."

"Good. Thanks. So, you don't have a husband." He narrowed
his eyes. Like, I maybe didn't have a husband, but I had a lover.
Like, I may have said I didn't have a husband but probably I was an
inveterate liar. I asked how the dinner was coming along and he
went back to the kitchen. We ate the spaghetti and the burned
meatballs and our two salads and Gus poured us the whole awful
bottle. We found ourselves back on the ugly couch, drinking brandy.

"I really wish you'd gotten my letters," Gus said.

I AM NOT AN expert in normal sexual behavior. I've had my crushes,
flaring and fading in a week, and most nights I dreamed about sex
with everyone from Ozzie Patterson to General MacArthur. De-
spite that business with Dr. Snyder, things had stayed pretty quiet
for me in that department. I had Danny and a man who loved me

and shared the cooking and I was surrounded by married people. I wanted something slow and romantic and even a little frightening. I wanted us to hold hands and find ourselves unable to let go. I wanted Gus to kiss me on the neck up to and around my ear (which I always thought I'd like) and back down to the nape of my neck, under my ponytail, and then a string of warm kisses along the top of my shoulder, where he pushed my sweater aside. My head would fall back against the yellow brocade and slowly, slowly, like opening a present, Gus would undo the buttons of my cardigan. He would carry me to his bed, never mind his bad leg, and unzip my pants and I would slip out, naked and smooth as the day I was born. He would kiss every part of me, my breasts and between my legs, and at last my sensible body would surprise me. It would do new, wild things that were as different from cooking and comforting and managing as can be. Waterfall of desire, is what I was hoping for.

In the event, Gus was drunk, following his own uneven tune. He kicked over the brandy bottle and we righted it and mopped it up and the whole room smelled like a French accident. Gus pulled my sweater over my head and it caught on my earring. I sat upright with my hands in my lap, like a woman on a bus in a bad neighborhood, except that I was just in my bra. He kissed me frantically, not always connecting with my actual skin. He had trouble with my bra and I thought he would tear it, so I unhooked it myself and let it drop to the couch. He tossed it on the floor, onto the brandy stain, and he kissed my breasts. He rubbed his face over them. I said, Ouch, a couple of times and he stopped. He looked at me, his eyes still unfocused, and I put my hands over my breasts. You scratched me, I said. He saw my face and my bare breasts and I think he did see me. He put his hands over his face and then he stood up. He handed me my sweater.

"You should go now," he said. "I'm sorry. You should go."

I pulled my sweater over my head and stuffed my damp bra into my purse. Gus was crying.

"I'm sorry," I said. I was sorry.

He opened his front door.

"I won't bother you again," he said.

FRANCISCO WAS SITTING UP when I came in.

"Awful," I said.

"You or him?"

I DID BETTER THAN average on my med school exams. I sent in my impressive transcripts and my stellar letters of recommendation and, waiting to become, I busted out as a psychic. I picked up M. Croiset's habit of saying things out loud, naming the creatures of the world, just because I liked the sound, and my clients leapt up, like trout, to agree with me, and see their happy futures unfolding. I was doing five readings a day, putting money in the bank, and I rented a saxophone for Danny so he could join the sixth grade jazz band. He wore a red vest every Wednesday evening for band practice. A friend of Ruthie's told Ruthie that Danny was cute. Wednesday nights, Francisco went to Society for Human Rights meetings, which were, as he said, lousy with old Reds and old Scotch and some new Judy Garland records and on Wednesdays, I couldn't settle down until they were both back home.

IT WAS WARMER THAN usual. The snow had left a few narrow white strips on the slick bright-green grass, as if spring were right around the corner. I had put away Danny's things and lain down to read the newspaper and fallen asleep. I dreamed that my father, younger and healthy, was in white tie (which would have suited him), carrying bottles of Champagne down a flight of glossy marble steps. They were slippery, so smooth light bounced off their rounded edges, but he walked confidently, with his shoulders back. He didn't look down. He tossed the bottles into two big ice buckets and looked in my direction and winked. I came toward him and the white flotsam of wherever we were brushed past me like tumbleweed.

"One's Champagne," he said. "One's egg cream. And I brought sandwiches." And floating near the ice buckets were dear Mrs. Gruber's fried-egg-and-cheese sandwiches, each in a soft white nest.

"Everything you need, as the chorus girl said to the vicar." He tapped his show-biz silver-topped cane a couple of times.

IT WAS ALMOST MIDNIGHT and I was in my pajamas and Gus was at the door.

I made us tea and we sat in the kitchen, saying nothing, watching it steep. I put out a plate of cookies, not that I wanted to.

"Are you mad at me?" Gus said, in the tone of a man who is sure he has every reason to be angry and the other person has none.

I was. I was as angry at him as if he'd been standing me up, night after night, in some fancy restaurant on Northern Boulevard.

"I don't know what you want," I said. "I don't even know you."

"You know me," he said. "I know you."

YOU KNOW ME.

I don't think the best beginning is loneliness or the memory of a man making you laugh while your sister is kissing his wife in the backyard or the strong feeling that if you do not leap now, unprepared and inept as you are, onto this buckling train, you may be sorry, but I don't think it's the worst.

Gus took my hand at the kitchen table and came forward to kiss me. I put my saucer over my teacup to keep it warm and Gus laughed. He did kiss me, not on the lips, but below my ear.

"Everyone's asleep?" he asked.

"I hope so."

We went up to my attic room and lay down on my bed.

"No one's seen me without my clothes for a long time," he said. "It ain't pretty."

I never wanted anything the way I wanted to see Gus without his clothes on and then to have him see me.

"Oh," I said, "please let me."

It was the end of winter and we were in layers. I put his sports jacket on the little wooden chair in the corner and then I came back to the bed. He kept his eyes on the ceiling.

"Look at me," I said. "I'm so glad to be seeing you."

"I hope so, kiddo," he said, and he closed his eyes.

The white shirt and all of its buttons, the undershirt, the belt, the pants, and then I was down to his boxers and shoes and socks, in which I'm pretty sure no man looks his best. I untied his black shoes and pulled off his socks. I had seen my father like this, and Danny. I had seen pictures of Michelangelo's *David*. Gus looked nothing like that.

"Getting cold here," Gus said.

I put my mouth on his smooth chest. He tasted like coffee. I kissed him from one shoulder to the other and down the dark line of his belly and I stopped, to gather my thoughts. I said his name.

Gus opened his eyes. He leaned up on one elbow and took off my clothes, one piece at a time, until I had on nothing but my underpants and socks. He kissed my breasts. Sorry for last time, he said. He kissed me through my underpants. I didn't take my socks off until the middle of the night. Everything surprised me and nothing frightened me.

Gus talked and I listened. He told me about the long march to Trutzhain and the Gypsy man he'd walked with and the people they had had to leave behind. I fell asleep and woke up, reaching for him. He was still talking, about a crippled boy on the ship that took him to Germany and about Greta and her two little girls. Anna and Carolyn.

We heard Danny's door creak open and we heard him pee into the toilet bowl. His footsteps stopped at the bottom of the stairs to my room and then I heard him get back into bed and leave his door open.

Gus got up and put on his boxers. He looked silvery and beautiful in the moonlight, released from his usual boxer's stance. His bad leg looked slim and elegant, like it balanced him. Gus smiled and reached for his glasses.

"I'll be right back," he said. "Wish me luck."

I fell asleep and woke up to Gus laughing.

"I met Danny," Gus said. "He could use some help with math, he thinks you should get out more, and we agreed that a bright moon, like tonight, makes it hard to sleep. I said that I had always found that a couple of cookies and a glass of milk helped. So we tried that. Also, you're low on cookies."

He lay down beside me, on the side of the bed I never slept on, and he lay on his back and sighed. He pulled me onto him. He talked about people in Pforzheim, about a man with no legs who got around in a cart, until I fell asleep again, my hand in his hair, his hand on my hip. I woke up at dawn and saw that he was crying in his sleep. I wiped his face with my hand and he curled around me, still sleeping, not an inch between us.

IN THE MORNING, WE tiptoed out of my room, absurdly, as if in my little house, another person wouldn't be noticed. Danny was dressed and sitting at the kitchen table. He stood up when Gus walked in the room.

"Good to see you again," Gus said. He stuck out his hand and Danny shook it.

"Do you want some breakfast?" Danny said. "Eva makes good pancakes."

Danny poured Gus a glass of orange juice. He acted as host and butler for all of breakfast. It was as if my father had entered Danny's body and soul. He poured coffee. He made remarks about the weather. He filled the sugar bowl and brought it to the table. Discreetly, he folded a napkin next to Gus's elbow and set a teaspoon on it. When Gus lifted the little bottle of syrup to pour on the pancakes, Danny put his hand on Gus's arm.

"Do you want that warmed?" he said, and cast an eye at me, as if to say, Hop to.

After breakfast, Gus washed and Danny dried. I said that I had some errands to run, and if Danny was not the nice boy that he was, and hadn't absorbed the Acton rule of good manners in the face of all, and if he didn't on top of that, love me, he would have said, Who's stopping you, lady?

Gus left his horrible apartment and moved in, with a suitcase and a box of books. He fixed the front step and fussed over Francisco's car until it purred and Francisco shook his hand. Gus slept on the couch for two weeks, in a gesture of something more benign than hypocrisy, but not much. Finally, Francisco and Danny sat us down on the second Sunday night and suggested that the following Friday would be a good day for us all to have our hair cut and our shoes polished and go to Town Hall, which we did.

Letter from Eva

220 Old Tree Lane
Great Neck
New York
April 2, 1949

Dear Iris,

Come home.

Your sister,
Eva

Telegram from Iris

TO: EVA ACTON
220 OLD TREE LANE
GREAT NECK, NEW YORK
MAY 2, 1949

ARRIVING SEVEN PM. BOAC LAGUARDIA AIRPORT.
CRYING ALREADY.

THERE IS A BLACK-AND-WHITE PHOTOGRAPH, WITH WHITE SCAL-
loped edges, in my red leatherette photo album, in Iris's padded
white leather one that has *IR* monogrammed in the corner, and in
a silver-plate frame that Danny took with him to college: five people on a wide, striped picnic blanket unrolled over thick green grass,
at the edge of the beach in Steppingstone Park. A fat, handsome
old man, dark, with beautiful silver hair curling over the collar of
his loose white shirt, smiles warmly. He lifts up a beer bottle, toast-
ing the camera. A younger—but not young—man raises his bottle.
You can see the condensation on it. The sun shines against his
horn-rimmed glasses and you can't see the man's eyes. His smile is
wide and a little watchful. A boy who might be eleven or twelve lies
on the grass, on his stomach, under the arc of beer bottles. His
horn-rimmed glasses are a little big for his face. He looks right into
the camera, his smile almost covered by his hands, his elbows buried in the grass. His round, bare feet stick up behind him, and on
one foot, someone has placed a blue-and-white Brooklyn Dodgers
baseball cap. The two women in the photograph lean in from opposite edges, making a canopy over the group. The taller woman
kneels, in light-colored slacks and a pale, sheer, sleeveless blouse.
You can see the edges of her lace bra underneath. Her dark hair is
piled up and she wears long, glittering earrings. She smiles and
you can see her white teeth. She dangles her sunglasses from the
fingers of one upturned hand, as if she's just been told to take them
off. In her other hand, she lifts a silver thermos in the air, toward
the center, and the long tails of the scarf around her neck billow out
behind her.

The other woman also kneels, arching over the group sitting
beneath her on the blanket. She wears dungarees rolled above her

ankles and a white blouse and you can see her bare feet on the blanket. Her dark hair is in a ponytail and her glasses shine on the top of her head. A pair of loafers is on the grass beside her. Her right arm is outstretched, her hand almost touches the other woman's. Her left hand rests on the boy's back and the man with the glasses' hand is on top of hers.

You can count four sailboats in the water behind them and there is a gull's wing in the upper right corner of the photograph. The sun is directly overhead, behind great sheets of cloud, and the light falls evenly on them, on the picnic basket almost hidden behind the old man, on the one gull approaching a ball of waxed paper, on the listing boathouse, on the smooth pale sand, on small whitecaps breaking in the distance, on everything we see.

AUTHOR'S NOTE

This is a work of fiction, from beginning to end. To the best of my ability, I have worked from the particulars and facts of geography, chronology, and customs of the time. I have also moved things and people, adjusted and reconfigured both, when it suited the story.

ACKNOWLEDGMENTS

My editor, Kate Medina, continues to be one of the luckiest breaks of my life, writing and otherwise. My agent, Jennifer Rudolph Walsh, is, always, a generous and serious reader, a gifted, relentless advocate and excellent company. My dear friend, Phyllis Wender, has always given me great support and continues to do so.

I want to thank the MacDowell Colony, at which I made any number of wrong turns, and a few right ones. I also thank Wesleyan University's Olin Library and its resourceful and exceptional librarians.

I also wish to thank my very dear friend, and twin, Jack O'Brien, and his Imaginary Farms, which have given me safe haven, comfort, and more joy than one can imagine, while sitting at a table, in a barn, facing a wall.

I am very lucky in my friends and family, all of whom know lots of things I don't: Dr. Sydney Spiesel helped me with all medical questions, and infallibly; Jane Stern, divine interpreter of road food and the tarot, was generous with her time and talent; my niece Karina Lubell and her husband, Romain Mareiul, are responsible for any good use I have made of idiomatic French and are in no way responsible for my gaffes; scholar and novelist LaShonda Barnett provided expert and creative research as I was getting this book under way and she also provided the soundtrack for much of the writing.

My reading family, Kay Ariel, Bob Bledsoe, Alexander Moon, Caitlin Moon Sorenson, and Sarah Moon, all read with care and kindness and well-crafted criticism. Michael Cunningham gave me a much-needed boost and, as he does, Richard McCann helped me through the last, dark hour.

I must thank my dear cousin Harold Bloom, whose brilliance shines a light on all writers, past and present, and who helped me, with tea and wit, to find a better way to put almost anything.

Jennifer Ferri is the best. Period.

Finally, I thank my husband, Brian Ameche, for giving me everything I have ever hoped for.

ABOUT THE AUTHOR

AMY BLOOM is the author of *Come to Me*, a National Book Award finalist; *A Blind Man Can See How Much I Love You*, nominated for the National Book Critics Circle Award; *Love Invents Us; Normal; Away*, a *New York Times* bestseller; and *Where the God of Love Hangs Out*. Her stories have appeared in *The Best American Short Stories, O. Henry Prize Short Stories, The Scribner Anthology of Contemporary Short Fiction*, and many other anthologies here and abroad. She has written for *The New Yorker, The New York Times Magazine, The Atlantic Monthly, Vogue, Slate*, and *Salon*, among other publications, and has won a National Magazine Award. She teaches creative writing at Wesleyan University.

www.amybloom.com
Facebook.com/AmyBloomBooks
@AmyBloomBooks

Amy Bloom is available for select readings and lectures. To inquire about a possible appearance, please contact the Random House Speakers Bureau at 212-572-2013 or rhspeakers@randomhouse.com.

ABOUT THE TYPE

This book was set in Adobe Caslon. William Caslon released his first typefaces in 1722. His types were based on seventeenth-century Dutch old style designs, which were then used extensively in England. Because of their incredible practicality Caslon's designs met with instant success. Caslon's types became popular throughout Europe and the American colonies; printer Benjamin Franklin hardly used any other typeface. The first printings of the American Declaration of Independence and the Constitution were set in Caslon. For her Caslon revival, designer Carol Twombly studied specimen pages printed by William Caslon between 1734 and 1770. Ideally suited for text, Adobe Caslon is right for magazines, journals, book publishing, and corporate communications.